GRAVE REGRETS

DAVID MASSENGILL

MONTAG

First Montag Press E-Book and Paperback Original Edition November 2022

Copyright © 2022 by David Massengill

As the writer and creator of this story, David Massengill asserts the right to be identified as the author of this book.

Montag Press ISBN: 978-1-957010-19-9
Design © 2022 Amit Dey

Montag Press Team:

Editor: Kate Sargeant
Author Photo: Stafford Lombard
Cover: Rick Febre
Managing Director: Charlie Franco

A Montag Press Book
www.montagpress.com
Montag Press
777 Morton Street, Unit B
San Francisco CA 94129 USA

Printed & Digitally Originated in the United States of America
10 9 8 7 6 5 4 3 2 1

For Kevin O'Brien

"Massengill's mixture of relatable, contemporary characters, urban legend, creeping horror, and multiple perspectives is a deft and winning one. Told with crisp prose that carries both the onion-peeling plot and a vivid personality, *Grave Regrets* is a mystery-horror that confronts, among other things, just how much our past can haunt us. It deserves a place on the nightstand of any Bentley Little or Richard Matheson fan, or anyone addicted to the CreepyPasta corner of the Internet."

—Mike Robinson,
award-winning author of *The Prince of Earth*
and the *Enigma of Twilight Falls* trilogy

"*Grave Regrets* is yet another first-rate thriller from David Massengill, who has been making a habit of creating skillfully written stories that keep you hooked from the first word right up to the last. With his latest, Massengill has crafted a pulse-pounding tale set in and around Seattle. The novel offers varying perspectives about the horrors of a past left unresolved, and how those horrors can manifest in the present day. *Grave Regrets* is a true page-turner with a conclusion that will leave you both satisfied and haunted."

—Jonathan R. Rose,
author of *Carrion*, *The Spirit of Laughter*,
Gato Y Lobo, and *Wedlock*

Praise for David Massengill's novel *The Skin That Fits:*

"...a great read, richly humid with atmosphere, tense, packed with paranoia. The characters are interesting and well-rounded, tackling some difficult social constructs. Subtle but distinct Lovecraftian undertones weave throughout."

—*The Horror Fiction Review*

"Cults, Cajun gators, and roly-poly fish heads as rendered by Jack Ketchum will be the least of your worries as author David Massengill evokes the kinographic horror to be found in Marisha Pessl's *Night Film* or even David Lynch's *Mulholland Drive*. Massengill builds on his previous work (*Red Swarm*) and is better than ever as our tour guide through this sickly-sweet southern Gothic."

—Mike Sauve,
author of *How to Market Your Grief Blog*

MAYA

Maya grabbed her friend Amy's hand as they neared three young men smoking cigarettes outside the Midnight Faith homeless shelter. The men didn't look homeless. They were skinny and couldn't have been much older than 21. They made the twitchy, unpredictable motions of tweakers. One of them leered at the women with yellowed teeth.

"I got something for you, Mama," the man said.

"Don't make eye contact," Maya muttered to Amy, whose hand was trembling. Amy lived in a gated community in Issaquah with her husband and their 14-year-old twin boys and spent most of her time on the suburban Eastside. She wasn't used to the grittier sights of Seattle.

Once they passed the men, Maya said, "I'm sorry. I probably should have picked a better neighborhood for dinner. Pioneer Square can get a little sketchy after dark."

"I'm glad we came here," Amy said. She gave a cautious glance over her shoulder. "We finally found a good Cuban restaurant. And I like to see you in your territory. You're the only one out of our high school friends who didn't end up in the Land of Soccer Moms."

Maya grinned and nodded. At 44, she did have a very different life from their friends. She lived in a condo on Capitol

Hill. She walked to her art director job at Cascadia Clothing Company. She had no kids even though she'd lived with three different guys during her adult years. Right now she was dating a man who was 12 years her junior. Overall, she was content, but sometimes she wondered what her life would have been like if she'd followed a more conventional path. She pictured a lakefront house with a dahlia garden, family dinners around a hand-carved oak table, she and her husband hiding Easter eggs for their toddlers to discover.

"Hey, Mama!"

Maya looked back at the approaching tweaker. He seemed to be addressing Amy.

"Mama, I got something for you." The man reached for Amy, and Maya swatted his arm.

"Back the fuck up," she said, stopping on the sidewalk. Amy gave her a shocked look.

"I was just going to offer a cigarette." The man sounded hurt. He retreated toward his two friends.

Amy shook off her stunned expression. "I think I can see his tail between his legs," she said. Both women laughed.

"There's Greg!" Amy said with relief. She pointed at a Subaru Forester idling across the street. It began drizzling as the two women hurried toward the vehicle. Amy's husband rolled down his window.

"Hey, good lookin'," he told Maya. "I always tell Amy I think you're the only one who hasn't aged since our senior year." Greg, on the other hand, looked considerably older. A pudgy, balding corporate lawyer had replaced the wide-shouldered teenage basketball player with the curling chestnut hair. Amy, too, let her looks slip. She used to be a petite, baby-faced ballerina, but her ass had expanded significantly and her eyes appeared puffy in harsher lighting.

Amy opened the passenger-side door. "She's got to look good for her 32-year-old boyfriend."

Maya smiled, although the truth of Amy's words stung slightly. She suspected Philip probably wouldn't stay with her if she stopped using her Sun-Kissed hair dye and let her natural gray grow in. She also thought he wouldn't appreciate her decreasing her hot yoga sessions from once a day to once a week.

"But time will come for us all eventually, won't it?" Maya joked.

Amy gave a concerned look in the direction of the homeless shelter. "Why don't we drive you to your car? I don't like the thought of you walking alone around here."

Maya watched the three tweakers disappear through the front entrance of the shelter. "I'll be fine," she said. "My car's just around the corner."

"Thank you again for dinner," Amy said. "Next time Greg and I will have you over. If it's too cold for Greg to grill, I'll make you my crab mac 'n' cheese."

Greg nodded. "Bring your guy if you don't think he'll be bored by us fuddy-duddies. We can pretend we're your aunt and uncle if you like."

"Or my grandma and grandpa," Maya said with a wink. "Drive safely, you guys." She continued past the Subaru onto the next block. She passed an ornate, old-fashioned streetlamp and a regal stone building that must have dated back to the late 1800s. She did love the character and mystique of Seattle's most historic neighborhood. She just needed to remember to visit it during the day—not after dark on a Tuesday night in October.

She glanced around her, then back in the direction of the homeless shelter one last time. She didn't see the tweakers, only two young gay men walking arm in arm and a woman in tattered clothes pushing her possessions around in a grocery cart.

Maya turned the corner and headed toward her Prius. The rain increased in intensity.

She noticed something rectangular stuck beneath the windshield wiper on the driver side of the car. Whatever lay on the glass was too large to be a parking ticket.

Maya lifted the wiper and picked up a wet paper object.

It was a magazine—the second-to-last issue of *Evergroan*, the literary magazine she'd created when she was a junior at Glimmer Lake High. The black-and-white cover showed a spiral made up of tiny pine trees.

She unlocked her car and lowered herself into the driver seat. She set her purse on the passenger seat and her keys on top of the bag. She stared down at the magazine with delight. Did Greg leave this for her as a gag? She hadn't seen any issues of the magazine for at least 15 years. She'd kept them in boxes in her parents' garage, and her mother embarrassedly admitted she'd donated them to a Goodwill in Lynnwood.

Maya flipped through the pages until she reached a creepy illustration of a man with long tree branches for arms. He stood on the edge of a forest. He wore dirty mechanic coveralls and had a long, distorted face that resembled a crescent moon. He had no hair. Beside the illustration was the title of the accompanying story: "Spindly Arms."

John Larsen's name appeared beneath the title. Maya hadn't been particularly close with John, who was a little blander than most of her friends. He was one of those golden guy high achievers most people liked. But she did appreciate the bleakness and the weirdness of his writing, and she also didn't mind that the local newspaper reprinted "Spindly Arms" on Halloween of 1992. The *Glimmer Lake Gazette* mentioned that the tale had originally appeared in *Evergroan,* a literary magazine edited by Glimmer Lake's own Maya Mathers.

Maya did recall the guy responsible for the illustration: Brandon Laurent of the dark eyes and perpetually tousled hair. She remembered how they'd ditched their dates at the Winter Dance and shared a forty of Crazy Horse behind the sciences building. They tried to fit their tongues inside the bottle at the same time, and soon Brandon's hand was up her frilly dress and her hand was down the front of his slacks. It was a one-time hook-up, but it was one she'd never forget.

She squinted in the dimness of the car to read the first sentence of the story:

> *Spindly Arms usually killed in the mountains near his home, but sometimes he came down to the towns of Western Washington to hunt people.*

Something scratched along the driver side of Maya's car.

"What the hell?" she whispered. It sounded like a stretch of pipe or maybe a piece of wood. She glanced in the side mirror to see who was next to the car, but raindrops obscured her view. She quickly pressed the door lock button and turned to look out her window.

She saw only the dark, wet sidewalk.

She suspected the tweakers had somehow followed her. Terrified, she reached to turn her key in the ignition.

But her keys were still on top of her purse. She moved to grab them and accidentally knocked the keys and bag onto the floor. "Shit," she said.

The scratching sound started on the opposite side of the car. Maya stared in horror as the scratching continued from the rear door to the door just across from her.

The doors are locked, Maya told herself. *No one can get in.*

She bent over the seat and felt the possessions scattered across the shadowy floor. Lipstick. Gum. Office keycard. The turquoise rubber heart Philip had given her.

"Keys!" Maya lifted the keys and held them in the streetlamp light coming through the windshield. She located the longest one, which would make her car start. Thankfully, the scratching had stopped. She imagined trying to reach Amy and Greg, but she guessed they'd already be on I-90, speeding toward the safety of suburbia.

She heard a heavy exhalation in her backseat.

Maya screamed when she saw the long, moon-shaped face staring at her in the rearview mirror. She reached for the door handle. Her hand opened in a spasm as something sharp and jagged tore through her throat.

JOHN

John was staring at a patch of gray on top of his head when Vivian called his name from downstairs. He combed his fingers through his hair and squinted at the many silver strands mixed in with the brown. How did this happen all of a sudden? When he'd turned 40, only his temples were gray.

"John!" Vivian shouted, sounding alarmed. "You need to come down and see this!"

John left the bathroom and hurried through the master bedroom of the two-story Madison Valley home he and his wife, Karin, had bought in 2008—the year before she died. Sometimes it seemed surreal that he was now sharing this house with Vivian Chiang, his high school love whom he hadn't talked to once between their senior year and last summer's 25-year Glimmer Lake High School reunion.

"John? This is important."

"Coming!" John found Vivian downstairs, standing before the small TV on the kitchen counter. She wore a faded blue sweatshirt and neon-yellow running shorts that curved around her butt perfectly. John placed a hand on the back of those shorts.

"Stop," Vivian said, brushing away his hand. "Watch this."

A Jeep commercial ended, and a blonde anchorwoman stared solemnly at the camera.

"We now bring you the story of a homicide that happened in Pioneer Square last night. Police found 44-year-old Maya Mathers dead in her car near the intersection of Yesler Way and Firehouse Alley at approximately 1 A.M."

"Oh, god," John said. "Maya from high school?"

Vivian nodded and glanced back at him with saddened eyes.

The anchorwoman's voice continued as the image of a beaming woman with long, sandy hair filled the TV screen. John recognized Maya's almond-shaped eyes and freckled cheeks even though he hadn't seen her since 1993. She stood on a sunlit trail winding through a desert landscape.

"Police say her throat was slit, but they haven't released any other details about the murder. They're asking any witnesses to come forward."

John scowled. "There's got to be more than that." He pulled his smartphone out of his pocket and Googled *Maya Mathers murder Pioneer Square*. Near the top of the list of results was a *Crime Scene Insider* blog.

John's eyes widened as he read the post from October 22, 2019. He read a portion of the blog aloud: "A tree branch was resting on top of Ms. Mathers's body. Her cell phone was in her hand, and it displayed an Internet site that features horror fiction stories posted by the public. The story of the day was about 'Spindly Arms,' a killer with tree branches for arms."

John gaped at his cell phone.

"John?" Vivian asked. "Are you all right? You're white as a ghost."

"Don't you remember?" he asked. "Spindly Arms! The man with the moon face. I invented him senior year."

"You haven't touched your food," Vivian said almost two hours later. John sat before the desktop computer in his upstairs den. He felt queasy as he clicked through various pages of the website *Bloody Bitz.*

"Come on," Vivian said, tapping a fingernail against the cold bowl of rice and curry next to John's mouse pad. "Have a bite, and then you should get to bed. You've got that meeting with your client tomorrow."

John rubbed his eyes and glanced up at Vivian. He once again clicked on the post titled "Spindly Arms." "I'm sorry. It's just...this is my story." He remembered how thrilled his teenage self had been printing out the final piece on his dad's dot-matrix printer. "But who the hell posted it? The byline says 'anonymous.'"

Vivian leaned over him and stared at the screen. "Anyone could have posted it. It looks like most of the posts on this site don't include the writers' names. That was the story that made it into the paper, right?"

John nodded. "The *Glimmer Lake Gazette,* back in the fall of 1992. But first, it was in the literary magazine Maya edited at school. I can't imagine many people having access to the *Glimmer Lake Gazette.* I Googled the paper and found out it went out of business in 2001."

Vivian placed her hands on John's shoulders and began massaging. "Listen, I'm sure the police are looking into this. I hope you're not feeling like you're in some way responsible for Maya's death. It's not like you posted that story. Somebody probably just came across it and loved it and posted it."

"And then someone else killed Maya and linked the murder to the story on the same day?"

Vivian lifted her hands from John's body. "Okay, so maybe it was the same person who posted the story and killed Maya. Some psychopath. But again, you had nothing to do with it. Do you want to tell the police you originally wrote 'Spindly Arms'?"

John closed his eyes and rested his head in his hands. He knew he wasn't to blame for Maya's death, but he hated that his short story was associated with the murder. "I guess I should tell the police. They'll find out eventually."

"Tell them tomorrow morning," Maya said. "After a night of sleep. They'll probably have all kinds of questions for you."

John nodded and went back to staring at the screen. Beside the story was a black-and-white illustration of Spindly Arms standing on a rock overhang, peering down at a distant suburban neighborhood.

"You know who drew that, right?" John clicked on the illustration to expand it.

Vivian hesitated before looking closely at the screen. "Brandon?"

"That's right. That's his style. Except that's not the illustration that appeared with my story in the magazine or the newspaper. This is a different one—maybe a new one."

Vivian turned her head and stared at John. "You don't think Brandon posted this, do you?"

"Why not? He went a little crazy after high school, didn't he?"

"That's silly," Vivian said. She looked away from John, and then she started for the door.

"You're not defending him, are you? He was my best friend for most of high school, and I'm not defending him. And it's not just because of what happened between you guys."

Vivian interrupted, "Maybe you shouldn't call the police until we talk this through some more. You're not thinking clearly."

"Are you thinking clearly?" John asked. Vivian didn't respond. She shut the den door.

John began his drive to Issaquah before Vivian was awake. As a senior sales representative for the medical device company Truetonix, he frequently made early morning visits to clinics around the Puget Sound area and beyond. Vivian was a manager of Ma Maison, a French-inspired home and accessories store in Seattle's Fremont neighborhood, and she didn't have to show up to work until 9:30.

Driving east on 90, John continued to obsess about Maya's murder and the fact that his Spindly Arms story appeared on *Bloody Bitz*. He thought of his and Vivian's discussion from the night before, and he was disappointed there'd been tension between them. That was the first time he'd felt any friction since they broke up in high school.

He'd immediately recognized Vivian when she arrived at the Everett hotel that hosted the 25-year reunion. She was stunning in her knee-length sleeveless salmon dress. Of course, her appearance had changed somewhat. Her hair was now short, framing her lovely face. She had crow's feet in the corners of her eyes, and those eyes revealed a weariness—maybe even a burden—he'd never sensed in high school. But her smile and dimples were the same, and her body felt just as good when he embraced her.

"We used to hug like this nearly every day," he told her. He experienced only relief from being in her presence once again. Gone was the pain of their final fight on that icy morning in December of 1992, when she'd confessed to him on Glimmer Lake's pebbled beach. Gone was the rage he felt when he screamed, "You're my girlfriend and you let my best friend fuck you!"

She looked deeply into his eyes as they stood facing each other in the hotel lobby. "Weren't we supposed to meet by a tree that isn't too far from here?"

John chuckled. He recalled the massive sequoia on which they'd carved their initials when they were teenagers. The tree was in a park in downtown Everett. They'd smoked a joint beneath the sequoia's limbs before going to see a riot grrrl band at a local all-ages club. "We said we'd meet there in 20 years if we were unhappy in our lives, right?"

Vivian smiled, and her troubled look returned. "So are we happy people since we didn't meet there five years ago?"

John glanced down at his shoes. "Happy?" He thought of repeatedly shouting his wife's name on that sunset beach in Maui in 2009, hoping he'd spot her bobbing head in the water. But he never saw her, and she never responded. "I don't know if I'd say that. Getting by, maybe."

Vivian slipped her arm around his and pulled him in the direction of the banquet room. "Well, help me get by a little tonight if you can. I'm not sure I want to see all these people."

John's cell phone began ringing in his car, and he realized he was almost at his exit. He glanced down at the phone and didn't recognize the number. He hit the speaker button. "This is John."

"Hello, John. I'm Detective Gabriel Garcia with the Seattle Police Department. I received the message that you called. I believe you have some information for me?"

John wondered if he should have waited until this evening to call the cops. That way he could have talked to Vivian about what he was going to say. But this morning while showering he'd felt compelled to immediately share everything he knew as if relaying this information would get Spindly Arms out of his head. And Brandon, too.

"I'd like to talk to you about the murder of Maya Mathers. I knew her in high school. I've also got a connection to that horror story that appeared online, and so does a former friend of mine."

John and Vivian didn't have a chance to plan what they'd say during their interview with Detective Garcia because the policeman showed up at John's house just after Vivian arrived home from Ma Maison. Detective Garcia was a wiry and frazzled-looking man who must have been in his mid-thirties. His short, black hair was wet and frizzy from the evening rain.

He sat with a remarkably straight back on the recliner in John's living room. John and Vivian were on the couch across from him. He asked them how they knew Maya, and he questioned John a little more about the background of the Spindly Arms short story. John mentioned he'd written the piece during his senior year, and it appeared in both Maya's magazine and the *Glimmer Lake Gazette*. He said he hadn't seen Maya since high school.

Detective Garcia brought up Brandon Laurent. "Tell me more about your relationship with him."

John noticed Vivian cross her legs and pull the hem of her dress over one knee, and the movement seemed like a nervous gesture. He told the detective, "The three of us were tight for most of high school. Like I said on the phone, Brandon did the illustration for my Spindly Arms story. I haven't seen him since senior year, though."

Vivian remained quiet. She nodded robotically.

"And why would you think he could be Maya's killer?" Detective Garcia asked John.

"I don't think that," Vivian blurted.

John ignored her. "There were rumors about what happened to Brandon after high school," he told Detective Garcia. "Some people said Brandon was on the streets in Seattle, that he'd lost his mind."

Vivian shook her head at John. "You don't think Brandon is capable of murdering Maya, do you?"

"I don't think he is. But how do I know?"

Vivian's cheeks reddened with anger. "This is your way of getting back at him, isn't it? For some reason, you've forgiven me for what happened 25 years ago, but you can't forgive Brandon."

Detective Garcia watched the couple with a confused expression.

"Brandon slept with Vivian our senior year," John explained, "when Vivian and I were first dating. But this isn't about that. This is about what happened to Maya yesterday."

"Bullshit," Vivian whispered. In a louder voice, she said, "I know Brandon wouldn't do this because he's not crazy. He's doing fine—maybe even better than you or me. I talked to him in August."

John frowned. "You told me you hadn't talked to him since we graduated."

"I told you that at the reunion, which was over a year ago."

"So you saw him?" John asked, feeling a lump in his throat.

"No," Vivian said. She suddenly looked as if she regretted sharing so much. "He called me. Somehow he got my number. I didn't tell you because I didn't want to open old wounds."

Detective Garcia raised a palm in a halting gesture. "It seems like we're getting off track here. Vivian, I'd like to call you to talk more about your discussion with Brandon."

Vivian nodded in assent.

"I'm going to try to get in touch with Brandon," Detective Garcia said. "It might take me a while because we have a lot of people to talk to. We've gotten a bunch of calls about the case, and, unfortunately, most of them have been pranks."

John wasn't listening closely to the detective. He kept thinking about Vivian and Brandon's secret conversation. When Detective Garcia rose to leave, John glared at Vivian and snapped, "The old wounds are open."

Acid reflux woke John at 3:12 in the morning. His esophagus was burning. He sat up in bed, pressing his hand against his chest. This was another one of the fun little life changes that came with his forties. He'd never experienced acid reflux when he was younger, but now fried, spicy, or greasy foods easily triggered it. So did too much caffeine. And stress.

He glanced at the side of the bed where Vivian normally slept. The comforter covered it in a smooth plane, and her pillow was undented. John didn't think she'd return to the house after he fell asleep, but he'd hoped. He picked up his phone off the nightstand and once again read the text she'd sent him after sneaking out this evening.

I'm staying at my apartment tonight. Today was a lot for me. I need some alone time and a good night's sleep. Let's have dinner tomorrow and we'll talk. This isn't just about what's been going on between us. The Spindly Arms thing is bringing up bad memories— not only what happened with Brandon, but that armless man. I do love you. XX

John had texted back: *I understand. Love u too.*

He didn't resent her for staying away tonight. When they began dating again a little over a year ago, they decided to go slowly in this relationship. They were old enough to know things can rot. She and her icy husband had divorced, and the pair shared custody of a bitter teenage daughter. John had lost his wife. John and Vivian agreed they'd give each other space when they needed it, and she'd keep her apartment until they were ready to move in together—*if* they were ever ready.

But they hadn't needed any space until now.

And it was all because of this fucking Spindly Arms murder. And Brandon.

After making himself a cup of chamomile tea for his heartburn, John headed into his den. He turned on his computer and peeked through the window blinds at the lamp-lit street outside. The rain had lessened into a mist. John shivered at the thought that Maya's killer was somewhere out there, and whoever that person was had read—no, had obsessed over—his story.

John typed the *Bloody Bitz* address into his browser, and he located the "Spindly Arms" post again. He read a few sentences:

His arms crept up the wall of the house, the branches making scratching sounds as they progressed. A light blinked on in the bedroom directly above Spindly Arms, and a teenage girl's face appeared in the open window.

"Who's out there?"

Scrolling down, John was stunned to see there were 742 comments. The most recent were "F-ing cool," "Scary as black Jell-O," "Spindly got naughty in Pioneer Square Tuesday night," and "Who's the author and artist???"

John left the page and went to Google, where he typed "Brandon Laurent."

He'd searched for Brandon in years past, and he never found any useful results. Tonight was the same. Google led him to a sixty-something tax attorney in Minnesota, an African-American folk singer in Tennessee, and a much-missed Columbia University philosophy professor who'd died of a heart attack in 2002. He tried Facebook and Instagram's search engines without any success. After visiting Vivian's Instagram profile, he was at least relieved to see she didn't have any Brandons on her followers' list. But who knew what his Instagram handle could be?

John reached for the senior yearbook that was on a shelf beside his desk. He paged through until he located Brandon's senior picture. Brandon smiled at the camera as if someone had just told him a raunchy joke. He had high cheekbones and thick, nearly shoulder-length hair. Though Brandon was no jock, the girls preferred him over most of the other guys in the class.

Lara Remmers had once explained, "He's good-looking in that devil kind of way."

John remembered how his fist had slammed into that face the same day Vivian told him about her infidelity. After hearing Vivian's confession, John drove to Brandon's house and shouted his supposed best friend's name until he came outside. Once Brandon was on the front lawn, John punched him and yelled, "I know what you did!" He forced his friend down onto the ground and held Brandon's bleeding face against the grass. Brandon muttered something about John being self-absorbed, and John shouted, "You fucked Vivian and I'm the self-absorbed one? Do me a favor and don't ever talk to me again. There's something seriously wrong with you."

A permanent silence did follow. John and Brandon didn't speak once for the rest of senior year, after which they took their separate paths in life—John to the University of Washington and Brandon to Crazyville.

Something tapped against the window, startling John.

"Shit," he sighed, eyeing the large brown moth pressed against the windowpane.

John shut down his computer and turned off the den lights. He inhaled and exhaled deeply as he returned to the bedroom, wanting to distract himself from his anger. He told himself maybe he'd hear from Detective Garcia tomorrow. Garcia had mentioned he'd call back if he had more questions or if there were significant developments in the case. Perhaps Maya's murderer was sitting in a cell right now, and John could once again forget about Spindly Arms and Brandon.

When John stepped inside the house after work on Thursday evening, he heard Vivian groan in the kitchen.

"Oh, no!" she said.

"What is it?" John called, dropping his laptop bag in the entranceway and rushing into the room.

Vivian stood in front of the TV, which showed two police officers escorting three people out of the front of a high school. All members of the trio wore long plastic masks shaped like a crescent moon and had tree branches protruding from their jacket sleeves.

"Has there been another murder?" John asked in a panicked voice. He felt a churning in his stomach.

Vivian shook her head. "Just vandals who spray painted the wall of a gymnasium. A bunch of teenagers around the city have started dressing up like Spindly Arms. It's some sort of sick fad—just in time for Halloween."

"What the hell is wrong with people?" John almost blushed when he remembered he was the creator of Spindly Arms.

Vivian turned off the TV. "The news said teenagers can't get enough of that horror fiction website. This morning the site posted over a dozen new Spindly Arms stories."

"Great," John said, pressing his palm against his face. He was annoyed that Detective Garcia hadn't phoned today to give him an update. Were the police going to sit on their hands with this case?

Vivian hugged him tightly. John was relieved to have her home with him again. He wrapped his arms around her back and breathed in her scent. She smelled of mint and coconut and something deeply calming. He kissed the top of her head before their bodies separated.

"Anyway, I want us to have a nice dinner together," Vivian said. "I made us Mexican." She motioned toward the stove, which held a pot filled with refried beans and a skillet containing simmering bits of chicken and onion.

"I'm a lucky man to have you in my life again," he said.

"We're both lucky, John."

Soon after they started eating, Vivian asked, "How old do you think that man was?"

John gave her a questioning look.

"The armless man," she said.

John nodded. "Oh. Him. The armless man." The man who became the inspiration for Spindly Arms.

Even though they called him the armless man, he did have arms—prosthetic ones that were an orange-ish brown that didn't match his pale complexion.

John thought of how the armless man had lived in the sketchier part of Glimmer Lake, where most of the houses were ramshackle and mossy-roofed and had chain-link fences bordering their overgrown yards or the car parts that made up their yards. The man was stocky and bald and had bulging eyes that narrowed when John drove by in his dad's Buick to deliver the *Glimmer Lake Gazette* every Friday. The man often wore dirty coveralls and black boots that looked like they could easily crush a person's head. He had two Doberman Pinschers, which he kept chained to an apple tree in his small yard. He also had a surprisingly beautiful and sexily plump wife with wavy black hair. Whenever John saw her outside the house she was wearing a nurse's uniform. He remembered Brandon once saying, "White stockings are hot. How did she end up with that crusty old monster?"

"I think he was at least in his early fifties," John told Vivian. He recalled her comment about the armless man in her text from yesterday. The man had once yelled at Vivian about something, frightening her, but John couldn't remember what. He didn't want to bring it up and spoil their dinner. "You don't think the armless man killed Maya, do you?" he asked with a dubious grin.

Vivian shook her head and dipped a chip into the bowl of guacamole. "I was just thinking about him. I remembered how you based Spindly Arms on him."

John didn't care to think about the character while he was eating. "Listen," he told Vivian, "I'm sorry I got...heated during our talk with the detective yesterday. I know we wanted to try to keep things light and easy in this relationship."

"It's all right," Vivian said. She set down her fork and looked deeply into his eyes. "I talked to the detective about Brandon before you came over. I didn't mention it earlier because I didn't want to bring up Brandon."

"Okay," John said, sounding nervous. Vivian looked like she was going to deliver disappointing news.

"Brandon called me in the summer because he wanted to make amends."

"Amends?" John asked with a furrowed brow. "For what?"

"He said he felt like he'd made my life worse at the end of high school because of what happened between us, and he wanted to apologize for that. He said he was making amends to a lot of people in his life."

"He didn't make amends to me," John said. He felt a hot knot in the center of his chest, and he didn't know if it was acid reflux, anger, or both. "Did he even mention me?"

Vivian looked down at her plate. "He didn't say much else. Just that he was doing well, and he'd gotten his life together. He called me from his sister's house. I guess she and her husband live in the same place where she and Brandon grew up. Brandon's mom moved-"

"You're changing the topic," John said. His voice sounded like a growl. "Did you two talk about me?"

"I told him you and I were together again. He didn't respond to that. But why should he?"

"It's like you don't think Brandon is worthy of any blame. He fucked up, Vivian."

"He's not perfect like you. A lot of us aren't."

"What's that supposed to mean?" John asked, throwing his napkin on the floor.

Vivian stood and took her half-empty plate to the sink.

"I don't like that we're fighting," John said. He remained seated at the table. "And we're fighting thanks to Brandon."

Vivian rinsed off her plate. "I don't like it either. But I guess we just have to accept that we're going to fight sometimes."

John gave a pondering look at the darkness beyond one of the kitchen windows. The windowpanes were once again wet with rain. "You know, Karin and I didn't have our first fight until we'd dated for two years. We rarely fought during our marriage."

Vivian dropped her plate, making a banging sound in the sink. She stared at John. "That's not fair. You know I can't compete with her. And I told you I don't want guilting in this relationship. I've had enough of that in my life." She rushed past John toward the staircase.

John understood he'd acted like an asshole. He cleared the table and considered making an apology. But then the thought of Brandon once again crept inside his skull. Brandon who'd betrayed him and ruined his and Vivian's relationship in high school. Brandon who was somehow hindering John and Vivian's relationship again 25 years later.

Tomorrow was Friday, and John had a meeting at an oncology center up in Mill Creek. After that, he'd drive north to Glimmer Lake, and he'd locate Brandon. He knew if he could look in his ex-best friend's eyes he could find out if Brandon had posted that story and illustration on *Bloody Bitz*. And regardless of whether Brandon was guilty of anything, John would tell him to stay the fuck out of his and Vivian's lives.

John's umbrella wouldn't open. Standing outside the Mill Creek Cancer Care Center, he tried to force the runner up the metal pole. "Damn it," he seethed. He gave up on the umbrella and sprinted through the rain to his BMW. He fell into the driver seat and watched the raindrops burst across the windshield. It was only 4:30, and the sky was already darkening. Despite the dimness, John noticed a pebble-sized crack in the glass.

Why was everything going to shit?

He unlocked his phone and looked with regret at the lie he'd texted to Vivian:

My niece needs help moving some furniture into her new apt. I'll probably have dinner with her in Edmonds. X

John had always told Vivian the truth, but he knew he couldn't today. She'd never approve of him seeking out Brandon. And John didn't want to risk fighting with her again. He needed their relationship to endure. He wasn't going to lose another love.

Pulling out of the parking lot, he once again felt that hotel manager patting his back on the twilit beach in Maui.

"I'm so sorry." The elderly woman had been crying while John's eyes were dry and wide and staring at the relatively calm ocean. "It makes sense the police think it was a rip current," the woman continued. "That can pull you so far out you don't have any strength to swim back. Your limbs seize up and...."

John hadn't believed the police. Something so horrible couldn't happen to Karin and him. They were on vacation in one of the most idyllic spots in the country. They were only in their early thirties, and they'd been married for just three years. They were working on having a baby, sometimes making love twice a day to double their chances.

"She said she was stepping out for a quick swim," John kept saying to the hotel manager. And eventually, he told her, "Tomorrow's her birthday."

But then John saw the body the Coast Guard fished out of the water, swollen from seawater with some kind of black, spiky weed entangled in Karin's long, blonde hair.

Yes, John deserved his life only to get better.

A year after Karin drowned, John lost his job at a commercial real estate agency. There were few positions available thanks to the Great Recession. He nearly lost his house as well. He only managed to cover the mortgage by cracking open his 401K and burning through most of his retirement savings.

But then he found the job at Truetonix. He got on antidepressants and joined a gym. He went to his 25-year reunion and, a decade after Karin's death, reunited with Vivian.

John glanced at himself in the rearview mirror. His hair didn't look so gray in the dark. He appeared younger than 44. Vivian had often told him he was on the right side of middle age.

"Things are going to be fine," he told himself in as confident a voice as he'd used this afternoon when he was describing Truetonix's latest CT scanner to a couple of nurses at the oncology clinic. He would find Brandon and establish a boundary, and then he'd go home to Vivian so they could only grow closer together.

John maneuvered the back roads of Mill Creek to reach Glimmer Lake. He figured he'd start his search for his ex-best friend at Brandon's sister's house. John was driving on residential streets in the poorer part of his hometown—the part where the armless man had lived—when he noticed a truck behind him. The vehicle was too close, and its brights were on, nearly blinding him when he looked in the rearview mirror. The truck came even nearer and began to swerve.

"Drunk idiot!" John said. He stepped on the accelerator, attempting to increase the distance between him and the truck. But it was difficult to drive fast because the terrain was hilly and the roads were curving.

The truck remained right behind John's BMW.

John pressed harder on the gas pedal as he reached the top of a hill, and he felt his car lift from the street. It landed with a skidding sound, and John nearly plowed into a mailbox.

John brought the car to a stop on the side of the road. He knew he couldn't keep this up without crashing. He was ready to unleash his rage if the intoxicated ass pulled over, but the vehicle sped past him. It was a black four-door pickup truck. John couldn't see any passengers because all the windows were tinted.

"Glimmer Lake fuck-up," he muttered.

John glanced around to figure out his location. He saw a sign for Creek Trail Road—one of the streets where he'd delivered the *Glimmer Lake Gazette* when he was in high school. He was only a couple of blocks away from where the armless man had lived. Curious about the current state of that house he used to dread, he turned onto the armless man's street.

John hadn't been in this part of Glimmer Lake in at least a decade, and he saw there'd been changes. Modern, boxy townhouses had replaced many of the dilapidated houses. Approaching the armless man's block, he realized all the houses were gone. Some of the lots contained the remains of homes: a crumpled brick chimney, a broken birdbath, a cracked garage door. A bulldozer and two excavators were parked on the unpopulated street. John drove past a large sign reading *Shady Hills Residential Community*. The sign showed an illustration of identical homes on a tree-lined road.

John wasn't a fan of cookie-cutter communities, but the new homes would look much better than what had been here before. *Good riddance,* he thought as he parked his car in front of what had been the armless man's property.

A flattened pile of mossy and muddy wood was where the house used to be.

John stepped out into the cool October air. The thudding rain had lessened into the typical Northwestern drizzle, and the dim daylight would soon give way to night. A low chain-link fence still lined the front of the armless man's property. John rested his hands on that cold metal—something he never would have dared do when he was a teenager.

The apple tree remained on the edge of the yard, but it was dead now. John could see scars on the trunk. The markings were from the Dobermans constantly yanking on their chains. John looked at the remains of the house once again. Only one story, the house couldn't have contained more than two or three bedrooms. Vivian had once mentioned the armless man and his wife had children living with them, but John had never seen any kids when he was delivering papers in the summer and fall of '92. He rarely saw the wife.

It seemed like the bald, glaring owner always saw John, though. When John drove by with his supply of *Glimmer Lake Gazettes,* the armless man would be sitting on his porch with his prosthetic arms hanging awkwardly over the sides of his canvas chair, or he'd be holding what looked like a tray of raw hamburger meat for his dogs to eat. The man never spoke. He just stared antagonistically enough to make John self-conscious when he threw the paper.

There was one afternoon when John had seen the man before the man could see him, and that was the time John realized the stranger had no arms. The day was in early summer, not long after John had first started delivering papers. The clouds looked like they were going to rain liquid charcoal. John parked in front of the man's chain-link fence to change the mix tape that was playing in his car. John heard a door slam, and then he heard the words "Bitch whore bitch whore bitch whore...." He saw the bald man storming around the front of the house.

The man wore his usual coveralls and a faded red T-shirt underneath, and where his arms should have been were two thick, pink stumps.

John dropped his cassette out of shock. He was suddenly terrified the armless man would see him and think he'd been spying. He ducked down in the front seat, fetching the tape from the floor. He still heard the man cursing, and then the words gave way to silence.

John sat up, figuring the man had gone back into the house. The front door was shut, but the toolshed to the left of the house had an open door, revealing the pitch-black space inside.

A flushed face with two bulging, angry eyes slowly emerged from the darkness.

The armless man stared back at John.

John turned his key in the ignition and sped away, his body stiff with fright. It was as if he'd witnessed a murder instead of a man's handicap.

John chuckled to himself now as he gazed at the patch of damp weeds where the toolshed had once been. Why had he, Vivian, and Brandon been so freaked out about the armless man when they were teens? The poor guy had probably lost his limbs in Vietnam or in some industrial accident. John and his friends had speculated about how the armless man might have become armless, but John never found out the truth.

Instead, John turned the unfortunate soul into the relentless anti-hero of a horror story. What was that one gruesome sentence he'd written?

Spindly Arms sat on the dead girl's chest while he chewed on her brother's dismembered foot.

John slipped his cell phone out of his pocket and put the camera on video mode. He filmed the ruined property from a dead apple tree to a soggy pile of wood, thinking he'd text the movie to Vivian with the words *He's long gone.*

But John didn't send the text because the image of a low battery appeared on the phone's screen. He cursed himself for forgetting to charge it overnight. He'd been too distracted with all that was going on. He hadn't brought his charger with him, and he'd need juice in the phone to call Vivian later this evening.

John turned his back on the property and headed toward his BMW. He hoped that the next person who lived on this lot would have better luck than the armless man. He also hoped that if a paperboy ever took on this street again he'd never write a story that inspired a murder.

Lakefront Avenue divided the poorer part of town from the larger, middle-class section. It also served as Glimmer Lake's commercial center. Taking a left onto the four-lane road, John drove past Lakefront Avenue's various strip malls. Most of the stores had changed since the early '90s. Kozy's Pizza Parlor, which had hosted so many of John's birthday parties in the '80s, was now a Bartell Drugs store. The frozen yogurt shop where he'd had his first kiss—with Crissi Fenn, over a bowl of Berrylicious and Skittles—had become a pho restaurant. But John's favorite block was the next one. Now it featured a gleaming Safeway, but 25 years ago there'd been both the Evergreen State Arcade and a Blockbuster video store. In 9th grade, before they'd become interested in alcohol and weed, John and Brandon often emerged from that Blockbuster with a stack of movies to watch Friday and Saturday nights. *Alien, Taxi Driver,*

Drugstore Cowboy, Elephant Man, or anything directed by Brian DePalma, Wes Craven, or David Cronenberg. And there, on that next block, still stood the Lake Town Cineplex! The theater's three massive domes looked ancient like they were part of some centuries-old temple. The Cineplex had smelled of melted butter and sweat in the early '90s. John could only imagine how it stunk now. He and Vivian would regularly go there on dates in their junior and senior years, sometimes bringing Brandon along. John couldn't recall many films he'd seen in the Cineplex. Instead, he remembered his tongue connecting with Vivian's, his hands inching up her shirt and beneath her bra....

He glanced down at his phone, noticing that Vivian hadn't texted or called. Nor had he received word from Detective Garcia.

Feeling giddy from all the flashbacks, John almost turned onto the street that would take him past that cemetery where he and Brandon used to smoke pot out of apples, but he continued on Lakefront Avenue. He heard the words Vivian had spoken to him when he was reminiscing about some of their experiences in high school: "Nostalgia's a more powerful drug the older you get. I think our memories alter reality, giving it a glow that wasn't really there."

Vivian was right, and John also knew some memories would always remain in shadow, serving as dark pockets of pain. It was down the street from here, on the pebbled shore of Glimmer Lake, where Vivian had stopped skipping rocks with him on that bitingly cold December morning. She turned to him and said, "I had sex with Brandon."

John couldn't see the lake today because night had fallen. He took a right onto Maple Hill Street, which would lead him to Brandon's sister's house. Despite the crisp weather, his palms were moist with perspiration. Gone was his previous anger toward Brandon. Now he was just nervous. What exactly was he going to say when he saw his ex-friend for the first time in over 25 years? "Did you draw the picture of Spindly Arms that's on that *Bloody Bitz* site?" "Would you stay the hell out of Vivian's and my lives?" "Why didn't you ever make amends to me?" Or, even better, "Why'd you betray me senior year after we'd been best friends since 7th grade?"

John was trying to imagine what Brandon would look like now when he saw a man floating specter-like into the air above a distant, unlit corner.

Startled, John stepped on the brake pedal. He then slowly drove closer, squinting at the strange sight. The figure wasn't a man. It was some kind of scarecrow fastened to a pole. The corner was part of a pumpkin patch. A darkened sign read *Pumpkins Benefiting the Glimmer Lake Food Bank.*

"What the fuck?" John whispered when he saw the scarecrow wearing a white mask shaped like a crescent moon and had dangling tree branches for arms. One teenage boy positioned the pole from inside the pumpkin patch while two others stood beside him, laughing hysterically as they took pictures or videos with their cell phones. All three looked punkish in their undersized sweaters and black skinny jeans.

John pulled his BMW over near the corner and left the car, slamming his door shut. "What's the matter with you?" he asked the teens. "Don't you have any respect?"

The redheaded teen holding up the scarecrow gave him a defiant look. "We thought it would look cool."

"'Cool'?" John asked. He stepped over the small picket fence bordering the pumpkin patch. "The only reason you know about Spindly Arms is because a woman got murdered. Take it down!"

One of the other teens sneered and glanced at the redhead. "You better not post your Spindly story, Mike, or this guy's coming after you."

"No, you better not post it," John said. He grabbed the pole out of the redhead's hands and lowered the scarecrow onto the hay-covered ground.

"Fuck you, old man," the third teen said.

John winced at the insult, but he tried to ignore the teens. He went to the scarecrow and yanked off the plastic moon mask. He dropped it on the ground and stomped on it until it was flattened. The trio watched in awe.

After returning to the car, John was momentarily embarrassed by his outburst. He realized he'd overreacted. But he was an adult now, he told himself, and he knew a hell of a lot more than what you know when you're in high school. All you know then is how to be reckless and impulsive, and how to make mistakes.

Brandon's sister's house looked just the same as when it had belonged to Brandon's parents. The beige, 1970s split-level home sat on a hillside and had a Japanese maple tree in front and towering cedar trees in back. The exterior of the Laurent house wasn't exactly attractive, but the upstairs bedrooms had impressive views of the Cascades and Snohomish Valley. Some nights in junior high, John and Brandon used to stare out of Brandon's bedroom window with binoculars, pointing at moving lights that could be Russian spy planes or even alien aircraft.

John wondered if Brandon now lived in the bedroom where he'd grown up. That wouldn't be a sign of peak mental health, no matter what Vivian had said of Brandon.

John rang the doorbell and wiped his sweaty palm on his pant leg. He saw someone standing beyond one of the frosted glass panels that flanked the door.

"Who is it?" a girl asked.

"John Larsen. I'm looking for Brandon."

The door opened, and John was stunned to see the beautiful teenage girl who stood barefoot in the foyer. She wore a short green skirt and a shapeless black hoodie and had an enormous smartphone in her hand. She looked exactly like Christie Clifton, a sophomore girl John and Brandon used to lust after when they were seniors, except her curling red hair wasn't in a triangular perm. John expected a smirking 17-year-old Brandon to appear at the top of the stairs and tell him, "You've entered the Twilight Zone, buddy."

Instead, a sandy-haired, frat bro type in a polo shirt appeared. "Everything all right, Ash?" he called down to the girl.

She waved him away and turned back to John.

"Brandon's Jenn's brother, right? The artist?"

"Artist?" John asked, frowning. He pictured Spindly Arms on that rock overhang, surveying the suburban neighborhood. "So he's still making art."

The girl shrugged. "Jenn said he was an artist. I've never met him. I'm just house-sitting for Jenn and Dan. My mom's friends with Jenn."

"And your mom's Christie Clifton?" John asked, grinning. He wondered if Brandon had ever slept with Christie. Brandon rarely shared the news of his conquests. He wasn't like typical guys. After all, typical guys don't fuck their best friends' girlfriends.

"Christie Clifton *Lavis*," the girl corrected him. She stared up at him with the same round green eyes her mother had. "Do you know my mom?"

"A lifetime ago," John said. "I'd heard Brandon was living here. I was hoping to...reconnect with him."

The girl nodded. "He doesn't live here." She hesitated before saying, "My mom said he's got some serious issues."

John wanted to say a self-congratulatory "Thank you." Instead, he offered, "I know. Anyway, I'm sorry to bother you. Have a good weekend." He started for his car, feeling deflated.

"Hey," the girl said.

John paused on the path.

"I just remembered Brandon has a painting in the Valley Dew Coffee Shop. I don't know which one it is. Jenn mentioned he sold one of his paintings there. They might know where Brandon lives."

"I'm not familiar with that coffee shop," John said. "Can you tell me how to get there?"

The Valley Dew Coffee Shop was in a small commercial area that bordered Glimmer Lake and Snohomish. The house where John had grown up was just up the hill, but he didn't feel like driving by. His parents had moved to Arizona about a decade ago after they both retired, and he'd avoided his old home since then. He wanted to remember it the way it was. Whatever the new owners had done to it would seem like sacrilege.

Rain once again splattered John's windshield as he parked in front of the coffee shop. He sighed when he noticed the

CLOSED sign in the window of the shop's door. There were lights on inside, however, so he decided to check if someone might be wrapping up a shift. He left his broken umbrella in his BMW and ran beneath the awning that sheltered the entrance.

The door was locked, and John didn't spot anyone inside.

He did see dozens of paintings covering the walls. The artworks depicted snowy mountainsides, salmon maneuvering the rocks of a creek, and a Native American dancing ceremony.

And there, in the center of the paintings, was Spindly Arms.

"What the hell?" John whispered, his hair standing on end. The painting showed the nighttime view from his old bedroom at his parents' house. He could see the corner of the roof and the immense willow tree that divided his family's property from the neighbor's. Standing on the corner beneath the dim streetlamp was Spindly Arms, staring up in the direction of John's window. Spindly Arms grinned with his mouth open.

John shivered. He hadn't really thought Brandon could be responsible for Maya's death. But after seeing Brandon's illustration on that *Bloody Bitz* site and his painting in this coffee shop, John wondered if maybe Brandon had lost it. He was still depicting and obsessing over Spindly Arms 25 years after that issue of *Evergroan*.

Someone touched John's shoulder, and he jumped in fright.

A silver-headed middle-aged man gazed at John with a wide, amicable smile. He wore a gray V-neck sweater and had a significant paunch. An attractive thirty-something woman with dyed blonde hair stood behind him, beneath a pink umbrella.

"John Larsen?" the man asked. "No way. It's you."

John recognized the voice, and, after staring into the man's eyes a little longer, he placed the face. Norm Richter, his classmate. But in 1993, Norm had had stringy, shoulder-length red hair and bony limbs. He wore flannel shirts that were rattier than those of any grunge star. He was a "burner" who hung out on the park bench behind the humanities building, puffing on cigarettes during the school day and joints after 3:30 P.M. Though John had smoked pot, too, he'd done it only on weekends, and not enough to let it affect his stellar GPA.

"How are you, Norm?" he asked, sticking out his hand.

Norm shook it forcefully. "Really good, guy. This is my wife, Janie."

The blonde woman chirped "Hi," and John smiled in return.

"John here was the cream of the crop in our grade," Norm told Janie. "Brain, basketball player, an awesome writer. Not a low-life like I was. You still writing these days, John?"

John was grateful he had the night to hide his blush. "No," he said. "I gave that up a long time ago."

"Hey, we just came from dinner," Norm said, pointing at a softly lit restaurant on the next block. "We've gotta get to Bowl O' Rama. Our twin girls are in a competition. Can you believe that place is still there?"

John shook his head, picturing the time he'd gone to the bowling alley for a former girlfriend's Sweet 16 party. Brandon had snuck him a flask of Bacardi in the men's restroom.

"I'd love it if you came with us and had a beer. Just one. We can talk old times."

John gave a weak smile. "I shouldn't. I'm trying to find Brandon Laurent."

"Laurent?" Norm asked, scowling. "You still friends with that guy?" he asked with distaste.

"I haven't seen him in years." Curious about Norm's reaction, John asked, "Did you have a run-in with him or something?"

Norm ignored the question. "We gotta go. You sure you won't come for a drink?"

John glanced through the window at the unsettling painting. That was his only lead unless he pumped some information out of Norm. He offered Norm and his wife a friendly grin. "One beer? Why not? My car's just across the street. I'll meet you guys there."

John went to his BMW after Norm and Janie strolled away. He was unlocking his door when he noticed the truck parked a block up. He paused and stared at the vehicle.

It looked like the same truck that had tailed him earlier, but he wasn't certain.

You're being paranoid, he told himself, and then he started his car.

He was at the bottom of the hill when he checked his rear-view mirror and saw the truck's headlights blink on.

John glanced around the packed parking lot outside Bowl-O'-Rama. He saw several trucks, but not the one that had followed him. He seemed to have escaped it after he changed lanes on Lakefront Avenue. He was concerned about more than the truck, though. He couldn't shake that disturbing feeling that had gripped him after he viewed the painting of Spindly Arms.

He tried to listen to Norm spew all that he'd been up to over the past quarter century: starting Normz Bedz, which he turned into one of the largest mattress businesses in Western Washington; marrying Janie at an elegant resort on Orcas Island;

raising those two strawberry-blonde angels over in Lane 7 who were supposedly going to beat the hell out of their eighth-grade classmates. He said he'd hated to miss both the 20- and 25-year reunions, but he'd had to go on buying trips to China for his business. "At least I'm my own boss so I can bring Janie and the girls with me wherever I go," he said, wrapping his arm around his wife's thin waist. She kissed him on the cheek and went back to watching their daughters.

Seeing Norm's smug face, John had the idea that he and Karin and their family-to-be could have had a similarly comfortable life. But no, one of the biggest burners of his grade got that reward, while John experienced his wife's drowning, years of financial struggle, and the horrible reality that his only piece of published writing had inspired a murder. He might have to endure a second break-up with Vivian, too.

Thankfully, Norm didn't mention Maya. He must have missed the news. John wasn't going to tell him about their classmate's death. He glanced down at his half-empty glass of Guinness and decided now was the time to pry.

"So what did Brandon do to piss you off?" he asked.

"You really haven't seen him?" Norm asked. "You guys were so tight in high school."

John looked into his glass of nearly black beer. "Not anymore. I don't know what happened to him after high school. I heard he had some kind of a breakdown and was homeless for a while."

Norm looked confused. "When I saw him, he seemed more drunk than crazy. I ran into him about five years ago at the Tulalip Casino. I asked him what he'd been up to all these years and he said he was living in Leavenworth."

"Leavenworth?" John and Brandon had driven to the Bavarian-themed mountain town several times when they were in high school. It was about a two-hour drive from Glimmer Lake. They would hike or camp. And, of course, there was that time they'd followed the armless man to a farm outside the town.

Norm continued, "I told him about my mattress business and he said I'd turned into a 'fucking bore.' Asshole. Never grew up, that one."

"No, doesn't sound like it," John said, shaking his head. "He was probably jealous you had so much more than him." He thought how Leavenworth was a small town. He should be able to find Brandon if he drove there and questioned enough people.

"I'm sorry you stopped writing," Norm said. "You should get back to it. You were good."

"Thanks," John said. He'd been confident about his talent, too, when he was in high school. His ego was so bloated after his story came out in the paper that he was less than present for Vivian. He should have been more supportive when her parents kicked her out of her house for a week, exiling her for sneaking away on a camping trip with John and Brandon. Vivian spent the week at a friend's house, and she started hanging out with Brandon more often.

"That one Halloween story you wrote," Norm said. "The one in the *Gazette*. Now that was awesome."

John gave him a nervous look, waiting for Norm's lips to form the words "Spindly Arms." He never spoke the name, though.

"Did you publish other stories after high school?"

"None," John said. He'd written some while studying English at the UW and during the year after graduation. The tales were all literary fiction—mostly about his hometown, and inspired by Hemingway's Nick Adams stories and Sherwood Anderson's *Winesburg, Ohio*—but he couldn't find a single literary magazine that would take them. He stopped writing and, to his surprise, he never really missed it.

"I should probably go," he said, pushing away his glass of beer.

"You've got more to drink," Norm said.

John placed some cash on the tabletop. "I'm good. I've become a lightweight in middle age."

"Sucks what aging does to the body, doesn't it?" Norm asked. "But I love the effects on the mind."

"Me, too," John lied.

Once again in his BMW, John checked his phone. Vivian still hadn't called or texted. John thought about phoning her, but he considered exchanging silences instead. Did she sense he'd lied to her about going to his niece's? There was no way she knew he was searching for Brandon. John saw it wasn't even 6. He could probably be in Leavenworth before 9. He could find a hotel and ask around about Brandon tomorrow morning. If he found Brandon and detected any guilt about Maya's death, he'd call Detective Garcia. And if he didn't suspect anything, he'd simply tell Brandon never to contact Vivian again.

John nearly dialed Vivian's number to tell her the truth about what he'd been doing. Instead, he texted, *The move is taking longer than we expected. I'm going to crash in Edmonds tonight.*

Vivian immediately texted back: *Do what you need to. Love u.*

John felt a pang of guilt. He tried typing *Love,* but his phone's battery went dead. He started the car, figuring he could buy a charger somewhere in Leavenworth.

He wondered if he should buy some kind of weapon to protect himself, too. Who knew what kind of a person Brandon had become?

The moon appeared as John reached the steep stretch of Highway 2 leading through Stevens Pass. The constant rainfall had been unsettling when he was at the base of the mountains and the road was only a couple of lanes wide. His parents had often cautioned him about Highway 2 when he was growing up, calling it the "Highway of Death" because of the lack of a divider and the frequent fatal accidents that occurred on the road. But John was more spooked when he was higher up, among the moonlit Cascades. The jagged mountains had a pale, ghostly glow to them, and John remembered driving up here in his dad's Buick on a similarly bright summer night in 1992.

Brandon had been in the passenger seat that night, feeding alternative rock tape cassettes into the car to keep them entertained. They followed the black 1970s Pontiac that carried the armless man into the mountains.

While delivering papers on a few Friday afternoons, John had seen the armless man get into the Pontiac. A muscular man with a white crew cut always sat behind the steering wheel. John wanted to know who the crew cut guy could be and what the pair was up to. Ever since the day the armless man had stared angrily at him from the toolshed, John thought there was something sinister—maybe even criminal—about the armless man. And this stranger's shady behavior could make for an illuminating story on paper.

During their pursuit of the Pontiac into the mountains, Brandon said, "I don't know why he'd leave that sexy wife of his on a Friday night. She doesn't work on Saturdays."

"How do you know?" John asked, but Brandon never responded.

The Pontiac took an exit about a mile before Leavenworth. John followed, trying to keep an inconspicuous distance behind the car. When the Pontiac veered up a steep road that cut through thick forest, John braked and waited. He turned off his headlights before stepping on the gas. During the slow crawl up the hill, he spotted a Bavarian-style cottage on their right. A sign in the front yard read *Alpin Haus – FOR RENT.* The driveway was empty.

John glanced ahead at the Pontiac and watched the brake lights go red. The car was coming to a stop at the top of the hill.

"Let's park by this house," John told Brandon, pointing at the cottage. "We can walk up the hill and see what's what."

Brandon pulled a couple of bottles of Mickey's malt liquor out of his backpack, and they downed the drinks within minutes for courage. They were walking along the driveway when they heard the Pontiac descending the hill.

"Hide!" John said. They crouched in the shadows of evergreens.

The Pontiac drove past, and John noticed the armless man was no longer in the passenger seat.

"This is a bad trip," Brandon declared. "Maybe we should just leave the old guy alone and find a campsite and chill."

"We chill after we see what he's up to," John said. "I don't think he's just some poor old guy. I think he's an asshole with a secret that's worth finding out." He tugged on Brandon's arm, leading him through trees toward the road.

A farm was at the top of the hill. A metal gate marked the beginning of a gravel drive that led to a battered, two-story farmhouse and a lopsided barn. The moon showed the walls of the two structures were bone-white and peeling. The forest stopped at the ancient wooden fence surrounding the property's dry, overgrown pasture. In the back of the farmhouse were enormous poplar trees. Half of them looked dead, their spiky, leafless branches reaching toward the moon.

The armless man emerged from the barn.

"Duck down," John whispered to Brandon, and they both kneeled by the front gate.

The armless man wore his prosthetics and his usual coveralls. He stared up at the moon as he staggered into the middle of the pasture. He moved as if he were drunk. Despite the darkness, John recognized a wild look in his bulging eyes. The man stopped and shook off one of his arms onto the grass. He then tucked his remaining arm under his armpit and removed that limb, too. He lifted his head even higher toward the sky, and he shrieked at the moon for what felt like forever.

"Oh, god," Brandon spoke in a cracking voice. "Let's get out of here."

Though frightened, John said, "Wait." He continued staring at the armless man because he imagined a different figure standing where the man stood. This person had a long, white head that curved like a crescent moon, and sharp branches where arms should have been.

Spindly Arms, John thought.

And all of a sudden the armless man turned his head and gazed in their direction as if he'd heard John's thoughts.

John was momentarily frozen with fear. "Okay," he whispered to Brandon, "let's go."

They sprinted down the hill to the cottage and scrambled into the Buick. As they drove back in the direction of the highway, Brandon asked, "You satisfied?" His tone of voice was guilting.

John had the idea that if he looked in his rearview mirror he'd see Spindly Arms standing in the center of the road, watching them flee. The thought was chilling but in a pleasant way. Tonight he'd found inspiration.

"I am satisfied," he told Brandon.

John shook off his memories of the mountain farm and turned on his windshield wipers. The October drizzle was starting again. His BMW entered the small strip of civilization that was Leavenworth, Washington. He drove past Bavarian-themed hotels that had flowers cascading from their carved balconies and a diner with a sign displaying a Fraülein picnicking beside a mountain stream. Within minutes, he reached the heart of the town, which could have been a quaint village nestled among the Alps. Except when you looked around closely enough you noticed the gas station, the ice cream franchise, the Starbucks. The increasing rain dampened the charm and appeared to deter anyone from being on the streets. John watched a lone pack of teenagers roam in the direction of the gas station, probably hoping to somehow obtain alcohol from the mini-mart. John could only guess how boring it would be growing up in this tiny mountain town that was so far from a major city. It was tedious enough coming of age in Glimmer Lake.

He stopped at the gas station to fill up his tank and buy a phone charger. The clerk inside the mini-mart looked half-conscious and not much older than the teenagers who now wandered along the store's aisles. While paying for the gas, John asked him where the chargers were, and the clerk shrugged his shoulders and said, "We're out."

Irked, John didn't bother with a thank you. He got back into the BMW and continued a couple of blocks east on 2 until he saw a sign blinking the words *Wilkommen – VACANCY.* He pulled into the parking lot of The Zugspitze Inn, a multi-storied motel with a pitched roof and paintings of skis and sleds above the doors to the rooms.

While checking in, John asked the clerk if there was some-where other than the gas station where he could buy a charger.

The clerk—a skinny, seventy-something man whose cow-boy hat and turquoise necklace contrasted with the motel's Ger-man theme—squinted at the cuckoo clock on the wall and said, "It's after 9, and this is our off-season, so there's not much open. You could try Gunther's Sundries. They've got just about every-thing there. They're on the corner of Front and 9th."

John hurried into his first-floor room to use the bathroom, and then he walked quickly through the rain to the town's com-mercial center. He needed both a charger and something to eat. His last meal was lunch, and he felt faint.

Leavenworth's core consisted mostly of hotels, restaurants, and retail stores. John guessed Brandon lived on the outskirts, maybe in one of those small, cabin-like houses they used to see near the river when they'd go inner tubing in the summer. He had no idea where he should start asking about Brandon. He didn't think phone books even existed anymore. And if Brandon had managed to evade Internet search engines, surely he wouldn't be in the white pages.

Gunther's Sundries offered plenty of Halloween- and Bavarian-themed tchotchkes, ranging from black cat figurines to apple dolls to beer steins with Leavenworth scenery on them, but the grandmotherly clerk looked befuddled when John asked about phone chargers.

"You might be able to find one of those at Safeway," she said. "You'll have to drive down 2 a bit to get to the store."

"Thanks," John said, sounding less than grateful. He considered mentioning the name Brandon Laurent to her, but he doubted she'd have any useful information. Instead, he glanced around the shop in search of some kind of weapon. He reminded himself that Brandon could have turned into a drastically different—and perhaps even violent—person over the past 25 years. John noticed a Swiss army knife, and in the corner of the store was a bucket of baseball bats and hockey sticks.

But how likely was it he'd use anything? He'd never been in a fistfight in his life—well, except for the time he beat up Brandon in high school.

All he bought was an umbrella.

He continued along Front Street until he spotted what looked like a beer garden. Awnings with hanging orange lanterns protected the few diners from the rain. John stepped to a shack-like structure where he ordered a pretzel, a bratwurst, and a pilsner. He took one of the sheltered tables and tore into the pretzel. While sipping his beer, he noticed two people sit at the table next to his. One person was a girl who could have been in high school or college, and the other was a man who must have been her boyfriend. The girl immediately gazed downwards at her large smartphone, and the device cast a blue light on her pretty face and black, pixie cut. Her boyfriend looked like he was in his mid-twenties. He also had dark hair and was sulky-seeming and handsome in an Ashton Kutcher kind of way. The girl began tapping away on her phone, and then she looked at John and smiled.

John managed a grin in return.

The girl tapped again, and then her eyes became round and her lips parted. "They named the Spindly creator!" she told her boyfriend.

John almost dropped his glass. He set it on the table. He must have appeared startled because the girl turned to him and asked, "Have you heard about these stories?"

"Sure," John said, trying to sound nonchalant. He hated how Spindly Arms had become a craze for the younger generation.

"They finally put the author's name on the original post. Everyone's been wondering who wrote it." The girl glanced down at the phone's screen. "John Larsen," she read.

John felt beads of sweat forming on his temple. He forced a shrug. "Never heard of him."

The girl tapped on her device once again and smiled. "He's a character in the latest post, too." She read aloud, "'In which John Larsen tries to kill Spindly Arms on his mountain farm.'"

"I don't read that stuff," John blurted, rising from the table. He nearly knocked over his stool. "Garbage for the brain."

The boyfriend gave him a skeptical look.

John had eaten only half his sausage. He didn't bother clearing his plate because both his hands were trembling. He nodded at the couple and hurried out of the beer garden.

He avoided the light of the ornate lamps that lined Front Street and crossed the road to a dark park. Standing in the shadow of his umbrella, he glanced around at the mostly empty commercial district, expecting to see his ex-friend leering at him from some corner. Brandon must have posted that story about him going to the farm. John had never told anyone except for Vivian about the time he and Brandon had followed the armless man. But how could Brandon know he was up here? Could that have been Brandon in the truck in Glimmer Lake? John had checked for the truck on his drive into the mountains, but the largest vehicle he'd seen behind him was a Jeep.

John suddenly wanted so much to speak to Vivian and tell her about where he was and what he'd discovered while in the beer garden. He searched for a payphone, but there was none. He figured he could call her from the phone in his room. He was about to return to the motel when he noticed that Gunther's Sundries was still open.

He went inside and bought the knife.

"Brandon Laurent?" the clerk of The Zugspitze Inn asked, scowling. "Never heard of him. And I've lived here since '61—a year before they turned Leavenworth into a theme town."

"He's an artist," John said. "He paints pictures of this guy with a head shaped like a moon and tree branches for arms."

"Now wait," the clerk said, removing his cowboy hat and scratching his wispy white hair. "I saw something about that moon face character in the news today. Someone dressed up like him and murdered a Seattle woman, right?"

John didn't want to somehow lead the man to the *Bloody Bitz* website and have him realize one of the Inn's guests was the one who wrote the original Spindly Arms story. He told the man, "No, I think we're talking about two different things. Thanks anyway."

Leaving the office, John had the thought he could drive to the farm—if he could remember where it was. But he wouldn't be so stupid. He'd get out of Leavenworth first thing in the morning and head back to Seattle. Before the drive, he'd stop at Safeway and find a charger for his phone. He could call Detective Garcia as soon as he powered up his phone and accessed the man's number. He'd reveal that Brandon had most likely been following him.

Knowing he'd never be able to sleep in his current state of anxiety, John returned on foot to the mini-mart a couple of blocks away and bought a six-pack of beer. He checked the sidewalks along Highway 2 and the motel parking lot for someone watching him, but he didn't see anyone. He went inside his room, which had windows with views of the parking lot. He locked the door and drew the curtains.

John picked up the room's phone and dialed Vivian's number. The call went to voicemail. He didn't want to try to explain all that had happened tonight in a message. "It's me," he said. "Just wanted to say goodnight, and that my phone's dead. I'm calling from a landline. I'll call you first thing tomorrow. Love you."

He collapsed in the chair that was between the window and the queen-sized bed. He opened a beer and stared at the painting on the nearby wall. The paint-by-numbers work depicted a windswept lake beneath a cluster of snow-glazed mountains. The sky was twilight violet. Near the shore sat a small, dark log cabin with a smoking chimney.

John wondered what could have made Brandon go so crazy. Sure, Brandon had always been a little weird in high school, oftentimes spacy-eyed and talking about unusual things like how crows followed him home from school and how U.S. troops in the Gulf War discovered that Saddam Hussein possessed a crashed UFO. During the fall of senior year, some jocks started calling Brandon "Fag Laurent" since he'd gone to a Gus Van Sant movie with the only openly gay student in their class of 220 students. John knew Brandon had hung out with Devon because he felt sorry for him and he was intrigued by outsiders. But the verbal abuse continued for at least a month. And then in November—not long after John's story appeared in the *Glimmer Lake Gazette*—Brandon's dad died of a gunshot wound in a hunting accident. Vivian had encouraged John to spend more time with Brandon because he was suffering from the loss of his father and the homophobic slurs, but John probably didn't hang with his friend enough. He was too busy writing short stories he thought he'd publish in magazines across America.

Maybe Brandon's decline started in '93 or '94, after John had stopped talking to him. While John attended classes at the UW, Brandon supposedly wandered the streets of downtown Seattle, homeless and crazed.

But killing Maya? John still didn't believe Brandon would do that.

John's brain started feeling soggy while he drank his second beer. He was exhausted and not thinking clearly. He glanced at the digital clock on his nightstand. It wasn't even 10:30. When he and Brandon used to camp outside Leavenworth they'd be up until 2 or 3 in the morning. But that was when John could down 40-ouncers of beer and smoke more than the occasional joint.

Now he was a 44-year-old man.

He stumbled toward the bathroom. Before urinating, he glanced in the mirror. His hair looked grayer than ever, and he had dark pouches beneath his eyes. "It's all downhill from here," he told himself.

He soon crouched by the bookshelf near the foot of his bed, sipping beer and swaying while he perused the selection. He picked up a serial killer thriller set in Berlin and immediately placed it back on the shelf. He took a copy of Goethe's *The Sorrows of Young Werther,* which he'd read as part of an English class in college, and lay on the bed. He'd finished only a couple of the main character's letters to a friend named Wilhelm when he fell asleep. He dreamt that it wasn't an 18th-century German penning the passionate letters. Spindly Arms was scratching them out in blood, and they were all meant for John.

Sssccccrrrriiiittttsssscccchhhh.

John's eyes shot open.

Ssssccccrrrriiiittttsssscccchhhh.

The sound came from outside his room. Someone scraped something along the wall and across his door. Maybe a pipe, or something sharper.

The digital clock showed it was 12:42 A.M. John crept from the bed to the window. He was going to part the curtains just enough so he could peek outside.

BANG. BANG. BANG. BANG.

John jumped back from the window, his heart slamming against his chest. Who had pounded on his door?

He tiptoed to the door and looked into the peephole. Again, he saw no one.

"Who's there?" he called.

Nobody responded.

John was about to try to call the motel's office when he heard the screech of a car's tires. Someone sped out of the parking lot. John ran to his window and yanked open a curtain. He spotted the taillights of a car racing west on Highway 2, but he couldn't tell what kind of vehicle it was.

And something was burning on his windshield.

"Shit!" He opened his door and quickly glanced to the left and right outside to make sure no one waited for him. The walkway that ran beside the rooms was empty. An external stairway near his room led to the second floor. As he hastened toward his car, he craned his neck to check if someone might be hiding on the stairs. He seemed to be alone.

The burning object appeared to be some kind of pamphlet. He ran to a small tree near the edge of the parking lot and broke off a limb. Using it as a poker, he dragged the pamphlet off his windshield and stomped on it. About a quarter of it remained intact, and he was able to read a title in the light of the smoldering paper: *Evergroan.*

John gasped. This was the issue in which "Spindly Arms" had appeared.

A shadow passed over the burnt magazine, and John looked up at the rain clouds drifting past the moon. He felt a few drops on his head.

When he turned back toward his room he saw a masculine figure standing in the doorway next to his.

The man wore a yellow moon mask, a black sweatshirt, and cargo pants. A tree branch protruded from one sleeve of his sweatshirt. Sticking out of the other sleeve was a large carving knife.

John couldn't breathe. He realized he'd left his newly purchased Swiss army knife in his room. He finally managed to ask, "Brandon?"

The man stayed silent and continued to stare. John shouted, "Help! Someone help!"

The lights in all the rooms remained dark. Only three cars were in the parking lot, so John guessed only a few people were staying at the motel. The masked man remained in the doorway.

John plunged his hand into his pocket. He was grateful to feel his wallet and car keys. He hadn't taken them out before falling asleep. Fumbling with the keys, he glanced at the man. Whoever this person was slowly approached with the knife pointing at him.

Get in the car now! John told himself. He finally opened the door and fell into the driver seat. He turned the key in the ignition, watching the man looming over the hood. *You won't get me today,* John thought as he backed out of the parking space. He turned the front tires toward the street and slammed his foot against the gas pedal.

He was soon tearing down Highway 2 toward the commercial district. There had to be a police station among the hotels and restaurants.

He was about to turn left when he heard someone say, "Keep driving on 2."

John looked in the rearview mirror, his mouth gaping.

Another moon face stared at him from the shadows of the backseat. John also spotted the black silhouette of a carving knife. For a moment he believed the man from the motel had somehow teleported inside his car. But that was impossible, wasn't it?

"You should listen to Spindly," the stranger spoke in a raspy voice, pressing one side of the cold knife against John's cheek. The clouds above suddenly released a hammering rain against the windshield, and John felt a burst of warmth in his crotch as he pissed his pants.

The BMW was outside Leavenworth, traveling west between forested slopes.

"Where are we going?" John asked.

"You know where." That voice wasn't Brandon's. "Where does Spindly live?"

John thought of another sentence he'd written so many years ago: *Satiated, he retracted his wood fingers from the dead flesh and began the trek back to his farm.*

"I don't remember how to get to the farm," John spoke in a brittle voice. "I don't even know if it's still there."

"Take the next exit."

John did and drove across a mossy bridge arching over the freeway.

"Go right," his passenger said, "and then turn left and drive up the hill."

The road leading to the farm was similar to the one in John's memories, except the trees on either side were leafier and the colors of autumn. The rain lessened because of the overhanging forest. John glimpsed the Alpin Haus cottage on the right. The cottage was unlit, just like on that summer night he'd driven up here with Brandon. John guessed there'd be nobody inside who could help him.

"Don't slow down."

John felt the knife against his cheek again. It slid down toward his jaw.

Was this going to be it? Death in his early forties, when he was struggling to grow a relationship and had an uninspiring job? John wasn't even sure if he believed in God. He'd wanted to explore his spirituality, but he figured that journey would come in his fifties, when he felt more settled and wiser than this, and at least somewhat comfortable with middle age.

"Park in front of the gate."

John brought the car onto the top of the hill, where the rain once again splattered the windshield. He saw the thick bars of the metal gate ahead. Somehow the rickety wooden fence had remained standing on either side of the gate for all these years. The rain was too heavy and the night too dark for John to see the farmhouse or barn. He could only see where the gravel road vanished into blackness past the gate.

John refused to enter that blackness. He wasn't going to allow his life to end here, on this nightmare property. The universe could give him metastatic cancer or nudge him into a fatal car pile-up on his commute to work, but he drew the line at death at the hands of someone dressed like a horror fiction character he'd created in high school. He aimed his car for the center of the gate and pushed the sole of his foot squarely against the gas pedal.

"Slow down!" the man in the backseat said. "You're going to-"

Just before reaching the gate, John turned the wheel sharply to the left.

Please let this work.

The tires skidded in the rain, and the right side of the BMW careened toward the gate. John held onto the steering wheel tightly.

Metal slammed against metal and the windows on the right side of the car shattered. John heard his backseat passenger hit something with a groan.

When the car settled, the man seemed to be at least dazed if not unconscious. John didn't look closely. He shot out of the driver side of the car into the rain. His neck was sore from jerking during the impact, but otherwise, he felt strong enough. He sprinted away from the vehicle and descended the road he'd just driven up. He figured if he ran fast enough he could reach Highway 2 in 10 minutes and try waving down help.

He was nearly at the Alpin Haus when he saw the yellow headlights. He had the idea that the armless man sat in the car with his white-haired friend at the wheel, but he dismissed the ludicrous thought.

The vehicle pulled into the driveway of the Alpin Haus. John figured whoever was in the car had rented the cottage. He was relieved to see a young woman climb out of the passenger side.

It was the girl from the beer garden.

Her boyfriend opened the driver-side door.

John ran toward the couple. They both looked stunned by his presence.

"Please call the police," John told them. He motioned in the direction of the farm. "There's a crazy guy up there with a knife. I think he wants to kill me. He'll be coming down here for me soon."

The girl's look of surprise became a look of fear. Her boyfriend seemed calmer.

"My phone's in the car," the boyfriend said. He returned to the driver seat.

John glanced up the hill. He couldn't see anyone, but the dark and the rain affected his vision. He started toward the cottage. "Can we go inside? It'll be safer there."

"Oh, I don't know," the girl said, sounding confused.

John looked at the cottage, and he noticed something he hadn't seen while driving up the hill.

While the front of the cottage was intact, the sloping roof and at least one sidewall were burnt black. The building had been on fire sometime in the past.

John glanced at the girl again, his brow furrowed. "You're not staying here?" he asked. The girl had been so chatty with him about Spindly Arms in the beer garden, but now she was speechless. She looked from him to the interior of the car.

What was her boyfriend doing? An icy knot climbed John's spine as he recalled there'd been more than one person outside his motel room tonight. Someone had sped out of the parking lot before the first masked man revealed himself.

John knew he wasn't safe with these people. He started past the car toward the road, but the boyfriend jumped up from his seat and grabbed John by the arm.

"Just calm down, mister," the young man said, staring him in the eyes.

John shoved him, but the man didn't release John's arm. John told him, "Don't tell me to fucking-"

He felt a stinging pain in his neck, and he noticed the girl standing next to him. Clutching a syringe, she stepped back toward the car with an apologetic look on her face.

"What the-?"

"Open the back door," the boyfriend told the girl.

"What?" she asked.

"Open the back door!"

John felt his limbs go limp, and he couldn't stand. The boyfriend held him up. John looked at the Alpin Haus over the boyfriend's shoulder. The image of the half-burnt cottage began to spin in his head.

The boyfriend dragged John to the car and laid his body on the backseat. The couple peered in at him and then disappeared in the black, wet night. The door closed. John shut his eyes. He heard raindrops on the roof of the car, then two men's voices.

The door opened again, and John barely felt someone climb on top of his body. He managed to crack open his eyes, and terror ignited somewhere deep inside him, beneath all the layers of numbness.

The man with the moon mask—or was it Spindly Arms himself?—stared down at John with that long, yellow face. He held a machete before John's eyes and said, "The past finally caught up with you, John Larsen."

VIVIAN

After reading John's text about spending the night at his niece's, Vivian decided to go for a run. She was relieved he wouldn't be home tonight. They could both benefit from some space after the last few stressful days. Maya's murder and that damn Spindly Arms post had strained their relationship.

The rain was merely a mist when Vivian jogged through the wealthy Madison Park neighborhood, not too far from John's house. She always enjoyed running along one particular street with old mansions overlooking Lake Washington. The street seemed like a world away from the mediocre, middle-class cul-de-sac where she'd grown up in Glimmer Lake. On this Friday evening, the street was especially dark. Few of the homes had lights on inside, and one of the two streetlamps was out. The lake beyond the houses was black. Fallen leaves crunched beneath Vivian's sneakers. She increased her pace to reach a better-lit road.

John had suggested she not run at night. "Someone could hit you, and who knows who's out on the streets after dark," he warned. Vivian understood he was just being protective. He didn't want harm coming to her as it had come to his wife. But Vivian loved the freedom she felt on her night runs, and freedom was what she'd asked of John on one of the earliest dates they had after the high school reunion.

"My parents wanted me in a cage when I was growing up," she told him. "The good, smart, successful girl cage. And my ex-husband also tried to trap me. Ralph got to be the big-time optometrist with multiple clinics, and I got stuck being the stay-at-home mom taking care of our big beige house in Lynnwood. I've promised myself there will be no more cages."

"Does that mean you never want to get married again?" John asked, looking troubled.

Vivian squeezed his hand. "I'm not saying that. I want room to be my own person, and I don't want guilt. I overdosed on guilt during the first half of my life."

Vivian felt awkward sharing that with the man she'd cheated on in high school. But she hoped to strengthen their relationship with truth and her desire to be with him again. Guilt and impossible expectations were the foundation of her marriage to Ralph.

Vivian stopped running at the bottom of the hill that led to John's house. While walking the rest of the way, she evened out her breathing, as those self-help books she'd recently been reading instructed. She repeated in her head, *I want room to be my own person, and I don't want guilt. I want room to be my own person, and I don't want-*

A man stood beneath the light that illuminated John's front doorstep, his hand on the doorbell. He wore a tan leather jacket, and he had slicked-back blond hair and a mustache. He couldn't have been much older than 30. He turned away from the door and stared at Vivian.

Vivian paused at the beginning of the brick path that curved to the doorstep, her heartbeat quickening. After all, Maya's murderer was still at large. And what kind of a man went around ringing doorbells on a wet October night? She glanced at the nearby houses to see if any of the neighbors happened to be outside.

It was just her and this stranger in the mist.

"Can I help you?" she asked in a brusque, louder-than-usual voice, hoping the young techie couple in the townhouse next door might hear her and glance out a window.

"I'm looking for John Larsen," the man said. "My name's Philip. I'm Maya Mathers's boyfriend."

"Oh, my god," Vivian said, approaching the man. As she neared, she noticed his eyes were red and swollen. She reached out and pressed his hand with both of hers. "I'm so sorry about Maya. I went to high school with her, like John." Vivian thought she smelled liquor on Philip's breath.

"I know John went to high school with Maya. He's the one that wrote that fucked-up story."

Vivian released his hand.

Philip shook his head. "The thing I don't get is why he'd add his name to the post after Maya was-" His voice cracked, and he placed his hand over his eyes as if he were holding in tears. "That's just sick."

"John's name is on the post?" Vivian asked, frowning.

"He wrote the goddamn story, didn't he?"

The mist was turning to rain. Vivian said, "John wrote that story over 25 years ago when we were in high school. He didn't know anything about the *Bloody Bitz* website until...everything happened." She stepped past Philip and unlocked the front door. "Listen, John's not here right now. I could have him call you."

"No," Philip said. "I'd like to wait inside until he gets home if that's all right with you."

Vivian glanced over her shoulder at him. She didn't want to let this drunk, disgruntled man in the house. "I'm sorry, Philip, but-"

"John should be sorry," he snapped. "He's the one who wrote that story, and I want an explanation from him. The police aren't telling me shit."

Vivian turned toward Philip. She reached behind her back and opened the door a crack. She tried to sound as calm as possible when she said, "Please believe me when I say he didn't post that story, and he had nothing to do with Maya's death."

"I won't believe anything until I talk to him!"

Vivian quickly stepped backward into the house and shut the door. She turned the lock.

Philip's fists sounded on the other side.

"Someone knows the truth!" he shouted. "And I'll bet John knows more than you think!"

"Tell me your number and I'll have him phone you," Vivian pleaded.

Philip didn't respond. When Vivian looked through the door's peephole, she saw only the lit doorstep and the falling rain beyond.

She was relieved to be safe inside the house, but she was stunned by everything Philip had told her. She needed to reach John. She bounded up the staircase to retrieve her cell phone from the bedroom. On the landing, she glanced through one of the windowpanes. She saw Philip standing in the middle of the brick path in front of the house. She felt a chill when she realized he was staring up at her.

"I blame John until he gives me a reason not to!" Philip shouted. He continued through the rain to the sidewalk and disappeared from Vivian's view.

Vivian inhaled and exhaled deeply, trying to calm herself. She went into the bedroom and picked her phone up off the night table. The screen showed the time was 7:01. John should be able to take her call. She dialed his number and listened to the repeated ringing. She suddenly felt completely selfish for wanting space between them. Poor John must be suffering from this shit storm swirling around his story. And now someone had added his name to the post.

She finally reached his voicemail.

"John, it's me. Please call me back right away. Something's come up—something important I need to tell you about."

She then immediately texted him: *Call me ASAP OK? ?*

She considered showering to help her relax, but she was obsessing about what was on that horrible website now. She headed into John's den.

His computer screen soon displayed the *Bloody Bitz* site. Vivian stared at the landing page, which announced to readers:

NEW SPINDLY ARMS POST!

"Blood Crop"

In which John Larsen tries to kill Spindly Arms on his mountain farm

"What the hell?" Vivian whispered, scanning the post. She couldn't believe John had somehow become a character in the Spindly Arms stories. She looked at a list of "Post Topics" in the right margin of the screen and found "Spindly Arms" below the topics "Scarification" and "Sorcerers."

She clicked on "Spindly Arms" and discovered there were now 38 posts under that topic. She was appalled by how viral

Spindly Arms had become. She went to the first post. "By John Larsen" was indeed beneath the story's title.

Glancing at the comments, she noticed John's address and the text "Author lives here!" The source of the comment was someone who used the pseudonym PastHitsHard.

Vivian looked up from the screen at the rain-splattered window. She shuddered at the realization that the comment was probably how Philip had located John's house. John had been doxxed. Anyone could find this address just by visiting *Bloody Bitz*.

Looking back at the screen, she found her way to the contact page. The page merely informed readers, "The cooks want to hear from YOU," and included an email address.

Vivian quickly typed an email demanding the editor remove John's address and name from the website. She added, "It's irresponsible of you to jeopardize someone's safety like this."

She immediately received a response from donotreply@ bloodybitz.com:

> *Dear Submitter,*
>
> *Thank you for your ghoulishly delicious fiction. We'll serve it up to the public as soon as we can. If we find it indigestible for any reason, we'll hunt you down.*
>
> *– The Red-Mouthed Editors*

"Shit!" Vivian said, smacking the palms of her hands against John's desk. She wished she hadn't been so dismissive of Detective Garcia. She hadn't kept his contact information.

She tried calling John again, but she reached his voicemail a second time. "John, where are you? You need to call me. Your name is showing up all over that *Bloody Bitz* website."

She scrolled through past text messages to her contacts, seeking the message she'd sent to congratulate John's niece, Heather, on getting her JD from Seattle University. Finding the message, Vivian dialed Heather's number.

Nobody picked up.

"Hi, Heather," she said. "This is Vivian, your uncle's girl-friend. Would you please have him call me as soon as he can? It's an emergency."

She clicked the back button on the Internet browser and returned to John's original Spindly Arms story. She gazed at the illustration of Spindly Arms that Brandon may or may not have drawn. The man with the moon face stood on a precipice, staring down at a distant cluster of houses.

Vivian had been so proud of John for getting that story published—not once, but twice. And the second time in the *Glimmer Lake Gazette*. The story didn't scare her. It was the man who inspired Spindly Arms that made her forearms break out in little bumps. She didn't even like thinking about him now. His bug eyes, his purplish lips, his ratty shirt with the sweat-stained armpits. She'd caught him glaring at her on that first day she'd seen him when she was accompanying John on his paper route. The words "bad energy" came to mind.

The raindrops were now hitting the windowpane hard enough to sound like pebbles. Vivian wanted to take a shower, but she thought she should first double-check that all the house's doors were locked and the windows closed. She kept thinking about how John's address was available to the public on *Bloody Bitz*. She wondered if she should have pushed John harder on getting a dog—a big one—and decided that after her shower she'd head to her apartment for the night.

Clutching her phone, she went downstairs, where the only lit room was the kitchen. She considered turning on some other lights, but she didn't want to encourage Philip to return to the front door for any reason. She entered the dim living room and went to the windowed doors that opened onto the small backyard. They were secure.

Staring through one of the doors into the darkness, she imagined the armless man crouched in the shadows of the high hedge that divided John's house from the neighbors', watching her with those big, loathing eyes.

Stop creeping yourself out, she told herself. She checked the living room windows, making sure they were all locked. "Armless man" really was kind of a heartless moniker. She, John, and Brandon didn't use his real name. She couldn't remember that name, though Brandon had mentioned it to her once. The trio of friends focused only on what made him different from them. Just like those white assholes who'd teased her for being Asian when she was a kid.

Heading into the kitchen, Vivian recalled when she'd run into the armless man's wife in a line at the Glimmer Lake Grocery Mart, months before John's story came out. Surely, that woman had known the armless man's good qualities. The armless man's wife was wearing her white nurse's uniform, and she had three small children with her—two wide-eyed boys clinging to her thick but sculpted legs, and a sweet-faced baby sitting among the many groceries in her cart. The kids all had shocks of black hair. The woman had dark hair, too, and she was pretty enough to be a model if people had employed plus-sized models back then.

The woman turned to Vivian with puffy, tired eyes. "You look familiar," she said in a melodic voice. "You're with that boy who delivers our paper, aren't you?"

"John," Vivian said with a polite smile. "Your baby's a cutie."

The woman smiled. "That's Ben," she said. "I suppose he's my baby now. He's my husband's grandson. We just inherited him and the twins from my stepdaughter." She pressed two fingers against the crook of her arm. "She's got a heroin problem, wouldn't you know." Shaking her head, she added, "It seems to be the trendy drug these days."

Vivian blushed. She didn't know what to say.

"I'm not sure how we're going to raise them in our tiny house," the woman said with a frown. "But I'm a bit of a magician, so I'll make it work. Wait at least 10 years before you have a baby, okay?"

Vivian felt herself go red again and nodded awkwardly. She imagined how much her prudish mother would disapprove of the conversation if she were there. "You'll have more fun that way," the woman said, placing her items on the grocery conveyor belt. "Fun is undervalued. I know my husband doesn't value it enough."

Where were that woman and her family now? The armless man must be in his seventies. That woman couldn't be much older than 60. But her looks were probably gone, and her "inherited" children already around 30. Vivian thought of how John was always complaining that time speeds up the older you get.

And then the unpleasant name PastHitsHard entered Vivian's head. PastHitsHard, the creep who displayed John's address in a comment field on *Bloody Bitz*.

Vivian crossed the kitchen to the door that led to the basement. She opened the door and flipped the light switch, illuminating the basement. She slowly descended the stairs.

"Shit," she whispered.

She gaped at the one-pane rectangular window above the washing machine. The corner of the glass was broken. John's lawn mower had sent a small rock flying through the window some weeks ago. John kept talking about how he was going to replace the pane. Vivian thought that even if someone cleared out the rest of the glass, the window frame was too narrow for most people to fit through. Still, she shivered at the idea of someone squeezing through the broken window and slinking up the basement stairs.

So lock the basement door. Vivian reminded herself that John kept a key to that door on top of the refrigerator.

She glanced around the finished portion of the basement, a small space that included the washing machine, the dryer, a sink, and dozens of cardboard boxes. Vivian was sure many of John's dead wife's belongings filled those boxes, but she'd never dared ask him. She tried to avoid making John think about the past tragedy of Karin's drowning, and whenever John spoke of his wife Vivian felt envious of the woman who'd been a part of some of the happiest years of his life. Vivian was feeling increasingly antsy being down here, and she could hear the rain falling in the muddy backyard. She didn't want to peek inside the other, larger area of the basement, which was earthen with a ceiling of crisscrossing pipes.

Vivian hurried back up the stairs and immediately locked the door.

The house was beginning to feel too large without John there. Vivian grimaced when she thought of all those days and nights she'd wandered through the Lynnwood house while Ralph was away at one of his clinics. He'd asked her, "Why are you always talking about filling up your days with a job when you've got this incredible house most of the American workforce would dream about?" At least she had Maggie to keep her company in that house much of the time, and she never felt afraid, like she did tonight.

She checked her phone. Neither John nor his niece had tried to reach her.

The doors are all locked and John will call you soon. Vivian headed back upstairs, finally ready for her shower. She turned up her phone's ringer as much as possible and set the phone on the stretch of the bathroom counter that was within reach of the shower. While bathing, she kept the shower door slightly open.

The steaming hot water soothed her as it beat against the back of her neck. She longed for John, wishing he could be here with her, his arms wrapped tightly around her naked waist. During those moments when their bodies were so close together, Vivian thought what a miracle it was they'd reunited after that long-ago breakup and two-plus decades apart. Surely, that was true magnetism.

And now John was up in Edmonds. He could have driven home in just half an hour. Vivian realized that in the year they'd been dating, she'd been the only one who'd asked for nights away, when she escaped to her apartment for solitude. Until tonight, John had never requested any distance between them.

John had created a gulf between them once, though—in high school, after the publication of his "Spindly Arms" story. It wasn't a physical distance, but a mental and emotional one as John spent more time writing. As John had explained, he was a 17-year-old whose fiction had appeared in a town's newspaper. He'd written only a couple of short stories before, and those were assignments for his AP English class. What if he wrote as much as possible during his senior year? Surely, more newspapers and magazines would publish his work. Maybe a publisher would take on a novel of his before he graduated from college. At first, Vivian understood. But the distance became a problem for her after her parents kicked her out of her house.

She'd told them she was going to spend a Saturday night at her friend Lisa's house. Instead, she went camping near some hot springs in the Cascades with John and Brandon. She would have gone both Friday and Saturday nights, but John had wanted to write Friday evening. When John dropped her off at the mouth of her cul-de-sac, he even asked that she not call him later because he wanted to focus on his story-in-progress before returning to school on Monday. Vivian tried to shake off her hurt as she ran up the walkway to her house and unlocked the front door. The door wouldn't open because the chain was on the inside. Not wanting to disturb her parents, she went around the side of the house to access the kitchen door.

Vivian almost screamed when a small figure stepped out from behind a bush.

It was her mother, glaring and dressed in a black sweater and skirt. The woman had a dark aura of disappointment.

"You weren't at Lisa's," her mother said. She had a Chinese accent even though she'd moved to the States from Hong Kong when she was 20.

"I was at Lisa's," Vivian lied.

Her mother slapped her. "I talked to Lisa's mother. You were with the boy."

Vivian touched her stinging cheek. She hated how her mother always called John "the boy," never acknowledging that he was her boyfriend.

"Mom, I'm almost 18, which means I'm almost an adult."

Shaking her head, her mother said, "You want to run around on your own like a street tramp? Is that the kind of adult you want to be? Go ahead and do that. But don't bring your shame back here for a week." She turned away from her daughter and headed into the kitchen. Vivian tried to follow her, but the door slammed shut in her face.

"Mom," Vivian pleaded through the door.

Her mother responded, "You don't have it so hard. Back in China, if I did what you've done, my mother never would have let me come home."

Vivian started the mile walk to John's, tears wetting her cheeks. Partway, she remembered his request that she not disturb him tonight. She wouldn't be able to bear John being annoyed by her presence. She turned up the hill where Brandon lived. When she reached his house, she found he was home alone. Surprisingly, his eyes were also bloodshot from crying.

"What is it?" she asked.

"My dad," he said. "He's dead. He was hunting. Someone shot him by accident."

Vivian embraced him, and he held her tightly. She relished the hug even though they were both in so much pain.

"My mom's not here," he said. "She's with...his body. Will you stay with me?"

"Of course, I'll stay," she said.

DING. DING. DING.

Vivian's cell phone sounded on the bathroom counter. It had to be John finally texting her back. She hurried out of the shower and snatched up the phone. She frowned at the message from John's niece:

> *Uncle J's not with me. I didn't see him today. I'm about to get on a plane for a bachelorette trip to LA. I texted Uncle J telling him to call you right away. Let me know if I can do anything else to help.*

Vivian gripped the phone tightly. Where was John? He'd lied to her about where he went. Distressed, she dried herself and left the bathroom to put on jeans and a sweater. She thought of Brandon hugging her again, and she recalled what John had said earlier this week: "It's like you don't think Brandon is worthy of any blame. He fucked up, Vivian."

After dressing, Vivian sat on the edge of the bed, trying to center herself. She practiced the circular breathing described in her self-help books, and she was holding her breath when she heard the sound of breaking glass downstairs.

Someone was inside the house. Vivian inhaled sharply as adrenaline surged.

More glass shattered. Vivian thought the sound came from the living room. She pictured someone punching through one of the windowed doors and letting himself inside. Could it be Maya's boyfriend, Philip? She grabbed her phone off the night table and dialed 9-1-1.

"What's your emergency?" a female dispatcher asked.

"Someone's broken into my house," Vivian said, rattling off John's address in a shaky voice. "Please hurry."

"Where's that person now?" the dispatcher asked.

"He's downstairs. I'm upstairs. I don't know if he knows I'm here."

"Ma'am, please stay on the line while I get someone to come over there."

Vivian quietly descended the steps to the landing and peeked down at the foyer. She saw a beam of light rove across one wall and illuminate a mirror. Whoever was in the house must have had a flashlight.

Then there was a second beam, and a burst of light as if someone had taken a photograph.

"Are you still there, ma'am?" the dispatcher asked.

Vivian crept back up the stairs. She glanced around, searching for something she could use as a weapon. She thought of the pronged fire poker, but that was next to the fireplace downstairs. Whoever had broken in could have already picked it up. "I'm here, she said. "I think there's more than one person in the house."

"Have you locked yourself into a room, ma'am?"

"None of the upstairs doors have locks on them," Vivian said, sounding hopeless. She heard a male voice downstairs.

"Make it fast," the man told someone. "He could come back at any time."

The dispatcher spoke again: "Is there somewhere you can hide until the police get there?"

"I-" Vivian froze when she heard footsteps coming up the stairs. There was more than one person.

She ducked inside John's den and hid behind the door. A lamp on John's desk lit the room.

"Ma'am," the dispatcher said. "Are you still with me?"

"I can't talk anymore," Vivian whispered. "Please just send the police here right away." She hung up the phone and slipped it into her pants pocket. She spotted a pair of scissors in a mug beside John's computer. She came out from behind the door and grabbed them, and then she returned to her hiding place.

The footsteps sounded like they were getting closer. Vivian's breath quickened. She gripped the scissors tightly.

Someone entered the room and walked past Vivian's hiding place. He approached John's computer. Vivian could only see his back. He wore a black trench coat and a pale blue plastic mask that was pointed at the top.

Still wedged between the open door and the wall, Vivian turned her body so she could face him if he came at her. Her hip bumped against the doorknob, making a metallic rattle. *Stupid,* she cursed herself.

The figure turned around and stared at Vivian through the eyes of a crescent moon-shaped mask. Sparkly black beads bordered the eyeholes.

"Get out of here!" Vivian screamed despite her terror. She charged toward the figure with the scissors raised above her head.

"Holy shit!" the intruder said.

Except it wasn't a man's voice. It was a boy's voice. He stepped away from the computer, avoiding Vivian.

Vivian paused, and then she lowered the scissors.

"Get away from her, Trent," a girl said. "She's crazy."

Vivian turned toward the doorway and saw four teenagers—two boys and two girls—gazing back at her with open mouths. One of the boys wore coveralls and a button with a smiling moon face on it, and both girls had sticks poking out of the hair they'd tied atop their heads. Vivian guessed they couldn't be older than 16.

"Who the hell are you?" she asked. She felt a tight knot in her stomach.

"That's John Larsen's girlfriend," one of the girls whispered, sounding dazzled.

"Answer me!" Vivian yelled. "The police are on their way. You kids are going to be in a shitload of trouble."

"We're just Spindly Arms fans," the second girl said. "We were out front taking pictures of the house. We found the address on *Bloody Bitz*. We didn't break in. The man with the messed-up face asked us if we wanted to come in."

"What man?" Vivian asked, forcing herself to breathe regularly and willing her heart to slow. Goosebumps covered her forearms.

"He should still be downstairs," the boy in the coveralls said. "He held the door open for us. He told us we could take a look inside before his friend John got home."

Vivian felt an icy tingling along the back of her neck. "He's downstairs now?"

She exhaled when the siren sounded down the street. *Oh, thank you.*

"Cops!" the masked teen said. "Let's go!" He brushed past Vivian on his way to join his friends. Vivian instinctively grabbed at his wrist, outrage tamping down her fear, but he wrenched it out of her grasp. One of the girls pulled a phone out of her coat pocket and aimed it at Vivian. The phone flashed as it took a picture. The pack of adolescents rushed along the hallway and down the stairs.

"Wait!" Vivian called, chasing after them. She wanted them to tell the police about whoever had let them inside, and she also wanted them to face consequences for invading her home.

She was almost at the bottom of the stairs when she paused.

A twenty-something man with a shaved head and sores covering his face stood by one of the windowed doors in the living room, gloved hands hooked into his belt loops. He gave her a sinister grin, and he crunched some broken glass under the sole of his boot. Vivian thought about running back upstairs and finding a new hiding place. Before she could retreat, the man followed the last of the teenagers out the door and into the shadows of the backyard.

Vivian clasped her hands together in front of her while speaking to the two brawny young policemen. Her hands wouldn't stop shaking. She described the teenagers and the man with the sores on his face and reported what the kids had said about him. The officers determined the man had broken a pane of one of the windowed doors and reached inside and turned the lock. Vivian also told them about her and John's connection to the recent Spindly Arms murder. She shared the name of the detective who'd spoken to her and John.

"We've gotten complaints about other kids running around dressed up like this Spindly Arms character," one of the policemen said. "Must be because Halloween's almost here. Where's John now?"

Vivian was about to tell them that her boyfriend seemed to have disappeared, but then she thought he could have tried calling or texting her in the last half hour. "He was going to spend the night at his niece's in Edmonds," she said. "Would you excuse me? I'm just going to check if he called me back." She realized she'd set her cell phone on one of the stairs when she went to open the front door for the policemen.

She felt encouraged when she saw she had a voicemail. She didn't recognize the number, though. The area code was 509—an Eastern Washington area code. Relief sank in as she listened to John's voice on the phone: "It's me. Just wanted to say good-night, and that my phone's dead. I'm calling from a landline. I'll call you first thing tomorrow. Love you."

Vivian turned to the policemen with a smile. "John left a message," she said. She realized she was beaming, and she tried to tone down her excitement. She didn't want to tell them about John's strange behavior tonight and draw suspicion to him in connection with the Spindly Arms case.

"Is he going to come down here?" one of the officers asked.

"Um, no," Vivian said. "He can't." She tried to think of an excuse for John.

"Is there someone else who can come spend the night with you?" the officer asked. "Or maybe you'd feel more comfortable staying at someone else's house? Any family in the area?"

Vivian thought of Maggie. Her 14-year-old daughter lived with Ralph in the house in Lynnwood. Maggie used to stay with Vivian in Columbia City as much as she stayed with her dad, but at the start of her teenage years, she seemed to develop an emotional allergy to her mom. Just last week Vivian had pressed her daughter about dropping out of the Halloween lip-syncing contest at her middle school, and Maggie snapped, "I don't fucking care about it!"

"You shouldn't drop out of commitments like that," Vivian replied.

"Why not? You did."

"Sweetie, we're not going to talk about this again. I know the divorce-"

"Dad said it wasn't a real divorce. You just quit him. Like when people give up something because they don't want to put the effort in anymore."

No, Vivian wouldn't be calling Maggie for company tonight.

"I have an apartment," she told the policemen. "I'd planned on spending the night there anyway."

The officers nodded, and one of them offered to stay with her in the house until she was ready to leave. Vivian thanked him and scrambled to assemble an overnight bag. Upstairs in the bedroom, she glanced out the window at the dark and empty street. She wondered if more Spindly Arms fans would skulk about in front of the house tonight, taking pictures while she slept in Columbia City. The idea made her shiver.

Around midnight, she lay in her bed, staring up at the ceiling. In addition to worrying about the home invasion, she kept thinking about that 509 area code John had called from. Why would John be in Eastern Washington? Was it possible his work had unexpectedly requested he visit a clinic east of the Cascades? He would normally tell her about a sudden change in schedule like that.

Vivian had attempted to call the number from John's house, but he hadn't answered. She reached for her cell phone and tried again even though it was late. No one picked up.

Vivian had finally nestled under her comforter and was on the verge of falling asleep when her phone sounded.

DING. DING. DING.

She was thrilled to see a text message from John:

> *Meet me at Glimmer Lake Bowl-O'-Rama at 4:30 tomorrow afternoon OK? I've got a surprise for you. Sorry I've been incommunicado. I've been superbusy. Can't text or call you before we meet because my phone's just about out of juice. X*

Vivian frowned at the odd message. Why did he send that when he'd called earlier and said his phone was dead and he'd speak to her in the morning? Why couldn't he charge his phone? And why would he want to meet at that bowling alley? Vivian hadn't been there since she was in high school, and she didn't think she and John had ever gone there together. That message didn't sound exactly like John. He often used the words "been superbusy" in his texts to her, but there was something unusually upbeat and aggressive about this particular message.

Vivian was at least relieved she'd finally see him tomorrow. She was longing for his presence more than ever. She responded: *K. Have much to tell you. Let's try to talk before 4:30 if possible. XX*

John didn't text back. Vivian watched the glowing screen until it timed out and went dark. She shut her eyes, but she knew she wouldn't be able to sleep.

By 4 o'clock Saturday, her red Honda Accord sped north on I-5 toward Glimmer Lake. The rain had temporarily stopped, but the clouds looked like they were about to drop ash on the Northwestern landscape. Crossing Seattle's Ship Canal Bridge, Vivian glanced in the direction of the Cascades and Eastern Washington. The weather kept her from seeing the mountains. She once again wondered why John would have ventured so far east last night. He must have been searching for Brandon and somehow ended up there. Why else would he have lied to her about going to his niece's?

John's suspicion of Brandon deeply irritated her. She understood Brandon's illustration appearing on the *Bloody Bitz* website was odd. But that picture didn't warrant thinking Brandon had slit Maya's throat.

Brandon always had a softness that John never had—and still didn't. Vivian loved the vulnerability aging had brought forth in John. She relished his midlife insecurity, his silvering hair, and the faint cracks that had formed beneath his eyes. But he'd never have that open woundedness she'd seen in Brandon when they were teenagers.

"He shot himself," Brandon confessed to her on that afternoon in 1992 when she went to his house. It was the day of his dad's death and the beginning of Vivian's weeklong exile from her own home. Brandon trembled while Vivian held him in the living room.

"I lied about the hunting accident," Brandon said. "That's what my mom says we should tell people." He wept, and Vivian hugged him more closely. "My mom found him in the basement—on his rocking chair. He did it by putting a gun in his mouth."

"I'm so, so sorry," Vivian whispered.

"He'd been depressed for a long time," Brandon spoke between sobs. "My mom thought his pills were helping him. I tried to cheer him up whenever I could."

"It's not your fault," Vivian said, thinking about her own parents' coldness and how she'd decided that coldness preceded her existence.

Brandon stared her in the eyes. "Please don't tell anyone. Not ever. Not even John."

Vivian did try to get John to talk to Brandon, though. She told him how upset Brandon was over the death of his father, and she also mentioned the silly incident where some of the jocks called Brandon "Fag Laurent" for hanging out with the one openly gay student in their class. She never knew how much John consoled his best friend. He wasn't there for her enough during the week she couldn't go home. She stayed with her friend Tamara. John spent time with her, of course, but his writing distracted him, and she kept wishing he'd hurry up and finish whatever story he was struggling to put on paper. She wanted everything to go back to how it had been before the publication of the Spindly Arms story, when she, John, and Brandon were all so close and happy.

Toward the end of her week in exile, Vivian returned to her house. Her mother opened the front door and, though she seemed moved by her daughter's apology, she didn't let Vivian inside.

"You deserve the full punishment," she said, "and then we will forgive you. It will take one week for you to be a good daughter again."

"Please, Mom," Vivian said, but the door shut her out.

"We will see you on Sunday," her mother announced through the barrier. "After church."

Vivian slunk away from her house, her head hanging. But after she left her cul-de-sac, she lifted her face, which burned with anger. She was suddenly sick of trying to be the ideal daughter. What if she let herself be just the opposite?

She stole a bottle of whiskey from Tamara's parents' liquor cabinet and dropped the booze in her backpack. She tried stopping by John's, but no one was home. Brandon was at his house, moping around while his mother visited some of her deceased husband's relatives. Vivian showed him the whiskey, and he said, "Well, it is Friday. We can try calling John later on so he can join us."

They never phoned John. Instead, they drank and listened to that Bell Biv DeVoe album that always cheered Brandon up. While dancing in the living room, Vivian looked into those dark eyes that so many girls in their grade admired. She'd heard more than one classmate talk about wanting to run her hands through Brandon's dark brown mane of hair or kiss his "bee-stung" lips. And Vivian knew Brandon was far from a virgin. John had once called him "a pussy magnet." As she slipped her arm around Brandon's waist and sang, "That girl is poison," she wondered why Brandon had never tried anything with her. He could have at the beginning of the junior year before she'd started dating John. She brought the half-empty whiskey bottle to her lips, and as she gulped Brandon stumbled backward and collapsed on the couch. His eyes were tearing yet again.

"Oh, no," Vivian told him drunkenly. "Let's try not to be sad tonight. Let's just make each other happy." She sat on his lap, and before long they were kissing wetly, and Vivian reached under her skirt to pull down her underwear. "I'm here for you tonight, and you're here for me."

Vivian woke on the couch with a quilt over her. Needles of pain pierced her head, and her stomach churned. She saw Brandon sleeping in his briefs on the carpet below her. He had a large hickey on his neck. Bitter liquid came up from her throat, and she knew she was going to vomit.

She reached the bathroom just in time. After throwing up, she heard birds chirping outside the window above the toilet. It was Saturday morning. Today she was supposed to go to John's to help him with college applications. Tomorrow she was allowed to return to her parents.

Vomiting again, she knew it would take much longer than a week to burn off this new growth of guilt.

Raindrops pelted Vivian's windshield as she pulled into the Bowl-O'-Rama's parking lot. The lot was surprisingly empty for a Saturday afternoon. Vivian guessed the dark and increasingly chilly day was keeping people at home. At least she'd have an easier time finding John if the crowd was small.

She ran from her car to the bowling alley entrance. Cardboard witches and ghosts hung on the inside of the door. One ghost's long face reminded Vivian of the moon mask that the teenager had worn last night, and she tried to shake off the memory. She was so glad she'd get to see John in a few minutes. This afternoon she'd tried to call his cell phone and the 509 number he'd called from the night before, but she wasn't able to reach him.

The bowling alley had 12 lanes, a dining area, and a section where people could play arcade games and pool. Vivian didn't see John among the 30 or so people who filled Bowl-O'-Rama. She checked her phone, but there was no text message or voice-mail from him. Maybe he was running late, or he'd just stepped into the restroom.

Increasingly nervous, Vivian went to the dining area and ordered herself a cherry ICEE. She sat on a stool with a view of the entire bowling alley. Sipping the sugary drink, she remembered how she and John used to buy Slurpees at 7-Eleven before swimming in Glimmer Lake during the summer. They would laugh at their red or blue tongues, and then they would kiss, exploring each other's frosty mouths.

DING. DING. DING.

Vivian snatched her phone out of her purse and glanced down at a message from John: *Remember this place???*

Below the words was the image of a dead apple tree. A little triangle filled the center of the image. This was a movie. Vivian tapped the triangle with her index finger.

The camera roamed from the scarred trunk of the apple tree across an overgrown and weedy lawn. It stopped on a mossy stack of wooden boards and zoomed in on what looked like half of a broken door. The camera zoomed out, revealing a chain-link fence that bordered the yard.

Vivian realized she was looking at the armless man's property. The video made her squirm on her stool. She wondered what had happened to the armless man's house. And what had happened to him and his wife and the kids they'd taken in?

Vivian waited for John to text more. When no words appeared, she anxiously typed *I'm at the bowling alley where r u?*

Vivian winced when she saw his reply: *In deep shit—where I deserve to be. Wish you were here with me.* ☺

Someone tapped Vivian's shoulder, and she nearly screamed.

Standing next to her was a cute girl with short black hair. She looked like she could be somewhere between 16 and 20. The girl wore a charcoal-gray hoodie, a backpack, and skinny jeans. She held a book titled *Best Short Stories of the Twentieth Century*.

"Are you Vivian?" the girl asked.

Vivian nodded, and the girl handed her an envelope.

"Some guy told me to give that to the pretty Asian lady who looks like she's looking for someone."

"'Some guy?'" Vivian asked.

The girl shrugged. "A handsome man with salt-and-pepper hair. He has a mole here." She pointed to one temple—the same place where John had a mole. "Anyway, my dad's picking me up. I've got to go."

Vivian tore open the envelope while the girl headed toward the exit. Vivian pulled out a square of paper. Unfolding it, she saw it was the front page of the *Glimmer Lake Gazette* in which John's Spindly Arms story had appeared. Vivian spotted the date of the issue: *Friday, October 30, 1992.* On the other side of the front page someone had written in red crayon:

> *You're the cunt that gave him this newspaper. He wants to talk to you. You better be alone or John gets it. NO COPS. 321 Garden View Lane ASAP –Spindly*

Her heart pounding, Vivian looked for the girl who'd handed her the envelope. The girl had already left Bowl-O'-Rama. Vivian ran out into the parking lot. The rain had ceased, and she had a clear view of all the cars. She didn't spot the girl.

Vivian glanced down at the piece of paper, which she now clutched tightly. She realized John had never actually texted her. Someone else had his phone.

Once again, she read the words *He wants to talk to you....*

Was the armless man waiting for her at this address? She wanted to call the police, but she didn't dare risk putting John in more danger than he already was. And what if someone was watching her right now from a car in this lot? She could always dial 9-1-1 once she reached the location where John was held captive.

She hurried toward her car and typed the address into her map app so she could listen to directions as she drove.

"Turn left onto Shady Shore Boulevard," directed a man in a broad Australian accent. "In half a mile, take a right onto Black Cedar Road."

You're the cunt that gave him this newspaper.

It was true Vivian had delivered that particular issue to the armless man. John was going out of town with his parents for just over a week to visit his relatives in Florida, and he'd asked her to take over his newspaper deliveries on two Fridays. When Vivian got out of her family's station wagon the second Friday to throw the paper over the armless man's fence, his front door swung open.

"Hey!" he shouted, charging out of the house.

Vivian became paralyzed in front of the fence. She wondered if she'd accidentally thrown the paper on his lawn last Friday. John had warned her some customers complained about newspapers left on their grass.

The armless man approached the other side of the fence. He was only feet away from her. He had a pale complexion and reddish-purple smudge marks beneath his bulging eyes. His scowl caused a deep line to form on either side of his mouth.

"You and your boyfriend think this is real fucking funny, don't you?" he asked.

Vivian took one step back toward the station wagon. "I don't know what you mean, mister," she said.

"Spindly Arms," the man said, his voice cracking. It was then Vivian glimpsed the sorrow on his face. The emotion only appeared momentarily, but it made Vivian understand that John had somehow gravely wounded this man.

Vivian opened her mouth as if she was going to speak, but she had no idea what to say.

"Spindly Arms wears coveralls," the man said. "He's bald. He lives on a farm."

Vivian knew the armless man was the inspiration for Spindly Arms, but she'd never considered the armless man might read the story or recognize himself as the main character. She'd been foolish.

The man raised his prosthetic arms in the air. "Do these look like tree branches to you spoiled shits? These don't grow, and I barely have any control over them."

Vivian blushed. "I'm sorry," she stammered. "I- John-"

"Get the fuck out of here!" the armless man hollered. "Tell your boyfriend I don't want to see him or you or that other friend of yours ever again." Vivian guessed that the "other friend" was Brandon.

"Go!" The man slammed one of his arms down against the fence, and it popped out of the sleeve of his shirt and landed on the sidewalk before Vivian.

She stared with an open mouth at the artificial limb. She considered picking it up for the man, but she was too frightened. With a quivering lower lip, Vivian scuttled around the car and jumped in the driver side. She almost said "I'm sorry" again through the open passenger-side window, but she remained silent.

She sped away from the armless man's house, and she never went back.

"In half a mile, take a right onto Overlook Road."

Vivian's phone began ringing. She glanced down at the screen and saw that 509 area code again. She answered the phone by blurting, "Hello? Are you calling about John?"

"Vivian?" The voice was familiar, but Vivian couldn't place it for a moment.

"Brandon?" She was too agitated to drive. She pulled her Honda Accord over in front of a row of houses.

"Vivian, are you all right? Is John okay?"

"I-" Vivian felt like she was going to start crying. She managed to keep the tears from forming. "Brandon, where are you?"

"I'm in Chelan, where I live."

Chelan was just east of the Cascades. Vivian now knew why John had called from an Eastern Washington area code.

"John didn't find you?" she asked.

"I told you when we talked last summer I haven't seen John since high school. Was he looking for me?" Brandon sounded hopeful.

"I thought he was."

"Vivian, what's going on with all this Spindly Arms stuff? I read about Maya, and I found that website with the

Spindly Arms stories. There's one about John, and there's one about you."

"Me?" Vivian asked. Though the heat was on, the air in the car suddenly felt ice-cold.

"There's a post about Spindly Arms killing a 'pretty Asian lady named Vivian.'"

"Oh, god," Vivian whispered.

"Vivian, are you and John in trouble?"

"We're -" She remembered she was supposed to get to that address as soon as possible. What were they doing to John? "Brandon, I need to go. Let me call you back later."

"Vivian, do you need me? I can drive out there."

Vivian worried that John would be furious if she asked Brandon to come to her aid. She knew her concern might be irrational, but she felt it nonetheless. "If I don't phone you in an hour, call the police and tell them I disappeared at this address in Glimmer Lake."

"What the hell, Vivian? What's going on?"

"Brandon, please, I don't have the time to explain. Just write down this address." She read the address to Brandon.

"Vivian, what else can I do?"

Vivian thought of waking up on the couch in Brandon's family's living room and seeing him half-naked with that moth-shaped hickey she'd made on his neck. She also thought of a cold December morning on the shore of Glimmer Lake. "I have to go now," she said. "Goodbye, Brandon."

She turned the key in the ignition and continued along Overlook Road.

"Take a left turn onto Garden View Lane," the Aussie said. "In a quarter of a mile, your destination will be on your right."

Garden View Lane had fewer streetlamps than the other roads Vivian had taken. Houses lined the left side of the street while a stone wall ran along the right side. The limbs of willow trees hung over the wall.

"Your destination is on your right. 321 Garden View Lane."

"Wait a second," Vivian whispered as she spotted the iron fence interrupting the wall. She knew this place.

She gasped when she saw the sign on the fence: *Lakeside Cemetery.*

Vivian knew the cemetery because this was where John and Brandon used to hang out some days after their 7th-period math class. Vivian would often meet up with them afterward, maybe at the Lake Town Cineplex or the bus station where they would take the 29 from Glimmer Lake to the rock club they frequented in downtown Everett. John had invited her to the cemetery numerous times, but she always declined and said it creeped her out. It didn't really, though. She just wanted John and Brandon to have their own place for quality guy time.

Sitting in the driver seat, Vivian stared at the entrance to Lakeside Cemetery. Raindrops bounced off the spherical lamps that glowed dimly atop the entrance's two stone pillars. Past the pillars, the gravel path curved into darkness. Vivian suspected that path would lead her to a trap. She didn't turn off the engine.

She picked up her phone and texted John's number: *I'm here. What do you want from me? I'm not going inside the cemetery.*

Ellipses showed on her phone. Someone was writing a response. But then the ellipses disappeared.

Vivian typed, *Where's John?*

More ellipses appeared without forming words. What was the hesitation?

Then the screaming began. The voice was a girl's, and it came from somewhere beyond the reach of the entrance's lights. The shrieking grew louder, and soon someone sprinted between the pillars toward Vivian's car.

Vivian recognized the girl who'd given her the envelope at the bowling alley. The girl's short black hair was mussed, and mud covered her face. She waved at Vivian with wet, soiled palms.

Vivian hesitated before rolling down the passenger-side window—the one that was closest to the girl. "What happened?" she asked. "Are you hurt?"

"Are you Vivian?"

Vivian nodded. She recalled the girl had asked her that same question in Bowl O' Rama. "How did you get here? Is John here?"

The girl gripped the top of the car door with her dirty hands. "I don't know if John's still alive," she said in a hysterical voice. "He stabbed him! Just now." She pointed behind her, toward the cemetery. "John's still in there."

"Who stabbed him?" Panicked, Vivian turned off the car and stepped out into the rain.

"Spindly Arms!" the girl said, her voice a scream again. She moved away from the car and fled along the sidewalk in the direction from which Vivian had driven.

"Oh, John," Vivian whimpered. She ducked back inside her car to call 9-1-1. She knew that note to her had instructed her to come here alone, but she needed to reach the police if John was hurt.

"Someone stabbed my boyfriend," she told the dispatcher in a rushed voice half an octave higher than usual. "I'm at Lakeside Cemetery on Garden View Lane. Please hurry." After hanging up, she went to her trunk and removed an L-shaped lug wrench she could use as a weapon. She headed through the pouring rain toward the cemetery entrance.

"John?" she called as she passed between the pillars. Her shoes made an overly loud crunching sound on the gravel path. "John, where are you?" The cold rain quickly soaked her denim jacket and chilled her shoulders. She glanced from left to right, barely making out the gravestones and trees on either side of the cemetery's gravel path. She had no idea what she'd do if someone confronted her.

She thought she glimpsed a person moving between two trees. "I've called the police!" she warned in a loud voice. She gripped the wrench with shaky hands. "They'll be here any minute."

She hurried along the path, veering in the opposite direction of where she'd seen the figure. The path forked ahead. Beyond the intersection was a copse of trees, and Vivian saw flames flickering among the trunks. The leafy ceiling shielded the fire from the rain. Vivian headed toward the light.

"Do you even know his name?"

The man's voice came from where Vivian had glimpsed the shadowy figure.

She stopped at the intersection and looked behind her. She thought she saw someone leaning against a tree trunk, but she couldn't be certain. She raised the wrench, ready to swing it.

"Do you?" the man demanded.

"John!" Vivian screamed, hoping he'd respond this time.

"No, not John," the man spoke with irritation.

A police car siren sounded in the distance, and Vivian sighed in relief. *Please, please get here soon.*

The figure stepped out of the trees and stood in the middle of the path with clenched fists. He wore a black sweatshirt and black cargo pants and stared at Vivian from behind a yellow moon mask. Vivian was terrified he was going to attack her. But he hastened toward the pillars and took a left turn outside the cemetery, disappearing behind the wall.

As the sirens became louder, Vivian continued off the path, toward the now dwindling flames. The trees provided shelter from the rain. There were numerous graves among the trunks. Vivian maneuvered around crosses and other markers until she reached whatever was on fire. At first, she thought a small pile of paperback books was burning. But after knocking over the stack with the tip of her shoe, she realized these weren't books.

They were all the same copy of *Evergroan,* the literary magazine in which John's Spindly Arms story had first appeared.

The last glow of the fire lit the gravestone directly behind the stack of magazines. Vivian read the etchings in the stone:

Ed Granley

Nov. 12, 1939 – March 21, 1993

Vivian didn't recognize the name. Flashlight beams appeared in the distance, at the entrance of the cemetery. The police were here.

"I'm over here!" Vivian shouted, wildly waving her arms until a flashlight beam was in her face. She turned away from the light. It was then she noticed the gravestone beside Ed Granley's:

Phoebe Granley

March 2, 1957 – March 21, 1993

The pair had died on the same date.

Vivian screamed John's name one last time as the two police officers approached.

Though the stocky blonde policewoman had asked Vivian to stay nearby during their search for John, Vivian wandered away, stumbling among tombs in the rain. She didn't want to answer more questions. Her mind was racing, nerves in overdrive. She needed to find John. She kept yelling his name, and he never answered. She dreaded finding his bleeding body beside a bush or stretched along one of the gravestones. She cried out when she spotted a prone figure between two crosses. Thankfully, it turned out to be a statue of a woman lying peacefully with her hands folded over her chest.

Staring at the statue's untroubled visage, Vivian blurted, "She didn't have any mud on her clothes!"

"What's that?" the policewoman asked. She left the stretch of the cemetery wall where she'd been searching.

"The girl who told me someone had cut John," Vivian said, wide-eyed. "She didn't have any mud on her hoodie or her jeans. It was just on her face and hands."

"You're sure?" the policewoman asked.

"Pretty sure." Vivian imagined the girl dipping her hands in the mud and wiping it on her cheeks and forehead while Vivian's Honda Accord idled outside the cemetery. "And how did she end up here? I originally saw her at the bowling alley." The girl had seen John at some point because she'd described his looks when she spoke to Vivian at Bowl O' Rama. Could the girl have been part of some set-up to get Vivian inside the cemetery?

Following the policewoman back to the cemetery entrance and her waiting partner, Vivian told her of Maya's murder, John's link to Spindly Arms, and the events that had led her to the cemetery tonight. She also told the policewoman how Detective Garcia was investigating Maya's murder in Seattle.

"Are you going to stay in Glimmer Lake tonight?" the policewoman asked.

"I think so," Vivian said. She wanted to remain in Glimmer Lake if there was any chance John was here, but she didn't know where she could go. Her friends from high school had left the town decades ago, and her father had moved into her oldest brother's house in Silicon Valley after her mother died of a stroke a couple of years ago. Her oldest brother told her their father still wasn't willing to put their childhood home on the market. Though it was no longer occupied, the house was filled with possessions, and Vivian's brother said their father still paid the utility bills.

"We're going to try to reach Detective Garcia and talk to him," the policewoman said. "We'll call you in a bit and give you an update. We may have some more questions for you."

Vivian smiled weakly in appreciation. She glanced into the dark maw of the cemetery once more before heading to her car.

She thought of the masked man's question to her: "Do you even know his name?" She also remembered how those issues of *Evergroan* were burning in front of Ed Granley's grave.

Was Ed Granley the name she was supposed to know? And, if so, who was Ed Granley?

She shuddered when she recalled the words on the note she'd received at the bowling alley: *You're the cunt that gave him this newspaper. He wants to talk to you.*

Could Ed Granley be the armless man?

The Hungry Bear was almost as quiet as Bowl O' Rama had been. Vivian found the diner soon after leaving the cemetery. She sat in a window booth, removed her drenched denim jacket, and tried to dry her short black hair a little by running one hand through it. She glanced around the softly lit diner. Hanging from the cedar walls were old black-and-white photographs of Everett in its lumber town days, stuffed birds, and acrylic paintings of mountain and forest scenes. Vivian, John, Brandon, and their classmates used to pack the place on weekend nights, but on this Saturday evening only a young family, a couple of elderly women, and some truck driver types filled the space. Vivian wondered if Glimmer Lake was a dying town, or maybe it was just the establishments of her youth that were fading and would soon be gone. After all, why go to The Hungry Bear when Chipotle and Papa Murphy's were on the next block?

She looked down at her phone again and tried a new Google search: *Ed Granley obituary 1993.*

Her search yielded no useful results.

She typed in other keywords: *Phoebe Granley death, Granleys Glimmer Lake, Ed Granley veteran.*

None of the listed web pages led her to the armless man, and she didn't recognize anyone in the images associated with the searches. Vivian rolled her eyes, thinking of how in the '90s adults warned that everything on the burgeoning Internet was permanent. It turned out that erasing traces of local news was as easy as unplugging a server or deleting an archive. She remembered again how Brandon had once told her the armless man's real name. She recalled writing down that name in the journal she only occasionally used in high school. That journal was still in the closet of her childhood bedroom, hidden beneath a stack of yearbooks. She should find that journal tonight.

"You ready to order, miss?" the waiter asked. He was a lanky man in his sixties with wide, white sideburns and a goatee. Vivian appreciated how he'd called her "miss" rather than "ma'am." Being in the Hungry Bear really did turn her into a high schooler again.

"Could I get just some toast and a side order of bacon?" she asked, knowing she was too anxious to eat much. "And black coffee. A large mug if you have it."

"I'll keep the coffee coming," the waiter said with a dutiful nod.

Even though she was apprehensive about visiting the site again, Vivian navigated to *Bloody Bitz* on her phone. She needed to see the post Brandon had mentioned.

She grimaced when she read the following:

NEW SPINDLY ARMS POST!

"A Grave Night for Vivian"

A woman stops by a cemetery and, thanks to Spindly,
stays forever

With clenched teeth, Vivian read about the "pretty Asian lady" wandering among burial plots until she kneeled at the grave of "a friend she'd wronged in the past." Vivian tried to ignore the statement that "harm to others deserves hurt in return." She cringed as she read about Spindly Arms watching her from behind the trunk of a willow tree. He sent one arm slithering up the trunk and along a limb and then down and around her neck. He yanked her up from the cemetery ground, strangling her until she hung lifeless and swaying in the nighttime breeze.

"Coffee, toast, and bacon," the waiter said.

Vivian jumped at the words.

"Didn't mean to scare you, miss."

"Thank you," Vivian said with a smile. She bit into a piece of bacon and glanced back at the horror fiction post. She didn't need to read any more of that shit. She scrolled down past the post to the comments.

"Oh, no," she whispered.

A comment by PastHitsHard included the full address of Vivian's apartment in Columbia City and the words "can't hide from the readers."

Vivian decided she'd tell the policewoman about this as soon as the woman called with an update. And if the police-woman didn't phone in the next half hour, Vivian would call her. Vivian closed the web page and reached for her coffee. Sipping the hot, bitter drink, she stared out at her car in the parking lot. Rain hammered the vehicle. There was no going home to Columbia City tonight. She wondered if she'd be dead in the cemetery if she'd never contacted the police. That's what happened to her in the Spindly Arms post.

In the post that featured John, he died on a farm in the mountains. Was that what had actually happened to him—or was happening to him now?

Tears filled Vivian's eyes. She gulped more coffee as if she could swallow her despair, but the action only made the tears spill down her cheeks. She grabbed a napkin and wiped her eyes.

Once again, she regretted ever wanting space between her and John. And she wished she'd never argued with him when he voiced suspicion of Brandon. She should have just let him express his grudge. She'd wounded John by sleeping with his best friend in high school. Couldn't she allow his wound to open up again so he could heal it once and for all?

She remembered how she'd promised to call Brandon. If she didn't, he'd phone the police and send them to the cemetery a second time.

He didn't answer. Vivian left the message, "Brandon, it's Vivian. I just wanted to let you know I'm fine." She considered asking him to call her back, but she imagined John's reaction if he heard her make that request. "Take care of yourself," she said, and then she hung up.

She knew she was trying to prevent another conflict between John and Brandon. She'd never forget walking away from them when they fought on the front lawn of Brandon's family's home, the freezing December day she'd told John about sleeping with Brandon. She was certain telling John the truth would be the ruin of her and John's relationship, but she could no longer keep it hidden. John was relentless when he attacked Brandon, punching him in the nose and then pushing his bleeding face into the grass. John refused to stop even when Vivian pleaded with him from the sidewalk.

"I'm not going to watch you act like a child," she shouted. She sobbed as she walked away from the pair. Covering her face with her hands, she understood it wasn't just her and John's relationship that was over. She, John, and Brandon would all have to take separate paths into the future.

"More coffee for you, miss," the waiter said, filling up her cup again.

"Thank you." Vivian forced herself to eat another piece of bacon. She was chewing when her phone sounded.

DING. DING. DING.

She silenced her device and read the text on its screen. The message was from John's phone.

Vivian I'm bleeding real bad

Vivian felt faint when she imagined John stumbling around Glimmer Lake in a blood-soaked shirt. She heard that girl's words again: "He stabbed him!" But she was certain this couldn't be John texting her.

Where are you? she typed.

YOU SHOULD NEVER HAVE CALLED THE COPS YOU CUNT

Vivian stared down at her phone's screen in horror. She responded, *Who are you?*

Her eyes large with shock, she read the words that formed on the screen:

Hope your food tastes good. Eat something for John because his mouth is full of blood.

Vivian gasped. Someone was watching her. She glanced around the diner. The only remaining occupants were the elderly women and the truck driver types. She looked out the window again, searching for the creep who'd texted. Two spaces away from her Honda Accord was an old black Camaro with a yellow face hovering above the steering wheel. It was difficult to see that face in the rain, but then the visage jutted forward, nearly pressing against the windshield.

It was a large, rubber mask in the shape of a crescent moon.

And it was staring at Vivian.

Though frozen with fright, she had the thought John could be in the backseat of that Camaro. She couldn't just sit in this booth.

"Call the cops!" she barked at the waiter before rushing out of the Hungry Bear.

The car had already backed out of its space when Vivian reached the parking lot. She could only see the silhouette of the driver's head. There were no numbers or letters on the Camaro's license plate. The vehicle lurched forward onto the street and took a sharp left with the sound of screeching tires.

Vivian stood wet and shivering in the center of the parking lot until she felt her cell phone vibrate in her hand. She glanced down at the message on her screen.

Spindly will be in touch

The same police officers who'd come to the cemetery sat with Vivian in the Hungry Bear. The waiter brought her another mug of coffee and a bowl of blackberry crisp.

"On the house, sweetheart," he said.

"We still don't have any leads," the policewoman told Vivian. "I've called Detective Garcia, though, and I'm going to call him again and tell him about what happened here tonight and about your address being on that website."

"Thank you," Vivian whispered. She kept picturing John bleeding—on the backseat of that Camaro, in a dark and hidden nook of the cemetery, among some thorny cluster of bushes in Glimmer Lake. Or what if he was already dead? She felt the tears returning, and she cupped a hand over her eyes.

"Is there somewhere safe you can go tonight?" the policewoman asked.

John's house and Vivian's apartment were no longer secure. Vivian knew she could stay with Ralph and Maggie in Lynnwood if she asked her ex-husband. But Vivian didn't want to risk leading her stalker to Maggie. She was so grateful her daughter had Ralph's last name. She couldn't imagine what she'd do if she saw Maggie's name or address appear on that *Bloody Bitz* site.

"Is there any place?" the policewoman pressed Vivian.

"I'll find a hotel," Vivian said.

But as she left the diner, she knew there was something she needed to do first.

A car's headlights lit up Vivian's rearview mirror, and her fingers tightened around the steering wheel. She told herself the man in the moon mask couldn't be following her. She'd watched the Camaro speed away from the Hungry Bear and disappear.

But she couldn't be certain. She pulled over beside a brightly lit Craftsman-style home with a streetlamp in front of it and held her breath until the car passed.

It was a 1980s station wagon. Vivian exhaled in relief.

She continued in the direction of the cul-de-sac where she'd grown up, no longer fretting over every car that appeared behind her Honda Accord. She drove by the street that used to divide two farms where her family would buy fruit every September. She and her brothers sometimes snuck into the farms' apple orchards, plucking the Galas and dropping them into their backpacks. Now large, cream-colored tract homes occupied the land where the farms had been.

The houses near the mouth of the cul-de-sac were still the same. That beige one was where Claire Kapoor, Vivian's best friend from middle school, had lived. In eighth grade and the beginning of high school, Vivian and Claire had rebelled against the white culture around them. They dressed in hip-hop fashion and constantly listened to rappers like Ice Cube, MC Lyte, and Public Enemy. They even snuck down to Seattle one weekend to go to an Eazy-E concert. Then Claire's parents divorced and she moved to Tukwila, and Vivian started hanging with the two handsome white guys who sat next to her in chemistry class, Brandon Laurent and John Larsen.

Where could John be? Vivian teared up again as she parked in front of the pink colonial revival house where she'd lived for nearly 20 years. Columns framed the front door of the unlit two-story home, and the sloping roof and all window shutters were a matching dark green. Other than a few patches of peeling paint and a leaf-filled gutter bordering the roof, the house was in fine shape.

Much better shape than Vivian was in tonight. She wiped her eyes and left the car.

She knew her entry plan was unlikely to succeed, but she'd try anyway. Veering off the front walkway, she headed toward the side of the house. She passed the bush where her mother had once hidden and waited to prevent Vivian from returning home. Now the bush was nearly bare and probably wouldn't survive the house's next owners.

Approaching the kitchen door, she glanced in the direction of the backyard bench where she used to escape some late nights in high school. She would come out in her bathrobe, smoke for-emergency-only Virginia Slims, and fantasize about the day she'd escape this house and this mediocre suburban town and her parents' narrow old-world ways. She imagined eloping with John and living in a European city—maybe Amsterdam or Prague—where John would write fiction and she would start an interior design business.

But then the Spindly Arms story came out, Vivian cheated with Brandon, and the three best friends stopped talking to each other—at least for 25 years.

You could still move to Europe with John, she told herself.

But she couldn't do that if he was dead. Feeling a sob rising in her throat, Vivian returned to her original mission. She climbed onto the wooden railing of the stairs to the kitchen door and reached into the planter outside the window of the guest bathroom. She felt wet dirt and dead weeds at the bottom of the container. And then she felt the key to the kitchen door. It was still there.

"Thank you for your forgetfulness, Dad," Vivian whispered.

She winced after she stepped inside the house and turned on the kitchen light. She'd hoped her childhood home would be nearly empty, but her father had left so much in place. There was the toaster oven her parents had used since the '90s to heat their poppy seed bagels each morning. Hanging on the breakfast room wall was the smiling glass sun Vivian had given her mother for her 60th birthday. From the kitchen, Vivian could see the patch of living room wall that displayed her brothers' framed senior portraits. Vivian knew her picture wasn't hanging anywhere in this house. Rather than experience nostalgia in her childhood home, Vivian had that old, awful feeling that she was the fuck-up in the Chiang family.

Unlike her two older brothers, who were a doctor and an attorney, she had failed to attain a graduate degree. She lived with her parents for a year after dropping out of pharmacy school. Instead of criticizing her, her father continued to treat her as he always had—as if she were a naïve, feminine entity that occupied a household where the males were the only ones that mattered.

Vivian moved into the dark foyer and glanced up the stairway that led to the second floor and her family's four bedrooms. She knew she'd find her high school journal in her old bedroom. From the foyer, she could see the doorway of the master bedroom. That was the chamber where she'd felt the most grief on that momentous day a couple of years ago when she helped her father and brothers sort through her dead mother's possessions.

While clearing boxes of decades-old shoes her mother had worn only for holidays, weddings, and funerals, Vivian found one box that contained photographs. She picked up Polaroids of her mother looking so young and miraculously happy on Cannon Beach, in San Francisco, at the Grand Canyon. There were some letters from Hong Kong with grids of Chinese characters covering their pages. And, finally, under everything else, Vivian found a folded-up note her mother had addressed to her. The piece of paper read:

> *I should never have shut you out of the house as I did. A mother should not do that to her daughter. My mother was cruel to me in many ways, and I should not have been cruel to you. I should have let you grow how you were meant to. But I pruned-*

The note ended abruptly. Her mother never finished it or gave it to her.

Feeling as if someone had kicked her in the gut, Vivian stumbled out of the room and past her brothers, who asked her concerned questions she couldn't hear.

She kept thinking *I could have been free from this guilt years ago.*

Outside the house, she dialed Ralph's number with a trembling finger. When her husband answered, she said, "I want a divorce, Ralph. We've got Maggie, and that's wonderful. But we don't have anything else to show for our marriage. We've done this loveless dance for too long."

DING DANG DONG.

Vivian's memories dissipated. That was the sound of the doorbell.

But who the hell could be outside?

She tried to shake her panic by telling herself a neighbor might have rung the doorbell. Someone probably spotted her entering through the side of the house and wanted to make sure she wasn't a burglar. She approached the door and peered through the peephole.

"No, not him," she whimpered.

Leering in the dim outside the door was the man who'd broken into John's house. Vivian could see the constellation of sores on his face.

He thrust that face forward as if he knew Vivian was looking at him through the peephole. "Trick-or-treat, Vivian Chiang," he said.

And then Vivian heard the kitchen floor creak.

She turned toward the lit kitchen, her heart slamming against her chest. Did she leave the kitchen door unlocked? All she could see from here was the yellow refrigerator and the magnetic pad her father had left stuck to its face. The words *TO DO* were on the top of the pad.

DING DANG DONG.

Vivian cried out, and then she immediately covered her mouth. More than one person had come for her.

She dialed 9-1-1 as she ran toward the stairway. When she was on the bottom stair, a man in a moon mask flew out of the kitchen with a carving knife in one hand. He reached for Vivian with his free hand but didn't make contact. She shot up the stairs.

"What's your emergency?" a male dispatcher asked Vivian.

"Please-" She didn't finish her sentence because the masked man grabbed her leg and she fell with a bang. Pain exploded in her right knee. Her phone tumbled down the stairs.

"Get the hell away!" she screamed, kicking at her pursuer. One of her shoes made contact with the man's head, denting the moon mask so it had a distorted smile. He groaned and fell back against the wall.

Vivian scrambled up the stairs and limped down the hallway to her childhood bedroom. Her knee continued to ache. Slamming the door behind her, she glanced around for a piece of furniture she could use to block the door.

"Fuck!" she hissed.

There was nothing in the room. Her father had left the downstairs looking like it had for the past 30 years, but he allowed no trace of his daughter in her old bedroom. The closet door was open, and Vivian could see the closet's shelves were empty. No old sweatshirts, no college textbooks, no journal with the armless man's name in it.

Vivian headed for the window she used to sneak out of some nights when she was a teenager. Yanking it up, she heard the door fly open behind her.

"Help me!" she shrieked out the window.

The masked man hurried toward her, his big black boots treading heavily on the hardwood floor. Vivian tried to run around him to get to the hallway, but he shoved her against the wall where her bed used to be. Her head hit the surface, and she crumpled to the floor.

The masked man stomped toward her, his carving knife raised.

"Who are you?" Vivian asked in a hopeless voice.

"I'm Spindly Arms," he said, sounding furious. "I'm Ed Granley. I'm your past, and I've finally come to kill you."

Someone suddenly appeared in the doorway. It was the same girl Vivian had seen at the cemetery and the bowling alley. The girl's eyes were round with fear.

"Micah, don't!" the girl said.

The man glanced back at the girl, and Vivian took advantage of the distraction. She sprang up from the floor and raced to the partially open window. She lifted it all the way.

She had one leg over the ledge when the knife plunged into the side of her lower back. She screamed into the Glimmer Lake night, but no lights came on in the cul-de-sac.

BRANDON

Sunlight warmed Brandon's face as he lay in bed. He cracked open his eyes and gazed upwards at the early morning sky outside his window. Being able to see the bright blue heavens most days of the year was one of the many things he loved about Eastern Washington. The sky was probably gray or dripping rain in Western Washington on this autumn day, just like it would be most of the time from now through June. Of course, Brandon had received plenty of sunlight during the decade he lived in LA, but it always seemed like a grainy, brownish light.

In Chelan, the light was healing—and inspiring.

Brandon closed his eyes and let the sun penetrate his prone, naked body. *Right now you're living your best life,* he told himself. That was part of the mantra he'd been using during his Sunday meditation class. *Right now is the perfect moment.*

His eyes shot open when he remembered what he'd received in the mail yesterday. It was still on his dining table, where he'd dropped it in revulsion last night. He should have tossed it in the trash.

He rose from his bed and walked into the small kitchen area of the attic apartment he'd been renting for the past five years. The owners of the three-story Victorian house were a young

119

husband and wife who lived in Seattle and leased the downstairs on Airbnb when they weren't staying there themselves in the summer. This week Brandon was the only one in the house. He was glad of that because last night he'd shouted, "What the fuck?" when he opened the envelope, and then he kicked over a chair.

With its yellow cupboards and daisy wallpaper, the kitchen calmed him this morning. He reminded himself he was in a bright and healthy place in his life, and the dark times in his past couldn't overshadow his present. He had an art show opening this Saturday—his first in 15 years—and the exhibit featured the most positive paintings he'd ever created.

He picked up the glossy 8 ½" x 11" photograph from his dining table like he was handling a dead insect. *Look at it,* he told himself, *and then let it go.*

The picture was of a painting he'd completed while living in LA during his twenties. It was one of the *Spindly Arms at Work* series. The moon-faced man crouched on a leafy forest floor with a fellow's decapitated head cradled in his tree branch arms. Spindly Arms had a pensive look on his face. He was about to deposit the head in a hole in the ground. Brandon thought he'd titled the painting *The Planting.*

Nothing had accompanied the photograph of the painting. No letter or note, and there was no return address on the envelope.

You're in the now, and you're in Chelan, Brandon told himself as he brought the photograph to the garbage bin in the kitchen. *You're no longer in LA.* He dropped the photograph. He knew he'd overreacted last night by knocking over furniture. But he'd reached a place of optimism in his life after suffering for 20 years. He didn't need some prankster who'd probably known him in California reminding him of his negative days. The dark artworks. All those substances. The flirting with death. He once again wondered who could have mailed him the photograph. He'd known so many people in LA, and his constant intoxication during those years prevented him from clearly remembering most of them. And why the hell would anyone want to send him that picture?

Brandon yanked open all the curtains in his living room and let in the sunlight.

"Your art show on Saturday's going to be beautiful," he said as if he were trying to convince himself.

Just before 10, Brandon walked the few blocks to his job at Sustenance, a natural health foods store where he'd worked since moving from Leavenworth to Chelan five years ago. While strolling, he couldn't help but think about John. John had first described Spindly Arms to him after they followed Ed Granley up into the Cascades one weekend in the summer of 1992. They watched spooky Ed take off his prosthetic arms and roam around a farm outside Leavenworth.

"I picture Spindly Arms living on a farm like that," John told Brandon later that night, as they drank Mickey's malt liquor in front of a campfire. "His house has no furniture—only shadows, spider webs, and the occasional corpse. I'm going to write a story about him, and how he wanders out of the mountains in the middle of the night so he can hunt people in the suburbs. Do you think you'd be able to draw Spindly Arms for me?"

Of course, Brandon could do that. John was his best friend. He was all those adjectives you want to be called when you're in high school: intelligent, talented, good-looking. The Most Likely to Have His Shit Together a Decade After High School. Yes, he was also selfish and arrogant, but teenagers don't often equate those qualities to sin. Classmates from Art class had called Brandon talented, too, and more than one girl had breathed the words "fucking hot" while staring at him intensely. But Brandon usually felt like he was a small fraction of what John was worth. He covered up his insecurity by intentionally being weird, telling people stupid stories about how Saddam Hussein had a crashed UFO in a bunker outside Baghdad and claiming that in the year 2000 the Moonies were going to wage war against the Mormons.

Despite all his recent self-work he still felt regret when he thought about John. He'd fucked up by betraying his best pal in high school. He and John had been two creative friends, twin souls in a way. Brandon ruined their relationship by sleeping with Vivian. He caused all three friends to split apart.

Brandon wondered if John could have been the one who'd sent him the photograph of the Spindly Arms art. He dismissed the idea. Why would John suddenly mail him a picture of a character they'd co-created? They hadn't spoken in over 25 years. Brandon redirected his suspicion to whoever had broken into his family's house in the spring of 1993. The thief didn't touch any electronics or jewelry. Instead, that person stole all of Brandon's drawings of Spindly Arms. The thief also took a stack of *Evergroan*, the high school literary magazine that had featured John's story about Spindly Arms and Brandon's accompanying illustration. Brandon had multiple copies of the issue that included his illustration, imagining their future worth when he was a renowned artist and John was a best-selling writer.

But Brandon didn't create the painting that was in the photograph until years after the break-in. The person who sent this photograph must have known him—or known *of* him—when he lived in LA.

"What's the glum look about?"

Deeanne had asked the question. The 29-year-old regular customer at Sustenance stood outside the store with a case of ginger kombucha in her arms. She had thick, curling auburn hair that nearly reached her waist. Today she wore a short blue T-shirt that revealed her pierced belly button and the seahorse tattoo that began at her waistline and curved somewhere beneath her tight jeans. Brandon had often imagined her naked, sweating, and pressed against him in bed, but he always reminded himself he was on a celibacy kick. His temporary abstinence from sex helped him focus on his steps, and he'd been struggling with the ninth for a while now:

Make direct amends to such people wherever possible, except when to do so would injure them or others.

"I'm just wasting time dwelling on the past," he told her.

She smiled knowingly. She gave him that warm, penetrating look that often made him semi-erect. "I know you're going to release a ton with your art show," she said. "These are the 'amends' paintings you were telling me about, right?" "

Brandon nodded. Each color field painting made amends to someone he'd wronged with his substance abuse. One painter friend from Wenatchee had described the works as "what Rothko would have painted if he'd been happy." There were 14 paintings in all, and Brandon's favorites included the hazy orange triangle he'd made with his mother in mind; the red-flecked violet rectangle dedicated to Martiniano, his last roommate in LA; and the pink, heart-shaped smear that was his reminder of Vivian. He'd meant to create 15 paintings, but he couldn't summon the energy to make amends to John. At least not yet.

"I think I'm going to be in a stronger place after this show," Brandon said. And when he was in that place of power he'd contact John and complete his 15th painting.

"I know you will be," Deeanne said, smiling more widely. She neared where he stood on the sidewalk. "I'll definitely be at the opening. I'm bringing some friends who can afford to buy art."

Brandon was now close enough to her to smell her peach-like scent. He knew he'd ask her out soon.

"Have you ever painted a person?" Deeanne asked.

The image of Spindly Arms suddenly invaded Brandon's mind. The supernatural killer had blood splatter on the cheeks of his pale moon face. Brandon couldn't help frowning at the thought.

Deanne stepped away as if she'd sensed his discomfort. "I'm not criticizing your abstract painting. I was just thinking I'd be happy to model for you if you ever wanted to paint a person."

Brandon was pleased to have the vision of an unclothed and posing Deeanne replace his thoughts about Spindly Arms. Nodding, he said, "One day soon I'll take you up on that."

Deeanne smiled again and started across the street toward her car. "I'm being a flirt, aren't I?" she said, sounding apologetic. "Best of luck with your show, Mr. Brandon Laurent."

Brandon was restocking a shelf with agave nectar when he imagined hearing the voice from the past: "I'm being inappropriate, aren't I?"

Phoebe Granley had said those words in the same way Deeanne had apologized for being a flirt. It must have been mid-summer, 1992—after John and Brandon started calling Ed Granley "the armless man" and before John came up with the character Spindly Arms. Brandon was covering John's paper route that first day the armless man's wife spoke to him.

"Excuse me," she called when Brandon got out of the car to toss the newspaper over the armless man's chain-link fence. She appeared in the doorway wearing a bathrobe. In the past, Brandon had only seen the sexy older woman in her nurse's uniform. Today Brandon glimpsed one of her wide, white thighs in the slit of the robe.

"You're not the usual boy," she said, smiling.

"I'm taking on John's route for him today." Brandon approached her, glancing around for the two barking and drooling Dobermans that were usually in the front yard. He handed her the paper. He stared at her lovely oval face, which was framed by her charcoal-black locks. She must have been in her mid to late thirties. She wore heavy make-up, and the dark mascara accentuated her light green eyes.

"I was hoping to ask a favor of you," she said. "Would you mind coming inside real quick?"

Brandon soon followed her through the doorway. Her robe was cream-colored with a pattern of little pink roses. Brandon stood only inches away from her plump butt. He hoped she wouldn't spot the hard-on in his jeans. The house was sparsely decorated and had a depressing atmosphere. Brandon viewed a tiny living room with an old television, a weathered maroon couch, and a rocking chair that held a stack of *Military History* magazines. Beyond the living room was an unkempt kitchen with a couple of dirty bowls and a box of Honey Nut Cheerios on one counter.

"I'm Phoebe, by the way," the woman said, turning to Brandon. She squeezed his hand, triggering more sparks in his loins. "You look older than the usual boy. Are you in college?"

"No, I'm a senior. My name's Brandon."

"Almost college age," Phoebe said, sounding satisfied. She led him away from the living room and stood outside a closed door. "My husband, Ed, had to run out unexpectedly this morning, and he left the dogs in our bedroom. He usually ties them up outside."

Brandon didn't like the idea of being just a room away from the Dobermans.

"I need to get my clothes for work," Phoebe said, "and the dogs jump all over me and slobber on my outfit. Would you mind distracting them while I grab my stuff? They look scary, but they never bite."

"Um, sure," Brandon said, his erection wilting a little.

Phoebe cracked open the door. "You go first," she whispered. "Just keep them on the left side of the room."

Brandon reluctantly stepped inside the small chamber, which contained a queen-sized bed, a couple of night tables, and a large, decades-old dresser. Above the bed was a faded painting of a naked, Rubenesque woman sleeping among pink tulips on a grassy hillside. A bark sounded on the left side of the bed, and Brandon watched in terror as the two Dobermans rose from reclining positions and stared at him with their black eyes. He awkwardly raised his arms in distraction and said, "It's okay, it's okay" in a less than confident voice.

Phoebe hurried to the dresser and yanked open a drawer containing a couple of folded nurse uniforms. She lifted one out, and then she opened a higher drawer and removed a pair of white stockings and red lacy panties.

Brandon was once again aroused—until both dogs started to bark at him. It was as if they'd sensed his sexual thoughts. One tried to veer around him, and he stuck out his leg to block the dog. The Doberman growled at him, baring its fangs.

"Stop that, Whistler," Phoebe said. She rushed out of the room and said, "Come along, Brandon."

Brandon backed away from the snarling dogs. "Good boys," he repeated, and then he slammed the door shut.

"Thank you," Phoebe sighed, patting his chest.

Brandon tried not to stare at the pantyhose draped over her forearm. He gave his best slanted Han Solo grin. "It was nothing."

"The girls must go crazy over your lips," she said. "You've got Steve McQueen lips."

Brandon lost his forced composure and blushed brightly.

"I'm being inappropriate, aren't I?" Phoebe said. "I tend to do that." She opened the front door. "I should get dressed for work. The next time you come I owe you a soda or something. There will be a next time, won't there?"

Brandon tried not to trip as he stepped out of the house. Looking back at her, he said, "I'm covering for John again two weeks from today."

There should be a 16th painting.

Brandon snapped out of his remembrance. The inner voice was as intrusive as that horrible image of Spindly Arms had been earlier. Brandon squeezed the bottle of agave nectar, trying to ground himself. His thoughts were all over the place today. Maybe he should meditate after his shift at Sustenance.

The 16th painting would be for Ed Granley, and the ways you wronged him before you were a full-fledged addict.

Brandon placed the bottle of nectar on the shelf and descended the stepladder. He glanced around for a distraction, and he was grateful to see an elderly man gazing up at the jars of peanut butter.

"You know you can make your own peanut butter in our store, right?" Brandon asked. "Almond butter, too. Let me show you."

Brandon sat on the shore of Lake Chelan after his shift, his eyes closed and the late-afternoon sun warming his face. He knew it was the Spindly Arms painting that had triggered his negative thoughts. But now he was centered and present again. The lowering sun made the blue lake sparkle and turned the gently sloping hills that surrounded the town a pastel brown. Brandon would go home, prepare the chicken and avocado salad that always made him feel healthy, and then finalize the plans for his art show.

The sky was orange by the time he reached his street. He walked beside the picket fence of the Victorian house where he lived. Sunset had turned the violet outer walls a dark purple, and the front yard's remaining flowers had lost their colors. Brandon pushed open the gate and stepped onto the curving stone path. The path split at an apple tree, leading to either the house's main front door or the external staircase that rose to the entrance of Brandon's attic apartment.

Brandon spotted a piece of paper dangling among the apple tree's withered fruit.

He plucked the paper out of the tree. The light was too dim for him to see what was on the paper, but he scowled when he felt it was glossy and the same size as the photograph he'd received in the mail yesterday. He hurried up the stairs to his apartment and unlocked the door. After flipping on the kitchen light, he hissed, "Shit!"

He stared down at a photograph of another one of his old Spindly Arms paintings. This one showed Spindly Arms descending the dark driveway of a well-lit ranch house. The man's tree branch arms dragged on the cement and left a bright red bloody trail behind him. Brandon recalled painting it soon after he'd moved to LA.

He guessed whoever was harassing him had found the images online. Brandon had managed to sell some of his Spindly Arms paintings in coffee shops, bars, and restaurants in Southern California. The purchasers could have posted pictures of the artworks on the Internet in an attempt to sell them or just display them.

But who was it that had entered his yard and left the photograph for him to find? Brandon shivered as he peered out the window at the darkening garden.

"You lived in LA? I thought you said you hit rock bottom and got clean in Leavenworth." Ray puffed on the second Marlboro he'd smoked since picking up Brandon and driving him into the hills above town. Stressed over the Spindly Arms images, Brandon had called his newest AA friend and asked if he'd be up for a drive and a talk.

"I did get sober in Leavenworth," Brandon said, "when I was 39. But during my twenties, I lived in LA." Brandon's mom couldn't afford to pay for college, and he didn't earn enough money for continued education by bagging groceries at the Glimmer Lake Grocery Mart. In the fall after he graduated from high school, he tried living with a cousin in downtown Seattle. But he was underemployed and intoxicated too often for her liking, and he was still too close to Glimmer Lake. He remembered a blur of high school classmates approaching him on the street while he was disheveled and coming down from a long night at a rave in a Belltown warehouse. He heard one of the girls comment to her friend, "Oh, gosh, is Brandon homeless?"

"I thought I'd get into the thriving LA painting scene I'd read about in some art journal," Brandon told Ray, "but I didn't meet many artists. I mostly came across people desperate for acting and modeling work. And I spent a lot of time by myself and painted a lot of dark shit—the shit that was in my yard today."

"And you drank," Ray said with a nod, blowing smoke out of the window of his truck. "Just like I did in Portland."

"Drank," Brandon said with a nod. "Smoked pot. Snorted speed—and coke when I was around anyone wealthy enough to have it. And then there was the compulsive sex."

"So you think this person who planted that photograph is a ghoul from your time in LA?"

Brandon imagined one of his painted images of Spindly Arms. The fiend was grinning and baring his pointy, bloodstained teeth. Brandon blinked repeatedly to get the image out of his head. "I have no idea who's doing this," he said.

"Well, I want you to know I've got your back, buddy. Anyone who fucks with you fucks with me."

"Thanks, Ray."

They reached a dead end high up on one of the hills. Ray pulled the truck over where they could look down on the distant pattern of glowing lights that was Chelan. "You feel any better, buddy?" he asked.

"I do," Brandon lied. He suddenly wished he were here with John instead of Ray. He could talk about how this Spindly Arms shit was coming up over 25 years after they'd fleshed out the character. He could tell him how sorry he was for sleeping with Vivian. He wouldn't try to explain it away by saying he was out of his mind after his father's death. He'd tell John his father didn't die in a hunting accident. The man stuck a gun in his mouth and pulled the trigger while Brandon and his mother were still in the house. He'd reveal that most times he came home from partying with John and Vivian, he kept drinking or smoking pot until he could barely stand up. He'd talk about what happened between him and Phoebe Granley, the woman who made him feel so much pleasure but also discomfort because of the massive age gap between them. And he'd share about the rainy day Ed Granley-

"You want to get something to eat?" Ray asked. "I discovered the chili cheese dog at Martha's Cafe. That shit'll make you forget all your problems."

Brandon remembered the chicken and avocado salad he was going to make himself tonight. The healthy meal could wait. "Sure," he said, "I could go for a chili cheese dog." He thought that after returning home from dinner he would try finding an email address for John, then decided he'd get through his Saturday art show first. That was just four days away. After that, he'd somehow reach John and make his last amends.

Ray started a third cigarette while the truck descended toward town. "I swear I'm going to quit these by the New Year," he said.

Brandon watched the orange glow at the end of the cigarette. Normally, he'd say something affirming, like "Take it easy and just stay sober." But right now he thought about how he wouldn't mind puffing on a joint.

Brandon lay on his bed in moonlight later that night, staring up at the dark clouds encroaching upon the glow of the half moon. He figured rain was coming from Western Washington. He didn't want to see the moon anyway. It kept Spindly Arms in his thoughts.

He remembered that night in LA that made him finally leave the city. His roommate, Martiniano, had just moved out of their two-bedroom apartment that was right next to the roaring 405 freeway. The building—the Sol Vista—looked like a 1970s motel, and Brandon and Martiniano's wood-paneled apartment had thick red carpeting and never enough light. Martiniano was a 30-year-old aspiring actor who occasionally got roles in commercials, and for the year and a half they lived together, he had an increasingly difficult time tolerating Brandon's substance abuse.

"Fuck him," Brandon had slurred to himself on that fateful night. He wandered into Martiniano's now-empty bedroom. The vomit-stained mattress was the only thing that remained in the room. He heard the words Martiniano had spoken after he and his girlfriend, Alicia, came home and found Brandon lying in puke on their bed.

"When I first moved in with you I knew you were a drunk. But you could at least manage your day-to-day life. Now you don't have a job or friends and you don't even fucking know where you are. You're stuck in this apartment with your alcohol and your creepy Moon Man paintings. It's like you've sealed yourself inside some kind of hell."

Brandon clicked off the light and returned to the living room. His Spindly Arms portraits leaned against the walls of the room, staring at the table in the center, which held beer cans, bottles of Bacardi, and Brandon's skull-shaped bong. Brandon collapsed on the couch and muttered, "'Moon Man' can live with me if you don't want to, fucking Martiniano. I've had plenty of people exit my life, and you're not the best of 'em."

And that's when Brandon heard the sounds coming from the bedroom he'd just left.

KNOCK. KNOCK. KNOCK.

The hair on Brandon's forearms stood up even though it was 70 degrees outside and even hotter in the living room. He tiptoed into the hallway that stretched past both bedrooms. The door to Martiniano's bedroom was wide open, just like it had been when Brandon left the room moments ago. The light was still off.

"That was the sound of the freeway," he told himself, and he stepped to the doorway and flipped on the light. "Nobody's in-"

Brandon shrieked when he saw the moon-faced man squatting on the stained mattress. Spindly Arms wore the black coveralls he had on in all of Brandon's paintings. His tree branch arms were lifted and curving in Brandon's direction as if they were ready to embrace him. Spindly Arms grinned a sharp-toothed grin and stared at Brandon with his black beady eyes. "How about we make one last painting?" he asked. "We'll make it so dark you'll want to blow your brains out when you see it."

Brandon sat up in bed in his attic apartment and wiped the sweat off his forehead. He hadn't thought of that horrible night in a while.

Because it was a delusion, he told himself. *A drunken delusion. You realized it the next day, the morning after you fled the apartment and slept in that littered park off Santa Monica Boulevard. You'd absorbed so much booze that it gave you hallucinations. It made you feel your greatest fear—that you'd go crazy like Dad and off yourself as he did. But you didn't off yourself. You're here in Chelan and you're 44, not 29, and life is so much better than-*

Brandon heard something fall over in the section of the house below his kitchen. That was the downstairs living room.

He hurried out of his bedroom and ran to one of the front windows. A black-clad figure dashed along the stone path and onto the sidewalk. Brandon thought it was a teenage boy, but he couldn't be sure.

Panic replaced his disturbing memories of LA. He continued watching through the window, wondering if anyone else would appear in the yard. The meth addicts who'd broken into the house last spring had been teenagers. They invaded the home just before the owners came for the summer. Brandon was supposed to be on alert for break-ins, and he was also supposed to lock all doors if he ever used the downstairs.

Did he lock the front door last night, when he'd had some people from AA over for the virgin eggnog and vegan pumpkin pie he'd gotten for free from Sustenance?

Be brave, he told himself as he quickly put on a pair of sweatpants and a T-shirt. *Whoever was inside the house ran away, and it was probably just a kid.* He grabbed a carving knife from a kitchen drawer and his cell phone off his night-stand. He called the police and reported the break-in while descending the outside staircase. The dispatcher said she'd reached officers on patrol, and they'd be there immediately. She advised Brandon to lock his door and not confront the home invader.

Could whoever had broken in be the same person who'd left the photographs of the Spindly Arms art? That thought was more discomforting than his suspicion about the meth heads. The drug addicts seemed mostly harmless. They were usually just roaming away from broken homes across Eastern Washington. Brandon worried that he'd been neglectful about locking the front door. He didn't want any animosity from the owners. He loved his attic apartment, and he doubted he'd be able to find an equally desirable place at the same price.

Nearing the front door, he called out, "The cops are on their way. If anyone's inside, you better come out now. You've got only a few minutes to get away."

He was grateful the front door handle didn't turn. He had locked the door.

He spotted the open window on the west side of the living room. Someone had pushed a garden bench against the wall beneath the window. One of the windowpanes was broken. He stepped onto the bench and peered into the darkness of the living room. He couldn't see anyone. He thought he smelled smoke.

Sirens sounded in the distance, and Brandon was no longer hesitant about entering. He stepped over the windowsill and walked into the center of the room.

His limbs tensed when he heard a crackling sound. He rushed to the fireplace and spotted the orange glow of something that had been burning. He kneeled and pulled out a small, partially charred magazine that was propped up against a log in the fireplace.

It was the issue of *Evergroan* that had featured John's Spindly Arms story and Brandon's illustration. Brandon stood with the magazine in hand. He recalled how that Maya girl had put out the magazine. Brandon couldn't remember her last name even though he'd hooked up with her once.

While eyeing the spiral of pine trees on the cover of the magazine, Brandon noticed the sketchbook resting on the mantel above the fireplace. The opened sketchbook showed a sloppy drawing of Spindly Arms crouched on the rooftop of a house.

"What the fuck?" Brandon whispered, lifting the sketchbook with a trembling hand. This was his sketchbook from high school. He'd lost it when the thief broke into his family's house during his senior year. But how did it end up here?

Brandon watched from one of the attic apartment windows as the police car pulled away from the curb. The two cops had been friendly enough, and they didn't show any suspicion of him. Maybe it was because they were rookies. Neither one of the men could have been older than 23. Brandon had told them with as straight a face as possible that the burglars hadn't seemed to have time to steal anything. They just opened the closet and cabinet doors in the TV room, probably searching for valuables. He pointed at the doors he'd yanked open himself just before the cops showed up. He said the burglars burned something in the fireplace, but he had no idea what it could have been. He'd hidden the blackened issue of *Evergroan* in the oven. As for the sketchbook, he'd tucked that beneath a couch cushion in the living room.

Brandon wasn't ready to tell the police about his harasser yet. If he mentioned the Spindly Arms art, he'd have to talk about his past in LA, and that was the past that involved a police record with a few charges of disorderly conduct. He didn't need the Chelan Police Department uncovering his embarrassing episodes of public drunkenness, and he especially didn't want the police discussing those episodes with his landlords. He would tell the police if his harasser did anything that was truly threatening. Hopefully, this break-in was the worst that person would do.

Brandon went from the window to his computer and searched for "John Larsen" on the Internet again. He wanted more than ever to email John. What happened tonight must have been the universe's sign that the two friends needed to connect again. He remembered how much he'd wanted to talk to John when life was at its lowest in LA. After imagining he saw Spindly Arms in Martiniano's bedroom, he had the terrifying realization that he and John hadn't just created a fictional character. They'd conjured something malevolent.

Disappointed with his Google search results, Brandon went to the Facebook landing page and stared at the empty password field. He guessed he'd be able to reach John if he were a member of the social media site. But Brandon had never joined because he didn't want people creeping out of his shaded past and trying to "friend" him, like the assholes who'd thrown the "pretty boy" and "faggot" insults at him in high school, or the countless addicts who'd encouraged his substance abuse in bars and nightclubs from Everett to Vegas.

Brandon pictured lifting an icy beer to his lips right now, and the thought made his mouth water. He shut down his computer and glanced around his apartment in a panic, feeling like the walls and ceiling were inching toward him. He needed to get out of his apartment and out of this town so he could find balance again. He had to maintain his sobriety no matter what. He also wanted to be far away from whoever had been harassing him. If he returned on Friday he'd still have time to prep the show. He called his friend who ran a spiritual retreat center in the Sun Lakes area.

"Amethyst?" he asked in a shaky voice when she answered. "Is it all right if I come to stay with you for a few nights?"

"Are you okay, Brandon? You don't sound it."

He glanced down at the sketchbook he'd dropped in the trash along with the two photographs of his Spindly Arms paintings. He could see a portion of the curving moon head and one beady eye. "I've been going through some freaky stuff," he said. "I'm having some cravings. I've got a big art show coming up this weekend, and I need to be clear for this new time in my life."

"You know I'm skilled at helping with new beginnings," Amethyst said.

Brandon did know that. But he wondered if she could help cut away the malignant past.

Looking in the rearview mirror, Brandon got a final glimpse of the Desert Silence Center. The two-story, red-walled structure was built to resemble a traditional Thai house with a steep gabled roof and stilts lifting it above its rocky lakeside location. Brandon had spent the last three nights and two days at the center, trying to live mindfully through meditation, healthy eating, and counseling with his friend Amethyst, whom he'd met at the "Spiritual Sobriety" workshop he attended in Bellingham last year.

He told Amethyst all about his harasser and the Spindly Arms artworks that were haunting him once again. During one of their chats over a cold brew, Amethyst stroked a gray dreadlock and watched him with those ever-smiling brown eyes of hers. "Sounds like your shadow side wants you to look at him."

"Shadow side?"

"The dark part you don't normally like to look at. We all have one. He may have been more powerful in the past, but he'll always be in you. He needs your attention right now. He won't leave you alone until you give him that."

Brandon's Corolla rose out of the canyon that contained the Desert Silence Center and the largest of the Sun Lakes. The sun was setting on the high-desert plateau he'd cross to reach Chelan. Speeding past the darkening wheat fields, he thought about how he'd initially struggled to explore the deeper, spiritual meaning of his plight after speaking with Amethyst. He couldn't focus on his shadow side when he kept wondering who'd planted those images of Spindly Arms and had the gall to break into the house.

His anxiety weakened but remained constant during the happier moments of his retreat: meeting that elderly lesbian couple from Mendocino; wading into the icy lake when the sun was at its hottest each day; wandering among the tall, shade-giving poplars that bordered the property.

While completing one walking meditation session, Brandon pondered his years in Leavenworth, where his shadow side had probably been its strongest, and where Brandon had been his drunkest.

He'd chosen to move to the town because it wasn't too far from Glimmer Lake and his sister, who lived in the house where she and Brandon had grown up. She'd moved in after their mother went to cohabitate with her best friend in Florida. Brandon also picked Leavenworth because he remembered all the times he and John had camped by the river and talked about how cool it would be to reside in the town. With the German architecture and surrounding mountains and countless hiking trails, Leavenworth might as well have been in the Bavarian Alps. It was so different from Glimmer Lake, a bland American suburb with strip malls and track housing and small hills soggy from the incessant drizzle.

For some reason, Brandon had ignored the fact that Spindly Arms's fictional home was on a farm just outside Leavenworth. Brandon had wanted to leave behind his thoughts and painted depictions of this sinister entity, so why the hell did he come to the place where he and John had first given form to Spindly Arms with their imaginations?

One drunken, delirious night after renting a single-bed-room cabin outside of town, he realized the answer: Spindly Arms had tricked him into moving here. Spindly Arms would try to convince Brandon to kill himself. After all, Brandon was in his thirties, and his dad had put a gun in his mouth when he was 38. Dropping his bottle of vodka, Brandon stumbled out of the cabin and wandered through black pine trees that began to glow from a supernaturally pink sunset. He had the heart-piercing realization that Spindly Arms wanted him stuck in an alcoholic loop. The definition of insanity is to do the same thing over and over again while expecting different results. And Brandon understood on that morning that if something didn't change he really would kill himself—or get himself killed.

Brandon now spoke aloud to himself in the car: "You got yourself out of that dark loop, and you'll get yourself out of this one."

He completed the drive from the Desert Silence Center to his home in Chelan in a little over an hour. He parked his car and gazed up at his attic apartment with dread. The Victorian was a black silhouette tonight except for the small stove light glowing beyond Brandon's kitchen window. Brandon couldn't believe he'd forgotten to leave on more lights before driving to the retreat center. An unlit house was an invitation to the creep who had left the Spindly Arms artwork earlier in the week. Brandon didn't need another scare on the eve of his art show. He reluctantly exited his car and headed toward the downstairs front door. He held up the flashlight on his phone as he approached the house. He saw nothing in the garden. Unlocking the door, he cracked it open and ventured inside.

Everything appeared to be the same as when he'd left town on Tuesday night. He once again heard the words Amethyst had spoken during his guided meditation session: "Scary things come, and scary things go—just like everything else in life. Breathe in that truth."

Feeling calmer, Brandon stepped out of the house and started up the external staircase to his attic apartment. His heartbeat quickened when he saw the large manila envelope resting against his front door. He snatched it up and braced himself for an image of Spindly Arms inside. But what he pulled out was a stack of flyers showing his *Martiniano* color field painting. The bottom of the flyer read:

Chelan's Own

BRANDON LAURENT

AMENDS – PAINTINGS

Waterway Gallery

Opening Reception Saturday 10/26, 5-7

The gallery owner had written on a Post-It stuck to the top flyer: *We've left these all over town. We're thrilled to show your work, Brandon. Break a leg! Marcia.*

Beaming, Brandon brought the flyers inside his apartment. He almost forgot to look for signs of a break-in. He decided the apartment was just as he left it, and he used a magnet in the shape of Lake Chelan to display one of the flyers on his refrigerator. Gazing at the piece of paper, he nodded and told himself tomorrow his life was going to get better.

He almost believed it.

The next morning Brandon was in his kitchen, adding oat milk to his coffee when the face appeared in the window above the sink.

Startled, he dropped the carton of milk on the floor. It splashed across one of his bare feet. "Fuck," he whispered. Glancing up, he saw the person blocking the morning sunlight was Deeanne. She stood on the small landing outside Brandon's front door, and she held a bouquet of sunflowers.

"I'm so sorry," she said. She cupped a hand over her mouth.

"It's okay!" Brandon said, relieved to see her. "I'll be right there." He threw a dishtowel on the mess and went to open the door.

Deeanne looked more gorgeous than ever this morning, watching him with those round emerald eyes of hers. Sunlight lit up her red hair, which she'd tied back into a large, floppy bun that fell over the back of her neck. She wore a green tank top, short pink shorts, and flip-flops. Her toenails were painted orange. She held out the bouquet for Brandon. "Good luck flowers for you," she said.

"Thank you," Brandon said, taking the bouquet. "Would you like to come inside?" He realized Deeanne would glimpse his messy, unmade bed, and the thought of her spontaneously slipping under its rumpled covers excited him. He remembered his temporary celibacy.

"I've got to drive my mom to her friend's in Manson," she said. "But I'll see you at your show this evening."

Brandon nodded. "Awesome."

"I don't mean to act like a stalker," Deeanne said with a nervous laugh, "peeking in your window like that."

"I'd rather you be my stalker than anyone else," Brandon said with a grin.

"Deal," Deeanne said, backing away from the door. "I should go." At the top of the stairs, she turned back to him. "Would you like to go out with me sometime?"

"Deal," Brandon said, smiling more widely. "I'd like that." He considered his celibacy again and thought, *Don't be so rigid. Pay attention to what the universe is bringing you.* "I'll see you at the show."

Deeanne looked pleased. "I'm more forward than most, I know," she said, and then she hurried down the stairs.

While wiping up the oat milk, Brandon thought that Deeanne wasn't even close to the most aggressive woman he'd encountered. He'd been prey to many a sexed-up woman in his drinking days, and he'd even let a couple of insistent guys suck him off when he was at his drunkest. And, of course, there was Phoebe Granley.

He'd trembled that second time he came to Phoebe's front door. He had the *Glimmer Lake Gazette* in his hand. He was expecting the armless man to appear in the doorway with those glaring bug eyes of his, or maybe he'd jump out of the toolshed and sic his Dobermans on Brandon.

But Phoebe opened the door when he knocked. She'd teased and sprayed her black hair so it was bigger than usual. Once again, her make-up was thick, and she wore red lipstick. She had on a blue tube top dress that accentuated her large breasts and wide thighs. Brandon didn't mind the love handles that showed beneath the tight fabric. He wondered if she was about to leave for a dinner date and her husband was going to appear behind her, forcing Brandon to speak the lie he'd rehearsed: "Today we're bringing the paper to people's doors because of the heavy rain."

The armless man didn't show, though, and Brandon remembered it was 4 in the afternoon—too early for dinner. But Phoebe couldn't have dressed up like that for him, could she? After all, she was in her mid-thirties and he was just a senior in high school.

"I'm happy you came," Phoebe said, taking the paper from him. "How about that soda I owe you?"

The living room seemed less depressing that day. Pink candles glowed atop the coffee table and a small bookshelf packed with thriller and romance novels. A red- and white-checkered quilt covered the maroon couch. The cream-colored carpet looked like it had just been vacuumed.

"Sit down and relax," Phoebe said, motioning toward the couch. "Ed went with his friend to the coast today, and I told him to take the dogs."

Brandon nodded and sat stiffly on the edge of the couch. He wasn't sure what to say, and he felt like he'd waded too deeply into something. But he did like how Phoebe looked at him as if he were a birthday present and there was only the wrapping keeping them apart.

"Tab or 7-Up?" Phoebe called from the kitchen.

"7-Up, thank you." Brandon glanced at the television, which was on mute and showing a soap opera. On top of the TV was a videocassette.

Phoebe entered the room with Brandon's can of soda and a glass of white wine for herself. Rather than sit in the rocking chair, she lowered herself right beside Brandon. He could feel her body heat, and he immediately went hard. Blushing, he took the 7-Up from her and sipped it.

"It's fun having a friend over to talk to," Phoebe said. "Most of my friends are busy with their kids or work or else they're just not that fun anymore. I like to have fun. I think I'll always be 19 inside, you know?"

Brandon nodded even though he didn't know. Phoebe continued to talk, and he watched her, noticing how she licked her lips after every sip of wine. She shared how bored she was with her nursing job, and how she'd originally gone into that job because she liked helping people, but now Ed and his moods and his expectations took up so much of her capacity for helping people that she felt like she didn't have much left to give.

"I feel like I need to put myself at center now," she said. "I need to recharge with some fun and some Phoebe time."

Brandon nodded dumbly again, and he questioned whether he should have come here. He was about to rise from the couch when Phoebe's eyes teared up. She shared how Ed wanted to take his three grandchildren into their house because his daughter from a previous marriage had a drug problem.

"I never wanted to be a mother," Phoebe said, fanning her eyes with one hand. "I always figured that since Ed was older than me and he had his injury and his ex-wife he'd never make me take the conventional route of having kids or keeping house. I guess I was wrong."

Brandon finished the last of his soda and nervously glanced down at his watch.

"Oh, god, listen to me!" Phoebe laughed. She squeezed Brandon's arm. "I'm not being fun. I'm being a bore." Her hand stroked his bicep as she said, "You can't go yet, though. I want you to watch something with me."

She shot up from the chair and went to the TV, where she picked up the videotape and inserted it into a VCR. "My friend gave me this. It's that Madonna video that caused all the controversy a couple of years ago. 'Justify My Love.' I never saw the whole thing, did you?"

Brandon shook his head even though he had seen it with John and some other friends. "Not the whole thing," he said.

Phoebe grinned devilishly and pressed play. She hurried back and sat down next to Brandon, closer this time.

Brandon grew hotter and hotter as he watched the black-and-white display of lace, leather, lesbianism, sadomasochism, and tonguing. He felt Phoebe's warm hand on his leg, and her face neared his. They kissed deeply.

She guided his hand beneath her dress. He nearly came when he realized she was wearing garters, just like the disheveled and platinum-blonde Madonna on the screen.

"You're not a virgin, are you?" she whispered.

Brandon shook his head.

"How old were you?" Phoebe asked.

"Fourteen," Brandon said. He remembered his older and distant cousin taking his hand and placing it beneath her bikini top while they lay by a river in Idaho.

Phoebe raised her eyebrows, obviously surprised by how young he'd been.

"She was my babysitter," he lied.

"Well, this'll be a lot better," Phoebe said, sliding her dress up over her thighs, "because now you're a man."

Walking to the Waterway Gallery, Brandon glimpsed his reflection in the window of a used bookstore. He wasn't normally vain, but he thought he looked particularly handsome on this afternoon of his art show. He wore a light blue Gucci suit he'd received more than a decade ago from a male model friend in LA. Brandon had carefully preserved the suit in a bag over the years. He also wore a pair of chestnut leather secondhand loafers he'd bought in Spokane when he was visiting the city with his sponsor. He'd slicked his lengthy brown hair back so it curled just a bit behind his ears. *Middle age suits you okay,* he told his image.

He was also pleased with the paintings that were awaiting inspection by the art show attendees. He'd prepped the show earlier today, and the large *Amends* paintings were towering and noble-looking on the white walls of the gallery. Marcia had insisted he leave by 1 so he'd have time to go home and rest before the show. She and her assistant were going to pick up the appetizers and wine at 3:30 and then set up.

"Come to the gallery at 5," she told Brandon, "when everyone else does. We'd like you to make your grand entrance that way."

A block away from the gallery, Brandon saw a small crowd of people standing outside the entrance of the historical brick building. Feeling a mix of anxiety and pride, he wondered how many would be coming this evening. He'd already thought about what he might say if Marcia asked him to address the attendees.

"I'm truly honored you're here to see my work. These paintings represent where I'm at in my life. I don't have much money, I don't have a significant other, and, at 44, I guess I'm technically 'over the hill.' But I'm happier and healthier than I've ever been, and I've reached a deep peace with the past."

Brandon noticed that some of the people outside the Waterway Gallery were frowning. He didn't recognize any of the people, who ranged in age from late twenties to mid-thirties. They glanced at him as he approached the building, and then they immediately looked away. Brandon saw Deeanne standing in front of the glass doors of the gallery. Her face was pressed up against one of the doors. She looked concerned.

"Deeanne," Brandon spoke. The crowd seemed to disperse away from him as if he were contagious.

Deeanne turned to him with a furrowed brow. "Brandon, I don't know what happened," she said, sounding apologetic. "I don't know who would do this." She seemed genuinely empathetic, but she, too, kept a distance from him.

"What is it?" he asked.

"You should go in and see," she said. "I'm going to take my friends to a restaurant so you can have some space. I'll find you later."

Confused, Brandon stepped toward the entrance. Marcia appeared behind the glass doors. She wore a sleek yellow dress and black high heels, but her graying blonde hair looked disheveled. Her smudged mascara showed she'd been crying. She unlocked one of the doors and opened it for Brandon.

"This is awful," she said. "I'm so sorry. Emma and I were gone for only an hour to get the appetizers, and then we came back to...this." Her eyes became glassy with tears. "I tried calling you, but you didn't answer."

"What is it?" Brandon asked. He looked past her into the main room of the gallery, and he gasped.

"I'll be out here so I can tell visitors to go home," Deanne said. "Come outside when you're ready."

Brandon staggered inside, feeling like his legs were about to buckle beneath him. Someone had pasted Spindly Arms drawings on all his *Amends* paintings. The drawings appeared to be the ones that had gone missing from his house in high school. Whoever had defaced the *Amends* paintings applied the Spindly Arms drawings by brushing a black, tarry substance along the edges of the smaller works. That person had also splattered blood-red paint all over the paintings and the walls of the gallery. A large red word appeared on each of the gallery's four walls:

THIS

IS

BRANDON'S

WORK

Brandon swayed from side to side, staring up at the ruined paintings in shock. All his healing paintings were defaced. He'd never be able to recreate the same artworks. He thought of the countless hours and powerful emotions that had gone into making those paintings. Who was it that hated him so much to do this?

Unable to look at the ravaged art anymore, he wandered outside the gallery to find Marcia. She was speaking to a pretty girl with short black hair. The girl couldn't have been older than 21 or so. She was holding up a large smartphone for Marcia to view.

Marcia turned to Brandon. She looked perplexed, and her eyes were still tearing. "Do you know anything about this?"

The girl showed Brandon the screen, which displayed his decades-old illustration of Spindly Arms standing on a cliff, peering down at a distant town. Brandon had just seen the same drawing on the *Amends* painting he'd made for his mother.

The girl tapped on a back arrow to reveal a website called *Bloody Bitz*. "Anybody in the public can post horror stories on this site," she told Brandon. "And Spindly Arms stories keep coming in. They're really popular. The first one was by this guy named John Larsen."

Brandon felt stuck in a nightmare as the girl spoke to him. She said a woman was murdered in Seattle's Pioneer Square neighborhood on Tuesday. Whoever did it left a tree branch on top of her body, and her cell phone displayed the *Bloody Bitz* site. The first Spindly Arms story went up on the site earlier that day.

"Did you draw those, Brandon?" Marcia asked. She motioned toward the Spindly Arms drawings covering the walls of her gallery. "The initials on them look just like the ones on your *Amends* paintings."

Brandon thought he might faint. "I drew them in high school," he admitted. "I don't know what's going on. I don't know who did this. I'm sorry, Marcia, but I need to get out of here. I feel sick."

"I'm going to call the police," Marcia said. "I'll have them call you so they can talk to you."

Brandon nodded. He no longer cared about his police record in LA. "I'll be glad to talk to them," he said. He teetered away from Marcia and the teenager, suddenly craving a drink.

Brandon's hands shook as he completed Google search after Google search on his laptop at home. He sat on the couch with his computer resting on his thighs. He learned that the woman who'd been murdered in Pioneer Square was Maya Mathers, the classmate who'd published *Evergroan*. Brandon felt a painful lump in his throat as he stared at one photo of Maya. She'd remained cute into her forties, and she still had that long sandy hair and freckled cheeks. Brandon hated himself for not remembering exactly when he'd slept with her in high school.

While scanning the Spindly Arms-related posts on *Bloody Bitz,* he saw there was one story about Spindly Arms decapitating John on a mountain farm, and another about the malicious character strangling Vivian in a cemetery. He knew it was time he contact the police. But first, he wanted to try to reach Vivian. He pulled his phone out of his pocket.

As the phone rang, he remembered how he'd almost called her to tell her about his art show. She'd sounded distant when he made amends to her over the phone in the summer, though, so he didn't call her a second time.

"Vivian?" Brandon asked when someone answered.

"Brandon?" Vivian sounded surprised—and upset.

"Vivian, are you all right? Is John okay?"

"I-" Vivian choked up. "Brandon, where are you?"

"I'm in Chelan, where I live."

"John didn't find you?"

Brandon had a moment of elation when he thought of his ex-best friend seeking him. He set his laptop on the couch and stood. "I told you when we talked last summer I haven't seen John since high school. Was he looking for me?"

"I thought he was."

"Vivian, what's going on with all this Spindly Arms stuff? I read about Maya, and I found that website with the Spindly Arms stories. There's one about John, and there's one about you."

"Me?"

"There's a post about Spindly Arms killing a 'pretty Asian lady named Vivian.'"

"Oh, god."

"Vivian, are you and John in trouble?" Brandon was ready to tell her about everything that had happened to him over the past few days.

"We're-" Again, she seemed to be on the verge of crying. "Brandon, I need to go. Let me call you back later."

Brandon suspected she was concealing something from him. "Vivian, do you need me? I can drive out there."

"If I don't phone you in an hour, call the police and tell them I disappeared at this address in Glimmer Lake."

"What the hell, Vivian? What's going on?"

"Brandon, please, I don't have the time to explain. Just write down this address."

Brandon hurried into the kitchen and grabbed a pen and pad off the counter. He scratched down the address she gave him, and then he said, "Vivian, what else can I do?"

"I have to go now. Goodbye, Brandon."

Brandon paced across his living room in frustration. He wanted to act, but he didn't know what to do. He was about to pick up his computer and start searching the Internet again when something smacked against his kitchen window. He flinched, and then he rushed to the window and peered out at the darkness of the night. He couldn't see much, but the light above his front door revealed a newspaper lying beneath his window.

He grabbed the carving knife off his kitchen counter and charged outside. He didn't see anyone. Whoever had tossed the paper must have thrown it from the stairway leading up to his apartment. He stepped to the railing and gazed down at the front yard. He saw no movement.

He picked up the newspaper, which was rolled up and had a rubber band around it. It was a copy of a *Glimmer Lake Gazette* from October 1992—the issue that included John's Spindly Arms story and Brandon's accompanying illustration. Brandon removed the rubber band and opened the paper. Someone had written in red pen on the page of the Spindly Arms story:

ARTISTIC FUCKER,

COME TO THE FARM ALONE. NO POLICE. IF ANYONE'S WITH YOU JOHN GETS IT.

—SPINDLY

Brandon dropped the paper as if it was covered in poisonous ink. He went back inside and tried Vivian again so he could tell her about the note. She didn't answer this time. Brandon hung up without leaving a voicemail. He knew he had to find that farm he and John had gone to over 25 years ago. It was where Spindly Arms began, and it was where something must end. The universe had previously been hinting that Brandon reconnect with John. Now it was screaming the message.

Brandon no longer wanted to call the police. The note instructed him not to bring any cops, and he could always phone them later. He needed to find John. He changed into a sweatshirt, jeans, and sneakers and pocketed his car keys. He picked up the knife again, and then he set it back on the kitchen counter. He returned to his bedroom and searched through a few weathered shoeboxes until he found what he wanted: the gun he'd bought in LA.

Driving on Highway 2, Brandon watched the sun sink beyond the distant brown hills. As the sky darkened, the trees on either side of the highway thickened.

Brandon wondered if he'd even recognize John if they passed each other on the sidewalk. Brandon had blood in his eye the last time they'd spoken to one another.

It was December 1992, on the small, sloping front lawn of Brandon's house. John had pulled up in his dad's Buick around twilight. Brandon watched from behind a living room curtain as John stood on the grass and hollered his name. John's face was red and his eyes puffy. He only stopped shouting when Brandon came outside. Vivian sat in the passenger seat of the car. She had a look of remorse on her face, and Brandon guessed she'd told John she and Brandon had slept together.

Brandon was only able to take a few steps toward his best friend before John punched him in the face. Brandon saw spots, and his left cheek throbbed with pain. "What the fuck?" he asked, and then John punched him again. Brandon's brow began to bleed.

"I know what you did!" John said, both his hands clenched into fists. He swung at Brandon again, but Brandon ducked.

John didn't miss a second time. He socked Brandon in the nose, and then he was on top of him, shoving his bloodied face into the lawn as he kneed him in the ribs. Brandon tasted a gritty blend of dirt and grass.

"Stop it, John!" Vivian called from the sidewalk. "I'm not going to watch you act like a child!"

"Then get the fuck out of here!" John yelled. He eased up on pressing Brandon's head against the earth.

With one swelling eye, Brandon saw Vivian walk away. She shot worried glances at the two of them, and then she covered her face with both hands.

"It's not just our fault," Brandon muttered after catching his breath.

"What'd you say?" John shot back.

Brandon knew he should be apologizing to his best friend, but he couldn't repress his resentment: "You're partly to blame, too. Maybe if you weren't so self-absorbed Vivian wouldn't have-"

"'Self-absorbed'?" John asked, scowling. He stepped back from Brandon and held his hands up in the air as if his friend wasn't even worth punching. He looked like he was about to start crying. Shaking his head, he said, "You fucked Vivian and I'm the one who's self-absorbed?"

"You've been acting like you don't even care about her," Brandon said. "Her parents kicked her out of the house and all you care about is your stupid writing. You're not even that great of a writer." Again, Brandon knew he shouldn't be saying any of this. But some rage surfaced from deep within him. Maybe it was because he felt like he couldn't tell John the truth about his dad's death, that John would be judgmental about the suicide in some way. Or maybe it was simply longstanding envy of John for being smarter, more talented, and better loved than him.

"Do me a favor and don't ever talk to me again," John said, starting toward his car. But then he stopped and swiveled toward Brandon. "There's something seriously wrong with you," he said. Glaring, he asked, "Did you know your dad told me he wished I was his son?"

Pain bloomed in Brandon's chest. His eyes started to tear.

"I never knew why he said that," John said. "But now I do."

Dazed, Brandon watched him stomp toward his car. John never looked him in the eyes again.

Brandon felt that decades-old pain in his heart as he once again focused on the road to Leavenworth. Brandon had healed so much through self-work, but John's comment about his dad was a wound that had scabbed over and never fully disappeared. Brandon knew what John had said was true. Because his dad would have stuck around if Brandon were a worthy son, wouldn't he?

Brandon imagined hearing the sound of whiskey pouring over ice cubes, and his mouth watered. He paid attention to his breath until the temptation passed. He was surprisingly relieved to see a trio of chalets on the hillside above the road and a Bavarian-themed hotel at the next bend. He was entering Leavenworth.

Even though the summer tourist season was long over, the town was aglow on this Saturday night. Brandon drove past the Korner Markt, where he'd bought his liquor, and fatefully bumped into Sharon, the motherly 60-year-old who turned out to be his first sponsor. "You look miserable," she told him that last time he lugged his grocery basket of bottles to the counter. "I was once a drunk," she said as she stood behind him in line. "I'll help guide you if you want to try a different way." That diner with the icicle-shaped lights hanging from its eaves had the backroom where Brandon attended AA meetings every Friday evening for nearly six months. And that bookstore—A Book for All Seasons—was where Brandon purchased all his spiritual books and the thank you cards he mailed to AA friends before beginning his new life in Chelan.

I'm starting over, he'd written in those cards. *And this new beginning would be impossible without you helping me plant the seeds.*

Brandon thought of Ray as he drove through the middle of town. Ray wouldn't hesitate to help him. And Ray had served in Afghanistan with the Marines. He could navigate dangerous situations. Brandon decided he should tell his friend where he was and what he was doing in case something went awry. He steered his car off Highway 2 and let it idle in an alley that ran between the bookstore and a beer garden.

He'd lifted his cell phone to his ear when the headlights blinked on behind him. Squinting in the rearview mirror, he realized a car was just in back of his. Brandon rolled down the window and waved for the vehicle to pass. The car didn't move, though, and its brights came on.

The rear of Brandon's neck prickled when he had the thought that whoever was behind him knew where he was headed—and wanted him to be on his way.

He aborted his call to Ray and set down his phone on the passenger seat. He continued along the alleyway. The vehicle remained in back of his as he took two right turns to get onto Highway 2 again. His palms were now sweating. Brandon eyed the glove compartment, which held his gun. The trailing car's brights finally went off. Brandon increased his speed, creating more distance between him and the car. Luckily, his pursuer allowed him to have some space.

Brandon passed the last of the Germanic buildings, and he was now in the darkness of the mountains, driving between steep, forested slopes. He spotted a sign indicating the exit for *Red Cedar Creek* was in 2 miles. He thought that was the exit he'd take to get to the farm. He glanced in his rearview mirror again and didn't see the car. It must not have come to the last curve in the road.

Brandon reached for his phone and dialed Ray's number. He heard Ray's voicemail.

"It's Brandon," he said. "I think I'm about to meet whoever was leaving me those nasty presents I was telling you about. I'm on Highway 2, heading just west of Leavenworth to a mountain farm. I think you take Exit 62 to get there. If you don't hear from me in an hour I'm in trouble. See ya, boss."

Brandon had only a mile to go until Red Cedar Creek. He once again wondered who could be waiting for him at the farm. Many people knew about his Spindly Arms paintings and could have left him those photographs, but only a few knew he'd been to Ed Granley's farm. John. Vivian. Phoebe Granley. Did Ed Granley know, too? Maybe because his wife had told him?

Brandon was still surprised by how much Phoebe had shared with him—the senior in high school she was fucking weekly. "I think he bought that farm as part of his midlife crisis," she said while they lay naked and side-by-side on her and Ed's bed. It was a November afternoon when Ed had taken the newly adopted kids to a circus show in Bellingham. She puffed on a joint and passed it to Brandon. "I mean what's he going to do on a farm when he doesn't have two good arms? His prosthetics only allow him to do so much." Phoebe also told Brandon how her husband's arms ended in stumps where his biceps should be. He'd tried the strap prosthetics, but they were too uncomfortable. Lately, he'd been using plastic cosmetic prosthetics that fit around the stumps.

"He's skilled with his feet and toes, though," Phoebe said, nodding and smiling as if there were one, sexual secret she wasn't going to tell Brandon. She turned to him with slightly bloodshot eyes and said, "I can't believe you guys followed him into the mountains in the summer. If he caught you following him now he'd find a way to kill you. Your friend pissed him off with that creepy man-with-the-moon-face story. He thinks your friend and that girl and you are all against him. 'Those fucking teens that deliver the newspaper.' I wanted to tell him you're much more mature than a teen and you deliver so much more than the *Glimmer Lake Gazette*." Phoebe tickled Brandon, and though he laughed he was uncomfortable about how relaxed she was about what was happening between them. He knew the sex sessions in her and Ed's house couldn't continue forever.

"He's not so innocent himself," she said, suddenly sounding resentful. She plucked the joint out of Brandon's fingers and brought it to her lips. "You know how I told you he used to work on fishing expeditions all over the world?" Brandon nodded.

"He lost his arms in Egypt."

Brandon listened intently. "In a boating accident?" he asked. Phoebe handed him the joint, but he didn't smoke it.

Phoebe shook her head and looked like she'd just tasted something bitter. "He told me some men—some 'crooks'—attacked him in a town on the Nile. But you know what? Whoever cut off his arms did a very clean and even job. I think Ed did something bad over there, and he got punished for it."

"Like what?" Brandon asked, his eyes wide.

Phoebe grinned and shook her head. "Curiosity kills cats, Brandon."

Veering onto the Red Cedar Creek exit ramp, Brandon thought about how he should have listened to her that day. He should have tried to end his fascination with Phoebe because, no matter how wildly sexy and impressively mature she was, she was also married and deeply unhappy in an infectious way. His troubles only increased during the affair. First came his dad's suicide, and then there was the sudden rift between him and John, and Vivian. And, finally, there was that rain-dumping morning in January of '93, not long after Brandon got his whupping from John.

When Brandon arrived at Phoebe's front door that morning, she looked flustered and as if she'd been crying. She pressed both hands against her temples. "I'm sorry, Brandon, but the kids are still here. Ed and I were fighting before he left for work, and everything's been...chaos."

"I can come back another day," Brandon said. He wouldn't have minded leaving. Lately, all he'd wanted to do was be at home by himself. "I won't be doing the paper route anymore, but I-"

"Stay," Phoebe insisted. "Please. I'm just going to run the boys down the block to the babysitter's. I'll be right back. You can wait in the house." She disappeared into the living room, and when she returned to the front hall she had a blue-eyed baby in her arms and two small, black-haired boys standing on either side of her. They were dressed in yellow raincoats and they couldn't have been older than 5 or 6. They stared up at Brandon with large, curious eyes, and he felt like they shouldn't be seeing him.

Before he could utter an excuse for going home, she said, "I'll see you in 5. Take your shoes off. Get comfortable."

Brandon reluctantly did as she requested, and he felt awkward as he sat on the couch barefoot, staring at what must have been her and Ed's darkly stained mugs on the coffee table. Toy trucks, fire engines, and police cars were strewn across the living room carpet.

The front door swung open minutes later, and Brandon shot up from his seat at the thought that the armless man had returned home. Phoebe said he worked at a car dealership that was a 15-minute drive from here. But it was only Phoebe, wet-haired from the rain and looking slightly crazed.

"I'm back," she sang.

"Who'd you tell the kids I was?" Brandon asked.

Phoebe gave him a dismissive wave. "I didn't say anything. The two older ones don't ever pay attention to anything. They won't think twice about you." She shook her head. "They're really little demons. Yesterday I caught them hurting the hamsters we bought them. Poking the poor things with a fork. I'm worried they're going to lead their little brother down the wrong path." She seemed like she was in one of her manic states where she would talk and talk.

Brandon approached the doorway. "I should probably go. Your morning's been rough."

"No," she pleaded. She placed a hand on each of his shoulders and guided him into the bedroom. "You're the one person who can calm me." She slipped a hand down the front of her jeans, and then she violently yanked down his sweatpants. Brandon couldn't deny his excitement.

Kneeling before him, she said, "You'll be ready again in a little bit. And then I want you to come inside me."

But Brandon never ejaculated a second time because Ed Granley burst into the house just as Brandon was climbing on top of Phoebe's prone and fleshy body. Ed swayed outside the bedroom, red and quaking. Panic-stricken, Brandon scrambled out of the bed and snatched his clothes off the floor. He realized there was no way he was getting past the armless man without knocking him over.

"The twins called me," Ed said. "'Auntie Phoebe's with a man at home,' they told me." He glared at Brandon. "Only you're not a man, are you? You're a fucking kid."

Brandon felt like he should respond somehow, but he could do nothing but gape.

"Tell me something," Ed said. "Did you think you could stick your dick in my wife without paying a price? Because you know she's a whore, don't you?"

"You bastard!" Phoebe snapped. She sat up in bed and threw a pillow at her husband.

Brandon didn't wait to watch the fight progress. He lifted the window and hopped out into the muck of a flowerbed. He didn't look back to see Phoebe, and he never saw her again. The last thing he heard was the armless man shouting at him from the window.

"I've got a horror story for you and your fucking friends! Just wait until I get your names!"

Brandon drove over a small bridge that traversed Highway 2. He wondered if Ed Granley could be the one holding John at the farm. Was this some kind of revenge plot against "those fucking teens" from the early '90s? It was possible, but Brandon doubted a man who must have been in his seventies could orchestrate all this.

At the end of the bridge, Brandon took a right and recognized the distant intersection. The road on the left would lead him up a steep hill, on top of which was Ed Granley's farm. He guessed if he took the low road he'd skirt the base of the forested slope. He stopped the car and glanced back across the highway. Near the start of the bridge, headlights illuminated trees. A vehicle was getting off Highway 2. Was it the same one that had been behind him in Leavenworth?

Brandon knew someone was expecting him to ascend the hill to the farm, so he turned off his headlights and drove straight ahead. He would reach the hilltop by climbing the forested slope on foot. That way he could scope out the farm. If he remained in his car, he'd be more vulnerable—especially if someone was driving right behind him. Past the intersection, he steered the Corolla off the road and onto a grassy stretch sheltered by trees.

He waited until he saw the headlights aimed upwards on the hillside road, and then he got out of his vehicle with a gun in hand. He hurried across the asphalt and entered the forest. Nervousness made his legs wobbly. He was glad he'd put on boots because his feet often sank into the mud. It must have poured here earlier in the day or the night before. He trudged up the hill in a zigzagging route for about 10 minutes before he spotted a clearing. He wondered if he was already at the edge of the farm.

But the building beyond the trees wasn't the farmhouse or the barn. It was the Bavarian-style cottage next to which he and John had parked when they followed Ed Granley up here all those summers ago. Venturing into the clearing, Brandon realized one side of the cottage and a portion of its roof had been blackened by fire. He heard a car coming down the road. He scrambled toward the damaged portion of the cottage and hid inside an exposed chamber. The narrow, charred space still stunk like smoke and exacerbated Brandon's feeling of dread. He gripped the gun tightly. The vehicle drove past the cottage. Brandon was sure it was his pursuer, probably wondering why he hadn't driven up to the farm as instructed. After the sound of the engine faded, Brandon dashed into the trees on the hillside above the cottage.

He hurried through the forest in the direction of where the car had come from. He soon stepped out of the evergreens and set his hands on that familiar rickety fence that bordered the farm. It felt like that summer night in 1992 again. The pasture was still brown and overgrown. The dark splotches on the farmhouse and nearby barn showed the structures were still in need of new coats of paint. The one change was that the trees of the apple orchard were now skeletal, their long, barren branches twisting in all directions.

And someone was moving among those trees.

Brandon's body tensed up as the figure staggered out of the orchard. The man was about 100 feet away. He wore a yellow mask in the shape of a crescent moon. He also had on a soiled button-up shirt that was partially tucked into stained khakis.

Brandon gasped when he realized the man's right arm was missing. He had a bandaged stump where a bicep should have been. Brandon noticed the rounded shoulders, and he somehow knew he was looking at a friend from long ago.

The masked head lifted slightly and then froze. The eyeholes were fixed on Brandon. Though Brandon couldn't see the eyes, he sensed the fear in them.

"John?" he called. He leaped over the fence and sprinted toward the masked figure. "What did they do to you, buddy?" His voice cracked when he asked the question.

"Brandon?" John responded in what was barely more than a whisper.

Brandon saw that John's one unharmed arm was constricted by a loop of rope tied around his waist. He also had a rope around his left ankle, snaking from John's leg to the trunk of one of the dead apple trees.

"I'm here, buddy," Brandon said, tucking his gun at the small of his back. He lifted the rubber mask off John's head and tossed it into a patch of weeds. John was clearly in shock. His eyes were glassy and round, and he had dark smudges beneath them. The rest of his face was bone white. Brandon noticed the stains on John's shirt and pants were dried blood.

Brandon embraced his old friend. "I'm going to get you help now." He pulled his phone out of his pocket to call 9-1-1, but there were no bars at the top of the screen. "Damn," he sighed.

Brandon untied the rope around John's middle, and then he crouched to free John's leg. Looking up at his friend's dazed face, he asked, "Is there anyone inside the farmhouse?" He glanced at the structure and spotted a dim glow in one of the ground-floor windows.

John mumbled something, but Brandon couldn't understand him.

"What's that, buddy?" he asked.

"Spindly Arms was a mistake," John said, sounding disoriented.

Brandon squeezed his friend's hand. "John, I need to know if anyone's inside that house."

"Drove away," John said. He pointed weakly toward the road. "Saw him drive away." He turned toward the house and spoke in a despairing voice, "Arm's in there."

Brandon scowled. He didn't want to venture inside the farmhouse, but he couldn't leave without John's arm. Was it even salvageable? He didn't know. If the house had a landline, though, he could call the police.

After removing the rope, Brandon stood and glanced around the property. He didn't see anyone else, and he wondered if the only person he had to be concerned about was in that car that had sped downhill past the cottage. He placed a hand on John's lower back and nudged him in the direction of the farmhouse. "Let's get you inside," he said. John showed no panic after hearing the suggestion, so Brandon guessed the farmhouse could be a safe place—at least temporarily. He took his gun out from beneath the waist of his pants.

They moved across the pasture, John shuffling rather than walking. Brandon tried to stay calm by not looking at John's bandaged stump, but he couldn't help glimpsing it a few times and noticing how blood soaked through the wrapping. He looked behind them in the direction of the road, and he was thankful no headlights cut through the darkness of the night.

Brandon checked for an address number on the front of the house. He could give that information to the police if he reached them. But the face of the farmhouse only showed disintegrating paint, filthy windowpanes, and lopsided shutters. When they reached the door, Brandon moved in front of John and pointed his gun ahead of him.

The door was unlocked. Brandon pulled it open and stepped onto a creaking floorboard. He listened for some noise in response to his, but the house was silent. He turned to John, who gazed blankly into the large, furniture-less space before them. Brandon said, "It doesn't look like anyone else is here."

"They've been dressing up like Spindly Arms," John said, still sounding like his mind was stuck in some other, nightmarish dimension.

Brandon led him inside the farmhouse and shut and locked the door. He glanced around the dim front room, which had a stone fireplace and a couple of faded paintings of bears on its walls. Near the fireplace were two crooked sleeping bags. Ahead of Brandon, a staircase rose to the second floor. The light in the front room came from two adjoining chambers, one of which appeared to be a kitchen. He figured there might be a phone in there. He cocked his head to listen for someone else inside the house, but the silence continued. Brandon felt like he could almost hear the pounding of his heartbeat, though.

"Come on," he told John and started for the kitchen.

A dusty ceiling light cast its glow on the sickly yellow cabinets and walls of the kitchen. A small, circular dining table occupied one corner of the room. The table held a half-full pot of coffee, two chipped mugs, and some candy bar wrappers. The coffee wasn't steaming, making Brandon think nobody had been in here recently. On the wall above the table was a calendar from 1993. The February photo featured a bikini-clad bottle blonde lying with legs spread on the prow of a yacht. Brandon didn't see a phone anywhere in the kitchen.

John was rocking side to side in the kitchen's doorway. Brandon pulled one of the chairs away from the table and instructed, "Have a seat."

John lowered himself into the chair as if he were decades older than 44. Brandon now saw the wrinkles around John's eyes and the gray that had crept into his hair over the past two decades. Brandon felt woozy when he glimpsed the wet redness at the end of John's bandaged stump. Brandon pulled open some drawers until he located a dishtowel. He carefully tied it around the stump.

"Can you tell me who did this to you?" he asked.

John shook his head and gazed into the dim front room. "What we did our senior year," he said in a solemn voice. "Two guys and a girl."

Brandon wondered if John was talking about their trio of friends in high school—John, Brandon, and Vivian. Brandon filled up one of the mugs with coffee, letting the liquid rise to the lip of the container. "I want you to drink as much of this as you can," he told John. He knew the caffeine might make John more conscious of his bodily pain, but he needed John to snap out of his daze. Whatever pain reliever he was on could prevent them from getting to safety. He slid the remains of a Snickers bar in front of John. "Try to eat this, too."

He watched John drink some of the coffee, and then he resumed his search for a landline—and John's missing arm. "I'll be right back," he said.

He used his cell phone's flashlight to search for a phone in the front room. The chamber truly was empty except for the sleeping bags. Clumps of spider webs lined the corners of the room. Brandon watched black spiders scurry away from the light of his phone, and he thought about how John had gotten the webs right when he wrote about Spindly Arms's home.

Brandon went to the house's other lit room, which turned out to be a small bathroom containing a sink, a toilet, and a bathtub. He winced when he spotted the blood splatter on the wall above the toilet. The bowl of the sink showed traces of red rivulets that had run into the drain. Brandon turned to the opaque yellow shower curtain concealing the tub and yanked the material aside. A dismembered arm lay in a puddle of blood. The arm was on top of a clear tarp that covered the bottom of the tub. Brandon retched. He set the gun on the back of the sink and bent over the toilet, waiting for his nausea to pass. *Breathe,* he told himself.

While he stared below him, he noticed the screen of the cell phone he still gripped in one hand. Bars appeared at the top of the screen. He'd be able to make a call. He straightened up and dialed 9-1-1. As the phone rang, he glanced into the mirror that was to the left of the toilet, just above the sink.

A man in a moon mask stared at him from the bathroom doorway. The man wore a black leather jacket and black jeans. He raised a machete. "Put down the fucking phone."

"What's your emergency?" a woman asked on the other end of the line. Though terrified, Brandon knew he needed to act quickly. He spun around and hucked his phone at the masked man. He then reached for his gun, but before he could pick it up the man punched him in the face.

Brandon fell forward over the toilet, and one of his elbows knocked the gun from the back of the sink onto the tile floor. His attacker was shoving him toward the tub. Brandon managed to raise his right leg and send the heel of his shoe into the man's shin. The man groaned and loosened his grip. His machete dropped to the floor with a clatter.

Brandon raised himself and broke away from the man's hold. He ran out of the bathroom and toward the kitchen, and he suddenly regretted he didn't try to retrieve the weapons from the bathroom floor. In the front room, he could see John was no longer sitting at the table.

"John!" Brandon called in alarm. He glanced back in the direction of the bathroom and saw John standing outside the door with a knife in hand. John must have heard the tussle and come to help. Brandon knew John would be useless in his current state. Brandon wished he still had his gun.

The masked man appeared in the doorway behind him, wielding the machete.

John started toward him with the knife raised, and the man lifted the machete as if he were going to hack off John's one remaining arm.

"No!" Brandon shouted, charging toward the pair. The masked man turned to him, and that was when John stabbed the fellow beneath his ribcage. The man howled. Brandon kept running forward and pushed the man toward one of the cobwebbed corners of the room as hard as he could. The wall caved in upon the impact with a loud cracking sound and an explosion of dust, and the man disappeared into a black hole.

Brandon heard a crashing noise as the man must have landed in the farmhouse's basement. Brandon listened for the sound of movement below, but he didn't hear anything. He couldn't be certain the man was unconscious.

John touched Brandon's shoulder. "I'm feeling more with it," he said, smiling weakly. "Thank you for coming." He glanced down at his bandaged stump, and fear filled his eyes. "I need to get to a hospital."

"We'll get you there, buddy," Brandon said. He returned to the bathroom in search of his gun and phone. Neither one was on the floor. The man must have pocketed them.

Brandon kneeled by the tub and wrapped up the arm in the piece of tarp.

"What are you doing?" John asked as he came to the doorway.

"We're going to get this back on you when we get you to a hospital," Brandon said, trying to sound confident even though he doubted any surgeon could make this fix. He hoped John wouldn't slip into another state of shock. "Come on," he said. "We're getting out of this hell hole."

Brandon placed his palm on John's back and led him toward the front door. John was still moving slowly, but he seemed more aware than before. Brandon's limbs tightened when the headlights appeared outside a window, across the pasture. A car was at the start of the farmhouse's drive.

"We need to go out a different way," Brandon said, hooking his arm around John's and pulling him toward the staircase. To the right of the stairs was a narrow hallway that brought them to a back door. On the side of the staircase was another door. Brandon guessed it must be a way to the basement. He once again listened for movement downstairs, but all was silent. He opened the back door and descended a few wooden steps to the backyard.

Thankfully, the moon was high and bright in the sky. Brandon could see the rusted ruins of a tractor in the backyard and the overgrown path that curved to an opening in the fence. He figured they could enter the woods and head downhill until they reached the road where he'd parked his car.

John tripped on the lowest step and fell on the path.

"You okay?" Brandon asked, lifting him onto his feet.

"I'm all right," John wheezed.

Brandon was anxious about how they were going to manage the steep hill when John could barely handle stairs. "Just hang on to me if you need to," Brandon said, holding John's dismembered arm close to his body. "We've got to move as fast as possible."

They were only about 30 feet from the house when Brandon heard glass breaking. He glanced behind them and saw the machete smashing through a slit window that was just above the weedy ground. The moon mask stared at him from the darkness of the basement.

Brandon watched with horror as the masked man punched out the remaining shards of glass and began to pull his body through the window.

"Go!" John told Brandon in a terrified voice. John somehow managed to trot toward the fence.

Brandon followed and glanced back once more. The masked man slid out of the window and into the moonlight. He rose to his feet without showing any sign of his knife wound.

Incredulous, Brandon asked, "Who the fuck is he?"

John pulled him by the arm through the opening in the fence. They entered the shadows of the forest. "I don't know who the three guys are," John said, traveling down the hill at an impressive speed. "Or who the girl is."

"There's a girl?" Brandon asked. And then he tripped over a tree root and tumbled down the slope.

AVA

"Summer can go away now," Ava said while walking through downtown Seattle with her mom. She wore a pale yellow sleeveless dress under a charcoal-gray hoodie. "I'm done with it."

"We're at the end of September, sweetheart." Ava's mom also wore a sleeveless dress, but hers was floral. Her pink heels clacked annoyingly on the pavement. "It's not even summer anymore."

"It's 86 fucking degrees."

Ava's mom stopped on the corner of 5th and Pine and grabbed her daughter's wrist. "I don't care if you're a senior now. You can't talk to me like that. And if you're so damn hot then why don't you take off that stupid sweatshirt?"

"Because I don't want to look like a rich Madison Park bitch who's going to Daddy's office tower rooftop for some dumb lawyer barbecue."

Ava's mom bit her lower lip and glared at her daughter. Ava always wanted to laugh when her mom made that face. She looked like a silly, middle-aged witch. Gone were the youth-inducing effects of the Restylane injections she received every January.

But Ava didn't laugh. She was too hot. And a boy—no, a young man—was distracting her.

177

He stared at her from the opposite corner. He was lean yet muscled and had tousled hair that was nearly as black as hers. It fell over his forehead. His eyes were coal-dark and simmering. His red T-shirt was faded, but it clung to his torso perfectly. A wiry man with sores on his face called to him from a bench in Westlake Park, and Mr. Simmering went to him.

But not before he grinned at Ava.

"Oh, sweetheart," Ava's mom said. She'd lost her angry expression. Her new smile was slightly mocking. "Surely, you're not interested in street punks."

"'Street punks'? Mom, that sounds so snooty."

"That's probably what he is—no matter how cute he may be. Wasting away his early adulthood by hanging out on the streets. No education or job or ambition."

Her mother's disapproval made Mr. Simmering even more intriguing. Ava repeatedly glanced at him as she followed her mom along Pine. The man kept his eyes on her while he sat by his friend. "If you think I'm elitist," Ava's mom said, "wait until you meet some of the women at this barbecue."

"So this is little Ava?"

Ava stood near the railing of the 22nd-floor balcony, grateful to have finally stopped sweating. She was staring down with fascination at the crowds of tiny people bustling along the sidewalks. She could see the block-sized Westlake Park from up here, but trees concealed the bench where Mr. Simmering had sat before. Ava turned toward a lovely, gray-haired woman in a sky-blue pantsuit. The fifty-something woman wore stylish horn-rimmed glasses and gazed at Ava with eyes the color of her suit.

Ava's dad lingered a step behind the woman. The lines on his forehead were showing. He had on that usual over-analyzing-things expression that detracted from his good looks. "You remember Beverly," he told Ava. "She's one of the partners at the firm."

Ava didn't remember her. "Hi," she said, and limply shook Beverly's hand.

"I wouldn't expect her to recall me, Daryl," Beverly said in a dismissive voice. "The last time I saw her she must have been in middle school." Beverly smiled at Ava. "And now you're on the verge of college. Any ideas about where you'd like to study?"

Ava wanted to go somewhere very far and very different from the little over-privileged enclave where she'd grown up. Somewhere that could satisfy her craving for experience. Somewhere that would fuel her writing. "I'm figuring it out," she said.

"Your father tells me you're certain you want to study English."

Ava nodded, and her dad added, "Ava's in AP English."

"I was an English major in college," Beverly said with a hint of pride. "Lots of attorneys are. The law profession requires a command of language."

Ava stared at the woman blankly. She began to dread the destination of this conversation.

"Perhaps you could intern at the firm next summer," Beverly said. "We need help with cleaning up the entries in our state law database. I'm sure you have the right skills for that."

Ava's father nodded eagerly, but Ava said, "I don't think I want to be trapped in an office next summer. I want to do some things."

"Oh, I see," Beverly said. "And what kinds of 'things' would those be?"

Ava shrugged again. "Some interesting things. You can't plan those."

Ava's dad's frown lines rivaled the lines on his forehead.

Beverly was grinning, clearly enjoying this challenge. "You've got all year to think about the internship, my dear. I'm guessing you're not going to become an interior designer, like your mother. You seem like you'll want a career with a little more...depth. No offense to your mother, of course."

Now Ava was the one frowning. "How is being a lawyer deep? You guys just argue whichever way someone pays you to, don't you? I'd rather have a strong opinion of my own."

Beverly laughed, but Ava detected a hint of resentment in that laughter. And Ava's dad was blushing at the age of 49. Ava once again became aware of being overheated. The weather was making her cranky and barb-tongued. She didn't want to be an asshole. She just wanted to get away from this barbecue and her parents. A waiter arrived with a tray of deviled eggs. "Appetizer?" he asked the trio.

"I don't feel well," Ava announced. She started for the coat check so she could retrieve her sweatshirt. "It was nice to see you again, Beverly. Thank you for the offer." She kissed her dad on the cheek and said, "I'll take the bus home. You and Mom don't need to worry about me."

Ava stepped out of the office tower and into the shade of 4th Avenue. The sun was weakening, but night's coolness remained hours away. Despite the lingering evening heat, Ava kept on her weathered gray sweatshirt, and she even slipped the hood over her head. Westlake Park was directly across the street. She ran through a break in traffic to the opposite sidewalk, feeling the sunbaked pavement through the thin bottoms of her flats. She just wanted to peek past the park's narrow-trunked trees and see if Mr. Simmering might still be around.

He sat on the same bench, and he was talking to an obese, unshaven man in a wheelchair. Ava glanced around the park. So many people looked like they were living on the edge of disaster: the messy-haired old woman curled up in a ratty sleeping bag on top of a cube-shaped sculpture; the round-eyed, Charles Manson-esque guy who clenched his fists and cursed at a pack of pigeons; the red- and puffy-faced men who sat at a table drinking bagged alcoholic drinks and playing checkers with filthy fingers. Ava knew her parents would want her to be nervous in such a setting, but she felt liberated—and she was fascinated by all she saw. This was stuff worth writing about. She told herself she'd just walk by Mr. Simmering's bench. She wouldn't make eye contact. She was aware of a quicker way to her bus stop, but she knew this was the way she had to go. She stared down at gum stains on the sidewalk as she strolled. When she was almost past the bench, she glanced at Mr. Simmering.

And he looked back at her. "Hey," he said.

"Hey," she said, pausing. Again, she was surprisingly calm as she stared at this man who must have been in his mid-twenties. She knew there was nothing that could prevent her from talking to him. "What's up?"

"What's up with you?" the man asked, smiling lopsidedly.

"I was just looking for my friends," Ava said, glancing around the park for her pretend pals.

"I saw you with some woman earlier. Was that one of your friends?"

Ava almost betrayed her embarrassment. Instead, she approached the bench and thought up a distraction. "I love your L7 T-shirt," she addressed the man in the wheelchair.

He pointed proudly at the shirt, which showed someone in a bloody-looking animal mask, and, beneath the band's name, the words *HUNGRY FOR STINK*. Splotches of dried mustard covered one sleeve. "My sister bought this at a concert," he said with pride, "a few years before she died. 1994. They played with Nir-, Nir- Nir-, Nir-." The man was stuttering and his eyelids fluttering. "Nirvana. I think it'll be worth a fortune."

Ava summoned a smile for the man, sensing something was wrong with him psychologically. He was a true character. She said, "I love all those riot grrrl bands from the mid-'90s even though I wasn't born yet."

"What year were you born?" Mr. Simmering asked.

"I'm 19," Ava lied with a grin, "in case you're worried."

"Why would I worry about something like that?" Mr. Simmering asked as if he were the Big Bad Wolf in Grandma's nightgown. Ava wondered what he'd think if he knew she was a virgin.

"I should probably go," she said. "My friends will be looking for me." She needed to cast out the hook to find out if Mr. Simmering was truly interested. She clenched her teeth as she started away from the bench.

"Wait."

Ava slowly turned back, thinking *Yes, yes, yes*.

"I'm Ben. And you're....?

"Ava."

"I don't think you should go yet, Ava. I don't have your phone number."

Ava touched her chin and stared upwards at the just-past-summer sky as if she were seriously contemplating something. She then looked at Ben. "How about you give me yours?"

Ava decided she'd forever associate her and Ben's relationship with autumn. The closer she and Ben got, the shorter and crisper the days became. The leaves of the trees in West-lake Park—where she and Ben usually met at the start of their dates—went from green to bright yellow, orange, and red. And then, in mid-October, the rains started. Usually, when the shroud of clouds covered Seattle each fall Ava would feel like her heart was contracting and hardening in preparation for the dim, depressing months ahead. But this year she sensed the water was loosening whatever it was that was stirring and blooming in her chest. She guessed this new sensation was affection for Ben and attraction to his darkness, his edginess, his belonging to an alien and potentially dangerous subpopulation. She also figured it was her strength—both as an adventurer in life and a writer in the making. She confided in Ben about her passion for writing short stories and some poetry, and that she'd never really had a "serious boyfriend" before. But most everything else she told him was carefully crafted fiction: that she was studying Creative Writing at the University of Washington, and her crazy class schedule was the reason she could only meet him a few days a week in the late afternoon, and on weekends; that she lived in an apartment on Capitol Hill, and he couldn't visit her there because her roommate/landlady was a "strict bitch" who never left home; that her parents were dead, just like his. "They died in a plane crash when I was 17," she told him without blinking. "Seattle to Vegas. I wanted to go with them on that trip, but my dad told me I was too young to gamble. That's kind of ironic, don't you think?"

The lies mostly thrilled Ava because they helped lodge her so deeply into this new cocoon of experience. But she did feel guilt about speaking untruths while Ben revealed so much of himself. When they strolled past the Gum Wall beneath Pike Place Market, he talked about how he and his two older twin brothers had grown up mostly in the foster care system. "You seem like you come from a good home," he told her. "We come from a bunch of shitty ones." He was reluctant about showing her where he lived in SoDo with his brothers because he insisted it would look like a "puke-stained shoebox" compared to wherever she lived on the Hill. He said he got by with income from odd yard work and construction jobs, but he was most financially comfortable when he was selling marijuana at prices that were just below what the pot shops offered. He became emotional that time they made out on a pier jutting into Elliott Bay, explaining it had been years since a girl had been interested in him without some agenda, like getting easier access to weed or being in the sphere of protection offered by his brothers.

Ava almost blushed when he said "agenda," but she reminded herself she did like Ben. This romance wasn't only about wanting to learn and write about his reality. And besides, isn't every relationship and friendship self-serving to some extent?

In the third week of October, Ben asked Ava if she'd like to come over to his place. Ava initially wondered if he was hoping to have sex with her. He'd been patient the two times she pulled his exploring fingers out of her underwear. The few guys in her high school she'd dated hadn't been so understanding with her pacing, and, red-faced, she told all of them they weren't worthy of being her First.

But Ben had another motivation for asking her to come home with him: "My brothers said they want to meet you," he said. "And I figure it's time you see how I live. It's not a way I want to live for much longer."

Ava nodded enthusiastically. While Ben crossed Westlake Park to say goodbye to Ollie, his pal in the wheelchair, Ava quickly called her parents' land line and left a soft-voiced message: "Hi, guys. I won't be home until late tonight. Alyssa and I are at the downtown library looking for books for a History class project."

"Watch it," Ben warned as he and Ava stepped off a bus onto 1st Avenue South. He pointed at a Ziploc bag on the sidewalk, and when Ava bent over that bag she realized it was full of syringes.

"This way," Ben said, leading her under an overpass. Evening was descending. They walked past mud-splattered tents and cardboard boxes sheltering homeless people. Beyond the overpass, they crossed a street lined with warehouses and fenced-off parking lots. On one corner was the Gull's Nest Motel, a two-floor, gray-painted structure with red doors and less-than-impressive vehicles parked in front. The building's hideousness gave Ava pleasant chills. Her parents and most of her classmates would panic if they saw her nearing such a dump.

"This is it," Ben said, motioning toward the motel.

Ava offered a comforting smile to signal there was no need for embarrassment. She grabbed his hand in front of the motel.

"It's kind of cool you live somewhere you can leave at any time," she said.

She remembered the exhilaration she'd felt when she "ran away" from home last spring. Her parents were on a weeklong island-hopping expedition in Greece, and they were without cell phone coverage or Internet access for days. Ava's best friend's mom and dad were periodically checking on Ava during her parents' absence. Midweek, Ava stole money out of the envelope of cash her dad hid under his armoire and took a train to Portland just after French class. She stayed in a Mexican-themed hotel in the Pearl District, wandered through Powell's Books every morning, attended a "Transgressive Cinema" film festival, and ate all her meals at food trucks. No loved one or acquaintance knew where she was, and she relished the independence and rebelliousness of her trip. When she returned to Seattle after a few days, she told her best friend's frantic parents she'd blame them for neglect if they ever mentioned her disappearance. She also told herself she'd go rogue even more strongly the next time.

Raindrops started falling as Ava and Ben climbed the stairway to the second floor.

The door to Room 21 opened before they reached the top stair. A man in a long-sleeved camouflage T-shirt and brown cargo pants stepped out onto the balcony. Like Ben, he had black hair, but it was buzzed. His body was a little thicker and more muscular than his younger brother's. His eyes were the same olive green, but they revealed a jadedness that Ben's didn't have. Ava noticed his feet were bare, and she couldn't help gawking at the parallel, slash-like scars on the tops of those feet.

"The scars remind me of where I come from," he said.

Ashamed that he'd caught her staring, Ava didn't know what to say.

He thrust out his hand. "I'm Micah, and I know you're Ava. We've heard all about you. Ben talks about you a hell of a lot."

Ava smiled politely and reached for his hand. Another man appeared in the doorway. He looked just like Micah except for a mangled right ear. He wore a black T-shirt showing the visage of Two Face, that *Batman* comic villain with half a normal face and half that resembled raw and rancid hamburger meat.

"Harley Quinn's my favorite *Batman* baddie," Ava said, making a thumbs-up gesture for the second brother.

"Hey, Ava," he said. "I'm Amos."

Ava guessed the twins were in their early thirties, but something about them seemed decades older and wearier. Ben looked like he'd had to trudge through some shitty times in his life, but he still appeared to be around his age—just over 26.

"Come on in, lovebirds," Amos said. Ava glanced back at Ben. He looked pleased about her meeting his brothers, but she also recognized the tenseness on his face. She figured it's normal to stress about your girlfriend meeting your family. She couldn't imagine how she'd act if she brought Ben home to her parents' Tudor in Madison Park. Inside the motel room, she surveyed the space. It had a popcorn ceiling, maroon carpeting, and the nostril-burning scent of marijuana and man sweat. The two double beds were carelessly made. A duffle bag crammed full of clothes lay on the foot of one bed. Beside the bag were a couple of yellow rubber masks in the shape of a crescent moon. The other bed held an ashtray filled with the remains of joints. An open magazine lay near the pillow. The outdated TV on the wall across from the beds showed some CSI show.

Amos grabbed a remote control off the night table and turned off the TV.

"Have a seat," Micah told Ava. He motioned toward the glider chair near the door.

Ava sat and Ben stood beside her. Ava spotted an upside-down crate in one corner. With a strip of purple silk over its top, the crate resembled some kind of altar. It held an old, propped-up photograph of a bald man who must have been in his fifties; a notepad darkened by scratchy writing; and a pistol in a glass box. Ava's back straightened when she spotted the weapon.

"Don't be scared," Amos said. He retrieved the box and brought it over to her. "It's a German Luger from World War II."

Ava noticed the Nazi swastika on the handle of the pistol and frowned.

"We're not skinheads," Amos said, "although we've known some. Micah and I just collect weird shit like this, and then we sell it."

Ava nodded and stared up at him. "Cool," she said. The gun still disturbed her, but it thrilled her, too. She was glad she had Ben next to her for protection.

"The maid didn't think the gun was so' cool," Amos said. "She's only cleaned our room once since we moved in. She's always in Baby Ben's room, though."

Ava looked up at her boyfriend. "You've got your own room?" "

"He's spoiled," Amos teased. "Too spoiled."

"I have to share it with Daniel," Ben said in defense.

"But Daniel's barely there," Micah said, "since he's tweaking 24-7."

"'Tweaking?'" Ava asked.

"Meth," Ben said.

Ava nodded and tried to conceal her discomfort. Of course, she knew about meth, but she didn't know anyone who'd done it. She guessed Ben had at least tried it.

"We let Daniel hang with us because we go way back," Micah said.

Ben set his hand on Ava's shoulder. He told his brothers, "So you got to meet her. I think she and I will go next door now."

Ava felt like she had more to explore before she left with Ben. She pointed at the open magazine on the bed and asked, "Good reading?"

"I don't know if I'd say good," Micah said. He fetched the magazine and brought it to Ava. "It's a fucked-up story that dates back to when we were kids."

Ava stared down at an illustration of a man with a moon-shaped face that was similar to the masks on the bed. He wore coveralls and had crooked, leafless tree branches for arms. He stood at the edge of a shadowy forest. The illustration was for a story. Ava read a random sentence: *Those blood-soaked arms reached over long distances, through dreams, and across the years.*

She spoke aloud the title of the story: "Spindly Arms." She glanced up at Micah. "It reminds me of *Bloody Bitz.*"

He gave her a questioning look.

"It's a website where anyone can post horror stories. My friends and I read the posts sometimes. I've written a few."

"You're a writer?" Micah asked, sounding impressed. "You didn't tell us that, Ben."

"I told you she goes to the UW."

Ava felt some guilt about Ben strengthening her lie. She knew she'd have to eventually reveal the truth to him if their relationship was going to last. "I'm majoring in Creative Writing," she said. "I'm not a bad writer if I say so myself."

"She could help us," Amos said.

Ben tightened his grip on Ava's shoulder. "Guys, let's not-"

Ava stood, freeing herself from Ben's touch. "Wait, I want to hear this. Help you guys with what?" She glanced at the masks on the bed again, wondering what kind of life experiences these brothers could offer her. Perhaps experiences that could advance her writing? Surely experiences that would get her even closer to Ben.

Micah took the magazine from her and smacked it with the back of his free hand. "The guy who wrote that story killed our grandfather—and our grandfather's wife, too."

"What?" Ava asked with raised eyebrows. Ben had mentioned his parents were dead, and his grandfather took care of him when he was a baby and his brothers were little. He said they entered the foster care system after their grandfather died. Ben never mentioned murder.

"Ritual murder," Micah said, glaring. "Three teenagers, including the guy who wrote this. It happened in 1993. We've finally tracked them all down, and we're going to make them pay."

"Are you going to tell the police?" Ava asked.

Amos began fidgeting with his mangled ear. "Ben didn't tell you?" he asked, giving her a crooked grin.

Ava glanced at Ben. He stood with his arms folded tightly over his chest. His eyes were on the carpet.

"We've got pasts," Micah said. "Amos and I have done time at Monroe."

Ava felt a cold prickling along the back of her neck. Monroe was a prison up north. She'd heard mention of it on the local news. "What'd you do?" she asked in a timid voice that probably made her sound much younger than a college student.

Amos's hand dropped from his ear. "Nothing compared to what that fucker did to our grandfather."

"The police won't believe us," Micah said. "But there are other ways we can make the truth come out."

"What if Ben told the police?" Ava asked.

Amos gave that wicked grin again. "Ben's not so innocent either. Thirty days in jail for a second offense of selling weed."

Ava turned to her squirming boyfriend again. She didn't appreciate that Ben had kept that bit of history from her, but he did mention he sold weed. She told herself jail wasn't as bad as prison, though she didn't know the difference. And all this new information was making her situation much more interesting. She was truly living life at 17. How many of her 12th-grade classmates could say that?

"What would you want me to do?" she asked the twins.

Micah tossed the magazine onto the bed. "We're figuring things out. We're talking to the woman who published the story. She's got valuable information on the three pieces of shit that killed our grandfather, and she's going to help us. We're going to make their lives fucking suck."

"Ava's not getting involved in this," Ben blurted. "I don't want to be involved in this." He took hold of Ava's wrist and tugged her toward the door. "We're going next door."

Micah blocked their path. "I think she is going to get involved. She's smart. She can write. She knows the Internet."

He told Ben, "If she's not in then you can kiss her goodbye and see her in five years."

"What are you talking about?" Ava asked, suddenly fearful. "Where would Ben go?"

"Ben will tell you next door," Micah said with a sneer. "He owes his big brothers, and if he doesn't pay up then he's going to suffer as much as we have."

Ben's room was cleaner than his brothers'. After turning on the lamp between the made beds, he led Ava toward a mattress and had her sit beside him. Rain hammered the balcony outside the room. Ben looked both remorseful and nervous as he peered into her eyes.

"I should have told you about jail," he said.

"Ben, it's all right."

"No!" he snapped. "My past is not all right. I've sold more than weed. I still do sometimes. Oxy. A little heroin—but only to people who look like they've used it before. And there's more."

"What is it?" Ava looked at him searchingly.

"My brothers were in Monroe for armed robbery. They hit up a dollar store. I was driving the car they were supposed to get away in."

Ava stared at him in shock.

"I didn't know they were going to rob the place," Ben said. "I swear. They told me they were just running inside to get a few things. While I was parked out front, I heard sirens and saw cop cars speeding up the street. I knew they were there for Amos and Micah. I freaked and took off." He stared at the floor with a tortured expression for a moment, and then his eyes met hers again. "My brothers say I owe them for their prison time."

"And if I don't help you then they'll turn you in?"

"I wouldn't put it past them," Ben said. He shook his head. "And the shitty thing is I've been thinking how I want to get a new life. Meeting you has been amazing, Ava, and it's made me want better things."

"It has been amazing," Ava said, and she meant her words.

"No more living in motels or squatting in abandoned houses," Ben said. "I want to move east in the future. Maybe Spokane. I'll get a real job. Maybe I'll fucking start going to church or something."

"Ben," Ava whispered.

"What is it?" He suddenly looked deflated. "You want to leave, don't you? Get away from this shitty motel room and shitty me."

Ava stood from the bed and faced him. She glanced around the chamber and then smiled at him. "This room isn't shitty. It's perfect. And you...." She reached for the hem of his long-sleeved shirt and lifted it above his stomach, past his chest. He raised his arms and allowed her to take the shirt off.

She gazed at his pale torso and his hairy nipples and the trail of black fuzz that went from his bellybutton to beneath his pants. She breathed in the smell of his musky odor and told herself to remember this moment.

"So you don't want to leave?" he asked.

Ava shook her head and unbuttoned her jeans. She slid them down past her knees. "I want to help you," she said, surprised by the confidence in her voice, "and I want to do it with you." Some of her friends had told her how much it hurts, and about the bleeding. While Ben went to lock the door and pull shut the curtains, Ava had the hope she'd feel pleasure.

But she wanted some blood, too.

Ava didn't see Ben again until the following Tuesday evening. The five-day delay wasn't because she regretted having sex with him. He'd been so tender with her in bed, asking if he was hurting her even after she whispered that he didn't need to speak. She avoided seeing Ben over the weekend because she needed to gain perspective on this new, life-altering experience with him and not get lost in it. Her heart was feeling a little too mushy after she untangled her naked body from Ben's and left his motel room. And she had questions: Would a lasting relationship even be possible with him after she'd told him so many lies? She wanted what they had to thrive. She felt a connection to Ben that was equivalent to something out of a Shakespeare play or Victorian novel she'd read in AP English—as if their relationship was about fate or shared past lives or something. His former crooked ways didn't concern her because she was certain he could straighten out like he wanted to. But when would she reveal the truth to him? After helping his brothers with this revenge plot she knew so little about? And what if he rejected her upon realizing she was just a 17-year-old from a wealthy WASP-y family in Madison Park?

Ava didn't only have questions about her relationship with Ben. She also wanted to know more about the twins and their criminal histories. She tried Googling them on her smartphone over the weekend—at night while she watched YouTube videos on the giant flat-screen TV in her bedroom, and on the afternoon she and Alyssa ate vegan ice cream cones on Capitol Hill. She recalled that Ben had said his last name was Lasaras.

But no useful results appeared on her screen. Not for Micah or Amos, and not for Ava's new boyfriend, Ben Lasaras or Benjamin Lasaras.

When she entered Ben's motel room on Tuesday, she was ready to ask him if he'd lied about his last name. She didn't say anything, though, because Micah and Amos were in the room with their little brother. Micah and Amos sat on one bed, and Ben was on the other. Ava's heart fluttered a little the moment she saw her new, darkly handsome boyfriend. All three brothers looked at her when she entered the room as if they'd been waiting for her. They gave her grave looks.

"What is it?" Ava asked. She momentarily worried they'd uncovered her lies.

"Remember how I told you we were in touch with the woman who published that story?" Micah asked. "The one who was feeding us info on the three fuckers who killed our grandfather?"

Ava nodded.

"She's dead. Amos was supposed to meet with her in Pioneer Square tonight. He found her in her car. Her throat was sliced open."

Ava cupped a hand over her mouth in surprise. She asked Amos, "Did you call the cops?"

He touched his ruined ear, which looked like a giant wad of bubblegum. "We told you we did time in Monroe. Ex-cons don't just happen to stumble on murdered people."

Ava nodded. "But it's not like you guys hurt anyone in the past, right?" She looked at Ben again, but he glanced away at the faded, anchor-patterned wallpaper.

"Stealing money from a dollar store isn't hurting people," Micah said, shaking his head. He looked annoyed by her questioning. "It's not like stealing lives. That's what those three fuckers did when we were kids—and again tonight."

"You're sure it was them?" Ava asked.

"We don't have time for all these questions," Micah said. "We need to act—and we need your help. Are you still up for helping us avenge the death of our grandfather, Ava? Ben told us you said you're in."

"You don't have to," Ben told Ava. His eyes now met hers. She was relieved to see the affection in those eyes.

"I've never seen you willing to give up so much for a girl," Micah said to his little brother, shaking his head. "You could daydream about her all the time if you were in Monroe."

"I'm in," Ava said. "But this is about avenging the death of your grandfather's wife, too, isn't it?"

"That's right," Ben said, giving her an appreciative look.

Micah was beaming, making Ava feel very useful. "We need you to put the Spindly Arms story and a drawing of Spindly Arms on that *Bloody Bitz* site you told us about," he said. "And we need you to do it in the next couple of hours. Can you do that without anyone being able to find out you were the one who put the story on there? Nobody can trace it back to you."

Ava thought of the loaner laptop she and her friends had stolen on a whim from the high school library before the last summer break. They were ecstatic—and somewhat scared—about the theft they'd committed. But nobody from the school even seemed to notice it was missing. Ava and her friends realized they didn't have much use for it, and Ava's friend Meaghan stashed it under her bed months ago.

"I can post that story without anyone knowing," Ava said. "But Ben will have to drive me to Madison Park."

Ben borrowed his brothers' black truck to take Ava. As they ascended the hill that led them out of downtown, Ava considered asking Ben if he'd lied about his last name. But she didn't want to irritate him. He already seemed like he was brooding. She guessed that woman's death was weighing on him. The murder was on her mind, too, but it was as exhilarating as it was disturbing. She wondered if the killers had also slit the throats of Ben's grandfather and the man's wife back in 1993. Ava had tried to talk to Ben about the ritual murder the night they slept together, but he didn't want to discuss it. She decided now was not the time to bring it up again.

Instead, she asked, "You probably don't remember your grandfather, do you? You said you were a baby when he died."

Ben shook his head. "I don't remember him. I remember Phoebe, though."

"His wife?"

Ben gazed ahead at the road. "I remember her singing to me. My brothers say that's bullshit because I was so young, but I swear I do. My brothers didn't like her."

"Why not?"

Ben ignored her question.

Ava couldn't let go of Ben's lie about his last name. "What was your grandfather's name?" she asked.

"Ed," he said. "Grandpa Ed."

Ava didn't prod further.

Ben asked, "Did your friend text back?"

Ava glanced down at her phone and found her message to Meaghan: *R u home? I need the laptop.* Meaghan hadn't responded. She and Ava weren't the closest of friends, so Meaghan might have been just ignoring her.

But when the truck entered Madison Park, Ava's phone vibrated. The screen displayed Meaghan's reply: *In bellingham for a crosscountry meet.*

Ava typed, *Really need the laptop. How can I get it???*

After a delay, Meaghan responded: *My parents are home but they'll kill me if they know I have stolen property.*

Ava didn't type anymore. She told Ben, "You're going to take a right up here."

Meaghan lived on the same street as Ava, but Ava's house was a couple of blocks down the winding road, closer to the lake. As the truck rolled past homes that many would call mansions, Ava considered telling Ben this was the neighborhood where she lived, and though she was still in 12th grade she would both graduate and turn 18 in just eight months.

Ava didn't disclose the truth, though. She pointed at a three-story Craftsman-style home and said, "That's the house." She'd lied to Ben and his brothers earlier by saying that Meaghan—the owner of the untraceable laptop—was also a Creative Writing major at UW, and she lived at home with her parents to save money.

Ben parked the truck beneath a canopy of yellow leaves in front of the house. "Should I come in with you?"

"No." Ava realized she'd sounded too adamant. In a softer voice, she said, "It'll be faster if I go on my own."

Ben looked as uncomfortable as she probably had when they walked past the homeless people's shelters in SoDo. He most likely wasn't used to being surrounded by the manicured properties of rich people. She wanted to touch his hand and say, "This is all a façade. These people seem like they have so much, but all they've got are their routines of corporate ladder climbing, conspicuous consuming, and supporting social hierarchy. They're barely living."

She left the truck and ran up the brick walkway to the lit front porch. She carried the plastic bag Micah had given her. She rang the doorbell.

Mrs. Hallbart's heavily made-up face appeared in the small window on the front door. Her dyed-sandy hair was tied up on top of her head. "Ava!" she said with an artificial smile. She opened the door.

"Hi, Mrs. Hallbart." Ava stepped inside the house. Mrs. Hallbart wore what resembled a yoga outfit. Her salt-and-pepper-haired husband stood in the large dining room to the right of the foyer among a cluster of Whole Foods bags. Dressed in business casual, he looked like he'd recently come home from work.

"Tom and I just got our food delivery," Mrs. Hallbart said. "We're trying to decide between risotto or something with quinoa. I'm afraid Meaghan's not here."

"I know she's not," Ava said, starting toward the staircase. "Meaghan said I could borrow a dress for a party I'm going to tomorrow night. I'm just going to grab it out of her room."

Before Mrs. Hallbart could speak further, Ava ran up the stairs and hurried inside Meaghan's palatial bedroom. She yanked an orange dress off a hanger in the closet and then pulled stuffed animals, stray socks, and shoeboxes out from under Meaghan's bed until she found the dated and scratched laptop and its power adapter. She wrapped the computer and adapter in the dress and deposited them inside her plastic bag.

Before leaving the room, she snatched a tube of lipstick and a couple of tinfoil-covered peanut butter cups that were on Meaghan's night table. She also pulled the book *Best Short Stories of the Twentieth Century* off a shelf and slipped it into the bag.

She found Mrs. Hallbart waiting for her in the foyer, looking slightly annoyed.

"I don't think you've been over here since you and Meaghan and Haley went to the Spring Fever dance in May. You didn't come to Meaghan's birthday party last month. I know Meaghan was disappointed about that."

Ava shrugged and thought, *Even after yoga, the bitch is still uptight.*

"Is that ginger beer?" Ava asked Mr. Hallbart, pointing at the glass bottles that stood among bags of kale and brussel sprouts on the dining room table. "I so love ginger beer."

"Take one," Mr. Hallbart said.

Ava smiled sweetly and entered the dining room. She plucked two bottles off the table. "It was good to see you, Mr. and Mrs. Hallbart," she said. "Bon appetit." And then she rushed out of the house.

In the car, she handed Ben a ginger beer and slipped the laptop partway out of the plastic bag. "Got it."

Ben gave her a tender look that reassured her about his feelings for her. He'd stick by her even after she finally spilled the truth to him, wouldn't he?

Twisting off the lid of the bottle, he said, "I'm sorry if I've been acting off around you today. I just don't want my brothers forcing you into anything. You don't have to do this for them—or me."Ava smiled at him. "I only do things I want to do," she said. She leaned over and pressed her lips against his. "Now let's drive to a coffee shop with WiFi. I feel like posting a horror story on *Bloody Bitz*. We owe it to that woman, and we owe it to Ed and Phoebe."

Two nights later, Ava stared at the screen of her laptop and announced with pride, "There are now 26 posts about Spindly Arms on *Bloody Bitz!*"

She sat in a corner booth of Merle's Counter, near the intersection of 3rd and Pike in downtown Seattle. The clientele of Merle's was only a little less sketchy than the lost souls who shuffled by on the stained sidewalk outside. But Ava felt safe because she shared the table with Ben and the twins.

"You done good," Micah said.

Ava nodded. She had done well indeed, she admitted to herself. She'd texted various high school friends and tweeted about the "crazy freaky scary" anonymous Spindly Arms story on *Bloody Bitz,* trying to draw visitors to the post. "And I created the profile PastHitsHard," she told the twins, "so you can comment on anything that appears on the site."

She brought the original "Spindly Arms" story up on her screen. Accompanying the tale was the illustration Micah had emailed her the night she posted the story. She stared at the black-and-white drawing of the moon-faced man standing on a cliff, glaring down at a faraway neighborhood. Though she considered herself a fan of both horror fiction and horror films, something about Spindly Arms seriously unsettled her. Maybe it was because a murderer had created the character, or maybe because the character was connected to at least three real-life murders—those of Ed, Phoebe, and the woman killed in Pioneer Square, Maya Mathers.

None of the brothers had given her the details of the ritual murder that occurred in 1993, but Amos told her the three killers had dressed up like Spindly Arms. Ava glanced at the plastic bag beside Amos. It contained two yellow rubber masks in the shape of a crescent moon—the same masks Ava had seen the first time she visited the Gull's Nest Motel. Ava had asked Amos about the masks when she first sat down in the booth, and he replied, "You fight poison with poison."

While the brothers picked at a plate of burnt French fries and talked about how they were seeking their meth-head friend Daniel, Ava once again looked up a crime blog about Maya's murder.

She reread the paragraph describing the scene: Maya's slit throat, the tree branch placed on her corpse, the clutched phone with the *Bloody Bitz* website on its screen. And the estimated time of the murder: Tuesday at 9:12 P.M.—about an hour after Ava had posted the "Spindly Arms" story on *Bloody Bitz,* and almost four hours after Amos supposedly discovered Maya's body. Ava had mentioned the time discrepancy to the twins, and Amos asked, "You believe everything you read on the Internet? Haven't you heard of fake news?" "

Ava couldn't ignore this point. Many of the sites that reported on the murder had differing details: the make of Maya's car, her age, and the type of murder weapon. And besides, why should Ava suspect the brothers killed Maya? Maya was the woman who was going to help them act on their plan of vengeance. The brothers' sole role that night was to manipulate the crime scene so it pointed to Spindly Arms—and that character's creator.

But the time discrepancy still bothered her, just like the possibly fictional name Lasaras and the fact that Amos and Micah would threaten to get their little brother into prison.

"Hey!" Micah snapped his fingers in front of Ava's face. "You spacing out on us?"

Ava looked at him, offended by his tone of voice. But she told herself that was how the twins talked to everyone, including Ben. She was relieved to feel her boyfriend's hand slide onto her thigh and squeeze her leg to comfort her.

"Did you hear what I asked?" Micah said.

Ava nodded. "You were saying Daniel's probably in Tacoma again."

"We want to know if you can spend the whole weekend with us, starting tomorrow afternoon. This is the weekend it all goes down, and we could use your skills."

"Your mad writing and tech skills," Amos said, nodding.

Ava's face glowed at the mention of her writing. She didn't like that the twins were pressuring Ben and her to help them, but she appreciated the men's praise. "I can do a lot more than what I did on Tuesday," she said. "I mean I just copied that story and submitted it and the illustration to *Bloody Bitz.*"

"You don't have to do anything, though," Ben said. He seemed unsure of his words.

Amos reached out and slapped his brother's left cheek. The slap was playful, but it looked like it stung. Ben touched his red face.

"Adventure's good for a relationship, Baby Ben," Amos said. "Let your girlfriend come if she wants to. She's doing this for you."

"That's the truth," Ava said. "Listen to your brother." She rose from her seat and reached across the table to grab one of the moon masks out of the bag. She pulled it over her head and sat back down, wagging a finger at Ben.

"What the fuck?" Amos barked. He yanked the mask off Ava's head, pulling some of her hair.

"Ouch!" Ava said. She looked at Amos with a pained expression. "I'm sorry." She regretted the whininess of her voice.

Micah offered her a consoling grin. "If we're not careful then everything's going to fall through. Can you be careful all this weekend, Ava?"

"I can," Ava said, sounding defensive. "I'm going to the bathroom."

On her way, she reminded herself she was following the twins' plan so she and Ben could be together and Ben could stay out of Monroe. And besides, the revenge plot—whatever it was—seemed justified so far. The brothers had reason to target those who'd murdered Ed and Phoebe.

Ava removed her phone from the front pocket of her sweatshirt. In the dark, stinky corner where the bathrooms were, she started to text her mom about spending the weekend with Alyssa.

Something bumped into the back of her leg, and she stopped texting.

She realized one of the tires on Ollie's wheelchair had knocked into her. Staring up at her, Ollie had a frown on his face and some kind of rash on his double chin. He wore an AC/

DC *Highway to Hell* T-shirt that looked like it had never been washed.

"I didn't know you were here," Ava told him. "Did you see Ben yet?"

He pointed at Ava. "Ben thinks his brothers are his allies, but they're going to fuck everything up for him. I'm afraid they're going to fuck everything up for you, too, too, too."

"Gotta go, Ollie," Ava said, pushing open the door of the women's restroom. She didn't have the patience for him. He'd seemed quirky the times she interacted with him before, but today he was not a character she wanted in the story of her life.

On Friday evening, Ava sat in the back seat of the old Hyundai Ben had borrowed from a friend at the Gull's Nest Motel. With her forehead pressed against the window, she watched the front entrance of Bowl-O'-Rama. Amos was in the driver seat, and Ben sat beside him. Micah had the brothers' truck. He'd been tailing a man named John Larsen through this suburb of Everett, Glimmer Lake. Ava wasn't sure if she'd ever been here before. She thought she and her parents had stopped in a Glimmer Lake Taco Time one spring when they were driving north to see the tulip farms in Mount Vernon.

"Here he is!" Ava said.

John Larsen left the bowling alley and crossed the packed parking lot to his BMW. Dressed in a brown blazer, a button-up shirt, and khakis, he resembled those corporate types Ava regularly saw bustling past Westlake Park. He was partially gray and handsome enough, but she probably wouldn't notice him if he passed her on the sidewalk.

She definitely wouldn't have thought of him as the kind of guy who would participate in a ritual murder. But who knew what he'd been like in 1993? And people conceal their true selves all the time, just like she'd been hiding her true self from Ben and his brothers.

Ava had Googled John Larsen on her phone when they first parked in the lot. She didn't find much. A picture of him on a website for the company Truetonix. He was a senior sales representative there. His name appeared on a list of attendees at the 25-year reunion for the Glimmer Lake High Class of '93. She also found a reference to him in an article about a woman who'd died by drowning in Hawaii over a decade ago. The article mentioned that *Karin Larsen's husband, John Larsen, never saw her enter the water.*

"Got you, fucker," Amos muttered. He backed out of the parking space just after John Larsen rolled out of his. "Now let's see where he takes us."

Ben called Micah on his cell phone. "We're leaving the bowling alley parking lot," he said. "Taking a right onto Shady Shore Boulevard. Looks like he's heading toward the 5 North ramp. We're on him."

Ava felt the hairs on the back of her neck rise up. She and the brothers were doing this! She didn't know exactly what they were doing. She only knew they were following John Larsen and Amos had brought the moon masks and she was going to write and post a story about Spindly Arms killing John Larsen. "The story's gotta make his skin crawl," Amos had instructed her. She hoped she wouldn't regret her participation, but she reminded herself that whatever happened this weekend would benefit both her relationship with Ben and her writing. And this adventure would be epic compared to her jaunt to Portland last summer.

Not long after getting on I-5, they traveled east onto Highway 2, heading toward the Cascades. Ben answered his ringing phone.

"You're betting on Leavenworth?" he asked Micah. "Yeah, I'll tell Amos. The farm it is."

Amos looked like he hadn't even heard the conversation. He glared ahead at the BMW as they sped along a narrow stretch of 2 over rolling, forested hills. Ava thought she saw his lips moving like he was talking to himself.

Ben turned around in his seat. "In the story, the killing happens on a farm," he told her. "A mountain farm."

Ava nodded. She opened the laptop and began typing. She'd already planned on having Spindly decapitate John Larsen. Now she knew that decapitation would take place in a barn. An owl would fly out as soon as John opened the barn door. Spindly would be standing in the darkest corner, his tree branch arms slithering through the shadows in John's direction. Blood would splatter hay.

She'd title the story "Blood Crop." She was proud of her quick inspiration.

"We also need you to add his name to the first post," Ben said. "Can you add his address, too?"

"I can add a comment using our profile name," she said. "PastHitsHard." She thought of the article about Karin Larsen's drowning and then tried to shake off her empathy for John Larsen. Karin Larsen didn't deserve to drown, but John Larsen probably deserved to lose his wife. After all, he did help murder Ed and Phoebe, didn't he?

"You posted the story?" Amos asked after Ava left the Leavenworth Public Library. He and Ben had remained in the car while Ava went inside to access WiFi. Micah had taken over shadowing John Larsen as the man moved about the mountain town.

"The story's up," Ava told Amos, showing him the *Bloody Bitz* post on the screen of her phone.

"I want you to rub that shit in John Larsen's face," Amos said. "He went into a beer garden a couple of blocks from here. Micah just called us."

Ava nodded, and Amos added, "Remember that John Larsen is a killer. He may not look like one, but he is."

Ben held her hand as they ran across the street. Outside the beer garden, he pulled her under an overhanging roof and kissed her. "You ready for this?" he asked. "It'll all be over after this weekend. Then you and I won't have my brothers up in our grills."

Ava shook off her nervousness and instigated a kiss herself. "Ready," she said, and they entered the beer garden.

"I'll get us a couple of sodas," Ben said. He went to the window where a woman in a feathered Bavarian hat took orders. The six occupants of the beer garden drank and ate beneath awnings with hanging orange lanterns. Ava spotted John Larsen in one corner, pushing a pretzel into his mouth.

She and Ben brought their Cokes to the table next to his. Ava wiped her sweaty palms on her pants, and she made sure the *Bloody Bitz* site was showing on her phone. She noticed how distressed John Larsen looked. Maybe "shifty" was a more appropriate adjective. She smiled at him, and he seemed to force a grin in return. She clicked on the original Spindly Arms post. Feigning shock, she loudly told Ben, "They named the Spindly creator!" Ben was supposed to exclaim something in response, but he released a weak "Whoa." Timidity seemed to be affecting his performance.

Ava knew she'd need to lead this interaction with John Larsen. She turned to him. "Have you heard about these stories?"

"Sure," he said. He seemed like he was trying to sound uninterested.

"They finally put the author's name on the original post. Everyone's been wondering who wrote it." Ava glanced down at the screen. "'John Larsen,'" she read, and then she watched John Larsen squirm on his stool.

"Never heard of him," he insisted.

Ava clicked on her "Blood Crop" story. "He's a character in the latest post, too." She read the description she'd added for the post: "'In which John Larsen tries to kill Spindly Arms on his mountain farm.'"

She was about to show John Larsen the screen of her phone when he blurted, "I don't read that stuff." He got out of his seat. Ava thought she spotted sweat glistening on his brow.

"Garbage for the brain," John Larsen said, and then he hurried out of the beer garden.

Ben grinned at Ava. "Nicely done," he said. "I'll text Amos and tell him he's outside. He was an antsy one."

"Probably because he's a guilty one," Ava said with certainty. She was invigorated by her impressive acting. She sipped her Coke and relished the sugar. She wanted energy for the next phase of the hunt. The Cokes continued as Ava spent the following hours in The White Owl, a 24-hour diner that was only two blocks from John Larsen's motel, The Zugspitze Inn. She was with Ben the whole time. Amos and Micah came and went as they prepared for whatever they were going to do to John Larsen. They didn't share the specifics of their plan, but they implied they were going to somehow get him to confess his part in the 1993 murders. Ava guessed they could pull a confession out of him without actually doing anything criminal. But when Micah showed Ben the syringe and said, "This'll knock him out flat," Ava knew they were going to take this further than what she'd expected.

"You're going to have Ben inject him with something?" she asked, her voice betraying her nervousness.

Micah shushed her as he held his vibrating cell phone to his ear. "Daniel?" he spoke into the phone. "You riled her up?" He paused, and then he grinned smugly. "No fucking way. You got them in the house? Perfect, buddy. I'm sure she's quaking." He left the diner again without speaking to Ava or Ben.

Ava peered across the table at Ben. "Nobody's going to get hurt, are they?"

"You'll be fine."

"I don't mean me, Ben."

"We'll be fine. Amos and Micah, they're smooth operators. They always have been."

Ava was concerned about what the brothers were going to do to John Larsen, but she told herself not to be. So what if they drugged him or beat his ass? He was a murderer, wasn't he? And the brothers were just ex-crooks who'd broken the law for money.

She still dreaded what was ahead of her tonight. Her body tensed up when Amos and Micah both entered the White Owl.

"Time to go to the motel," Micah said. "Here's what you need to do...."

Ava found herself eyeing Amos's wallet from the backseat of the Hyundai. Amos had just set the wallet on the dashboard before leaving the car with a moon mask over his head. That wallet could contain his driver's license, which would show his last name. Ben had claimed he didn't even have a driver's license.

It was 12:31 A.M. The car was in the parking lot of The Zug-spitze Inn. The rain had finally stopped, and all lights were out in the building except for those that lit the walkways outside the rooms. Ben sat in the driver seat. Micah had already broken into the room next to John Larsen's and was peering out at them from the open door. He also wore a moon mask, and it gave Ava chills even though she knew who was behind it.

"You're up for this, right?" Ben asked.

"I just have to light a magazine on fire." She tried to sound nonchalant about her task, but she still didn't want to complete it. She slipped on the plastic green witch mask Amos had given her and grabbed the issue of *Evergroan* off the backseat. She left the car and headed toward John Larsen's BMW, passing Amos on the way. He was picking the driver-side lock of the BMW.

Ava's heart pounded. With shaky hands, she slipped the issue of *Evergroan* under the windshield wiper and positioned the lighter beneath it. She clicked on the lighter, but the flame didn't appear.

"Shit," she whispered.

"Hurry," Amos snapped. He quietly opened the back door of the vehicle and crept inside.

After a few more clicks the lighter finally worked. One corner of *Evergroan* burned. Ava ran back to the Hyundai and sat beside Ben. She pulled off her witch mask and buckled her seatbelt. She knew they had to leave soon.

"There he goes," Ben said. They watched Micah step out of the room with a long tree branch in one hand. He scraped the branch along the outside wall of John Larsen's room, and then he pounded a fist against the door.

BANG. BANG. BANG. BANG.

"Time to wake up, fucker," Ben said. He turned the key in the ignition and slammed his foot on the gas pedal. The tires screeched as the Hyundai sped out of the parking lot.

Amos's wallet flew off the dashboard and landed between Ava's feet.

Delighted by her luck, she leaned forward and opened the wallet. She clicked on the lighter again, and the flame immediately appeared.

"What are you doing down there?" Ben asked.

"I'm having trouble seeing," Ava said as an excuse. She found Amos's license in one of the compartments and pulled it out. Her eyes widened when she read the name on the ID: *Amos Edward Granley.*

"Just calm down," Ben said. They were on Highway 2 again, heading in the direction of the farm where they were supposed to meet the twins.

"You lied to me!" Ava pointed at her phone, which displayed an article that had appeared in the *Wenatchee Daily Journal* six years ago. "Your last name isn't Lasaras. It's Granley. And your brothers didn't just steal things. They hurt a woman."

Ben nodded. "I know," he said in a solemn voice. "I didn't want you finding that article." He steered the car into the parking lot of a closed restaurant on the edge of Leavenworth. A sign on the side of the building showed a blonde woman in a Bavarian dress picnicking near a stream.

Ava read from the article: "'The brothers, who are both repeat offenders, face a 5-year minimum sentence for armed robbery and assault. The cashier of the Dollar Tree suffered a broken jaw. The assault occurred on the eve of her 50th birthday.'"

"My brothers have done bad things," Ben said. "I have, too."

"You haven't hurt a woman, though, have you?" Ava asked, sounding repulsed.

Ben shook his head. "I told you what I've done—what I'm going to stop doing." He stared ahead through the windshield. The rain had started again. It pelted the car's windows. "My brothers served their time, though," Ben said. "And you don't understand what we went through growing up, Ava. The fucked-up foster homes we were in—together and apart. Places like that can mess you up."

Watching him, Ava acknowledged to herself she couldn't relate to the Granley brothers' childhoods. She'd grown up going to private schools and expensive swim, tennis, and theater camps. Her parents took her to Europe every few years. They'd suggested renting a steamboat for a Sweet 16 dinner party on Seattle's Lake Union, but she told them she'd prefer they pay for her to go to Kauai with her friend Kaley.

Ava remained alarmed, though. "They broke a woman's jaw, Ben."

"And they were in prison for five fucking long years," Ben said. "I'm telling you everything was stacked up against us from the beginning, Ava. And we never would have gone through any of that shit in our childhoods if our grandfather lived longer than he did."

Ava became quiet as she processed what she'd read and Ben's defense of his brothers. She considered asking him to take her back to Leavenworth so she could find a bus home. But she reminded herself Ben hadn't attacked a woman. His brothers committed the crime.

"I didn't want you to get involved in this, Ava," Ben said. His voice was pleading. "But if you back out now Amos and Micah are going to make sure I serve as much time as they did."

Ava realized this was the first time Ben was asking her to help with the brothers' revenge scheme. He leaned over and kissed her deeply. His tongue on hers made her entire body relax and grow soothingly warm. She knew she couldn't leave Ben and get on that bus. She sighed.

Ben placed his hands back on the steering wheel. "We need to go," he said. "We're off schedule."

Ava didn't protest. She closed the article on her phone.

Soon after exiting the highway, they ascended a steep road that cut through thick forest. The rain came down the road in rivulets.

"The farm's at the top of this hill," Ben said. "We'll wait for my brothers up here." He motioned toward a cottage to the right of the road. Like most of Leavenworth's buildings, the cottage looked like it belonged in Germany. A sign outside identified the place as the *Alpin Haus.* Ben pulled the car into the driveway.

Ava was stepping out of the vehicle when she saw the man running down the hill toward them. Despite the rain and the dark, she recognized John Larsen.

"Careful," Ben told her. He opened the driver-side door and stood beside the car. He was closer to the man than she was.

"Please call the police," John Larsen said to them. He looked panicked and kept glancing behind him. "There's a crazy guy up there with a knife. I think he wants to kill me. He'll be coming down here for me soon."

Ava remained frozen by the open passenger-side door. She didn't know what to think. How did John Larsen get here? The brothers never mentioned they were going to take him to the farm. She thought they were just going to harass him— terrify him—at The Zugspitze Inn. Who was the man with the knife?

"My phone's in the car," Ben said. He disappeared from Ava's view. She was left staring at the agitated man.

John Larsen took a few steps toward the Alpin Haus. "Can we go inside? It'll be safer there."

She heard Ben whisper to her from the dark of the car. "Don't go," he said. "He's dangerous."

"Oh, I don't know," Ava told John Larsen. Her anxiety level kept climbing. Was he lying about the man with the knife? Did he recognize the Hyundai from the motel?

John Larsen looked desperate. He turned toward the cottage again, and something seemed to snag his attention. Ava realized why he was gawking. The building's roof and one of its walls were black from a past fire.

John Larsen frowned at her. "You're not staying here?" He sounded suspicious.

Ava wondered where Amos and Micah were. What if John Larsen had hurt one or both of the brothers? What if he was concealing a weapon? She glanced at the car again, and she saw Ben reaching inside the shoebox that was in front of her seat. It held the syringe Micah had given them.

John Larsen started back toward the road, and Ben shot out of the car and grabbed his arm. Ava knew in her gut the situation was going to escalate to violence, and she needed to act. She had to protect Ben. She hurried around the rear of the car toward the men.

Ben's right hand gripped John Larsen's coat sleeve. The syringe was in his left hand.

John Larsen shoved Ben, and Ben dropped the syringe. "Just calm down, mister," Ben said, still gripping John Larsen's arm.

Ava moved behind John Larsen so he wouldn't see her. She picked up the syringe and pulled off the cap covering the needle. She raised the syringe with a trembling hand.

John Larsen addressed Ben: "Don't tell me to fucking-"

He went quiet after Ava plunged the needle into his neck. He turned toward her. When their eyes met, Ava felt overwhelming regret.

He asked her, "What the-?"

"Open the back door," Ben ordered her.

"What?" Ava faltered.

"Open the back door!"

She finally did as told, relieved to break eye contact with John Larsen. When she saw him again, his head was bent to one side and his arms dangled above the ground. Ben dragged his limp body to the car and laid him across the back seat.

Ava experienced the nausea she felt whenever she rode a rollercoaster. Her illness became greater after she noticed the man in the moon mask striding through the rain toward her, a machete in his hand. She knew it was Amos or Micah, but it might as well have been Spindly Arms himself, coming to congratulate her for doing more than a writer should. For she hadn't just observed; she'd acted—and she'd acted badly.

Ava awoke with the sensation of something dripping on her forehead. Her eyes still closed, she pictured Spindly Arms standing over her, his white moon face smeared with blood. The crimson liquid ran down to his pointed chin and dribbled on Ava's face.

Her eyes shot open. Spindly Arms wasn't above her. She stared up at the charred ceiling of the second floor of the Alpin Haus. It was leaking. Raindrops were what fell on her forehead. She lay in a sleeping bag, and Ben was wrapped in a sleeping bag beside hers. Though he slept, he had an agitated look on his face. Rain poured in the morning gloom beyond a glassless window.

Ava unzipped her sleeping bag and crawled out of it. She still wore her gray hoodie and jeans. She located her sneakers near the foot of the sleeping bag and put them on.

She stopped tying the laces when a jolt of regret shot through her. She recalled sticking the needle in John Larsen's neck last night. Why the hell had she done that? Sure, she'd acted to protect Ben. But her actions could land both her and her boyfriend into a very deep and dark pit of trouble.

Amos had been the man in moon mask who came down the hill after John Larsen lay on the backseat of the Hyundai. Amos climbed inside the car with his machete and said something to the nearly unconscious man. Ava feared he was going to cut John Larsen, but her anxiety decreased once Amos shut the door and approached her and Ben. He lifted his mask and smirked at them. His mangled ear looked red and swollen. He held up John Larsen's cell phone and said, "Fucking jackpot."

Micah soon showed up in the truck. With a smug expression on his face, he peered through the Hyundai's window at John Larsen. "And we've still got hours of night ahead of us," he said.

Ava looked at Amos and motioned toward the backseat of the car. "He thought you were trying to kill him."

Amos waved his arm as if he were shooing her away. "Well, he's alive, isn't he?" He told Ben to get the sleeping bags out of the car's trunk. "You and Ava will sleep here while Micah and I take the fucker to the farm." Ben tried to protest, saying he wanted to drive Ava home. Amos grabbed him by the arm and yanked him toward the forest.

Micah pulled Ava aside. "Let's figure out where you guys are going to sleep," he told her. He fetched the sleeping bags and motioned for her to follow him to the Alpin Haus. While walking, she heard Ben and Amos arguing in the woods. She couldn't understand what they were saying until Amos yelled, "You gonna go against your brothers? Your flesh and blood?"

Ava turned back toward the forest, but Micah took hold of her wrist with a painful grip.

"You're not going to try to come between us and Ben, right?" he asked. "You know what we'll do if Ben doesn't do what we've asked him to do. And if you back out now...." He stared at Ava until she couldn't bear the intensity of his gaze.

"I'm not backing out," Ava said only so he would stop scrutinizing her. She asked, "You're not going to...kill John Larsen, are you?"

Micah grinned. "He deserves a lot worse than that. Why do you care about him? Didn't you already kill him in your story?"

Ava finished tying her shoelaces and went to the window. She peered down at the wet and weedy grounds behind the Alpin Haus. The truck was still outside, but the Hyundai hadn't returned. Ben had said the farm was just up the hill. Ava could walk there and find out what the brothers were up to. But what if John Larsen saw her again? She didn't have her witch mask on when they'd parked here last night. He could describe her to the police, and she'd end up with her own criminal record.

A hand touched her shoulder, and she cried out in surprise. She quickly turned around. Ben stood before her, sleepy-eyed with disheveled hair.

"This is the last abandoned house I ever spend the night in," he said, staring beyond her at the falling rain. He wrapped his arms around her and hugged her tightly.

Ava relished his touch. But it wasn't enough to distract her from what she'd done to John Larsen last night.

Ben asked, "Will you take class off next week and go somewhere with me? It'll be good for us to get away after this weekend." He slipped a hand inside the back of her jeans. "We can get real close again."

Ava wondered whether she'd be in a jail cell by Monday morning. Before she could reply, she heard Micah's voice.

"Ben!" he called from the yard. "Ben!"

"Be right down!" Ben shouted, sounding too dutiful for Ava's liking.

Ava picked up her cell phone from beside her sleeping bag. It was 7:32 A.M. Her parents would be up by now, peacefully eating their oatmeal in the breakfast room while they watched HGTV or listened to NPR on the radio.

"Hurry up!" Micah called.

The rain had weakened by the time Ava and Ben stepped out of the front door. Micah waited for them beside the Hyundai. He had dark, hook-like lines beneath his eyes. Amos wasn't with him.

"Hop in," Micah said. "We've got a lot to do today. And I need coffee."

Ava knew she was risking upsetting him by speaking, but she had to ask the question: "What'd you guys do to John Larsen?"

Micah shook his head in annoyance. He pointed at the trunk and told Ben, "Put the sleeping bags in there."

Ava kept staring at Micah until he finally responded: "He's where we want him. And no, he's not dead. Now we've got to deal with the two other fuckers. Let's go."

Ben went to the front passenger-side door. He gave Ava a sympathetic look, but it was clear he wasn't going to disobey his brother. Ava remained standing in the mud outside the car. She didn't want to step inside the vehicle, but she knew she had to if she wanted to keep the older brothers from turning against Ben and her. She told herself this experience would all be over by tomorrow, and she'd eventually be able to process it and understand it, and maybe one day write about it. But she remained uneasy about what was next in the revenge plot.

She buckled her seatbelt in the rear of the car, and Micah told her, "Brandon Laurent is next. He's the one who killed our grandfather's wife. Stabbed her in the stomach, over and over."

Ava glanced at Ben, recalling his affection for Phoebe. He stared through the windshield with glassy eyes.

"Brandon Laurent made the drawing for that story," Micah continued. "And he kept drawing and painting Spindly Arms for years after what he and his friends did. Is that fucked up enough for you to keep helping us out?"

Ava wondered why Brandon Laurent would keep making Spindly Arms art if he and the other two killers had dressed up like the character for the ritual murder. But she knew now was not the time to point out holes in Micah and Amos's stories about the murderers. Her eyes met Micah's in the rearview mirror. "That is fucked up," she said.

When he started the engine, she noticed three spots of dried blood on the side of his neck.

They drove east in the direction of Chelan, where Micah said Brandon Laurent lived. The rain had stopped, and mountain forest gave way to sparsely treed brown hills. After an hour of driving, Micah motioned toward a tiny town across a river. "We'll find a place to stop in Cashmere," he said.

They soon pulled into the mostly empty parking lot of a blue, boxy diner that looked like it hadn't been renovated since the early '80s. Pink letters on a neon sign above the front door formed the words *THE DESERT PLATE.*

Micah told Ben, "Give Ava her laptop. It's under my backpack."

Ava glanced at the open backpack in front of Ben. One of the moon masks protruded from the bag. She wondered what else could be inside. She wanted a clue to the brothers' complete plans for the weekend.

Ben handed her the laptop.

"Time for the next *Bloody Bitz* story," Micah said. "You can write it in the restaurant. In this story, you'll have Spindly kill another one of the three—Vivian Chiang, the cunt."

Ava winced at his last word. Her mother had once told her, "That's a hideous word. A misogynist's word."

Micah dug inside his pants pocket and pulled out a piece of paper. "Here's her address. Link it to the story, just like you did with John Larsen's address. You did that perfect, by the way."

Ava faked an appreciative smile and took the piece of paper. Micah's compliment would have meant so much to her just a day ago, but this morning it was merely a string of words. She asked, "What does Vivian Chiang look like?"

"Good-looking Asian lady. Same age as John Larsen and Brandon Laurent. Oh, and the story has to happen in a graveyard. She comes across the grave of someone she wronged in the past."

For once, Ava had little desire to write.

The only occupants of The Desert Plate were a trio of construction workers in yellow vests. Tan desert photographs and paintings hung from the turquoise walls. A glass case near the entrance displayed an assortment of muffins, scones, and doughnuts. A blond teenage boy who must have been a year or two younger than Ava stood behind the counter, gazing at his smartphone. He set it down on the counter. "What can I get you all?" he asked.

"You go ahead and sit and write," Micah instructed Ava. "I'll order for you. And make the story short because we don't have much time."

Ava nodded even though she was reluctant about completing her assignment. She glanced back at Ben for encouragement, but he only made brief eye contact before closing the door to the diner. She guessed the haranguing by Amos had rattled him. She started toward a table by the front window.

"Wait," Micah told her. He looked at the teenager. "You ever hear of Spindly Arms?"

"Sure! My friends and I read-"

"You see?" Micah told Ava. "You do good work when you're working with us."

Ava sat at the table and powered up the laptop. Staring at a blank Word document, she heard Micah say, "A black coffee and a doughnut for each of the three of us. The cheapest and most sugary doughnut you've got. Ben, you bring it when it's ready."

Micah passed Ava's table and sat at one of his own. His back was to her. He stared down at a cell phone with a gray protective case, and Ava recognized the phone as John Larsen's. She noticed the back of Micah's hand had a large, purplish bruise on it. Again, she wondered about all that he and Amos had done last night. And she once again considered what could be in that backpack in the car.

She began writing "A Grave Night for Vivian." Despite her tiredness and her anxiety over her involvement in the Granley brothers' scheme, she found the words eventually flowed. The writing was a welcome distraction from her current reality. She only took breaks to consume the coffee and doughnut

Ben had brought her. She imagined Vivian stumbling around tombstones until the woman located the grave of a friend she'd wronged in the past. Spindly gazed at her from behind the trunk of a willow tree. His arm slithered up the trunk and along a limb and then looped around her neck. Ava felt a mix of artistic delight and stinging guilt when she wrote about Vivian's corpse hanging from the branch, swaying in the nighttime breeze.

"You almost done?" Micah asked, and Ben gave her a questioning look from across the table. Ava finished adding Vivian's address in a comment by PastHitsHard.

"Done," she said. The story was rough, but it was enough.

"I've gotta piss before we go," Micah said. He rose from the table and handed Ben the car keys. He then moved toward the back of the cafe.

"You want me to get you another doughnut for the road?" Ben asked Ava as they started toward the door. "The one with sprinkles is awesome."

"Please," Ava said. She glanced through the window at the Hyundai. She knew now was her chance to look inside that backpack. "I'll take the laptop to the car. I feel like I need some air. Is it okay if I have the keys?" She looked Ben in the eyes, waiting for some sign of suspicion. She saw only affection. She was glad he was warming up to her again.

He handed her the keys.

Ava hurried across the parking lot. She glanced back at the cafe. She didn't see Micah, and Ben appeared to be talking to the teenager. She quickly unlocked the front passenger-side door and sat on the seat, her feet still on the pavement of the parking lot. She slipped the laptop under the open backpack and then rummaged through the bag.

Just beneath the moon mask was the notepad she'd seen on that altar in the brothers' motel room. Someone had filled the first page with small, slanted words. Ava read hungrily.

TO MY GRANDSONS—AMOS & MICAH & BEN: I'M WRITING YOU MY WISHES BEFORE I DIE & I WANT TO EXPLAIN WHY I HAD TO-

"Ava!"

Ava's head almost hit the ceiling of the car when she heard Micah's voice. She turned around and saw him leaning against the cafe's doorframe. He looked pale and dark-eyed. Had he seen her searching inside his backpack?

"Ben wants to know if you want another coffee," he said. "He's buying it because I sure ain't."

"Yes, please!" Ava called. She concealed the notebook with the mask, but not before she spotted the words *BEING A WHORE WITH BRANDON LAURENT.*

The Hyundai veered into the parking lot of the Sahara Breeze, a yellow, two-story mid-century motel on the edge of Chelan. The paint on the second-floor railing was peeling, and a few of the lower-level doors looked like they'd been burned in a fire. Micah said his and Amos's "Eastern Washington guy" was staying at the Sahara. "We've got to pick up stuff for the next part of the plan," Micah told Ava while parking. "Come on in and meet him."

Ava thought if she stayed in the car she could read through that notebook. "I'll wait here," she said.

"Suit yourself."

She frowned when Micah picked up his backpack and brought it outside with him. Watching Micah and Ben climb the staircase to the second floor, she wondered how much of what they'd told her about the ritual murders was true. Why would their grandfather write what he did in that notebook before becoming a victim of a ritual murder? He'd written *I'M WRITING YOU MY WISHES BEFORE I DIE....* What if he knew he was going to die in some other way? Ava Googled Ed and Phoebe Granley on her phone. When she didn't find any satisfactory results, she searched for the "Seattle Police Department." She dialed the "non-emergency" number.

A woman answered.

"I'm calling about the Maya Mathers murder that happened on Tuesday. I'd like to know what time it happened." According to the brothers' story, Amos discovered Maya's body around 5 P.M.

"Do you have a homicide tip, miss?" the woman asked. "I can transfer you to a detective."

Ava heard a motel door slam shut on the second floor. Startled, she ended the call.

Micah and Ben descended the staircase with a lanky, red-haired man whose face was clouded with freckles. The word *YENOM* was tattooed on his forehead. Micah carried beneath his arm what looked like a couple of large sketchbooks. He approached the car door closest to Ava and motioned for her to open it.

"This is Count Red," he told Ava after she opened the door. He tossed the sketchbooks on the seat beside her.

"Hey," Count Red said, leering.

"Hey," Ava spoke in a flat voice. She knew she was looking up at a true character, but she was finding the freaks and criminals much less fascinating and more intimidating than she had in the past weeks.

"Like his tattoo?" Micah asked. "He knows how rich he is every time he looks in the mirror."

Ava eyed the tattoo and realized its reflection would be *MONEY.* She faked a smile. "Yeah, cool," she said. Micah snorted with laughter, but Ben didn't seem amused.

"Anything Ava needs to know about Brandon Laurent?" Micah asked. "She's going to be the one talking to him."

Ava gave Micah a surprised look.

"He's spooked," Count Red said with a smirk. "I've been spooking him since Tuesday. You guys are going to have him shitting."

Ava remembered stabbing that needle into John Larsen's neck, and she felt a knot of fear in her throat. She asked Micah, "What do you want me to do now?"

The blonde, middle-aged gallery owner and her assistant came striding out of Chelan's Waterway Gallery in their heels and pretty dresses, and Micah perked up in the driver seat. Ava slumped down in the backseat. Her palms felt clammy. The Hyundai was parked in a small, mostly empty lot beside the old brick building that housed the gallery.

"Once they drive off," Micah said, "we go in. Ava, get the drawings."

Ava glanced down at the two sketchbooks filled with Spindly Arms illustrations: Spindly sitting with legs crossed on the edge of a blood-soaked couch, Spindly staring through a bedroom window at two teenagers with tangled limbs, Spindly stalking a woman down a steep and shadowy staircase.

"I don't want to go with you guys," Ava blurted.

Ben shot her a look. She hated seeing the disappointment in his eyes.

Micah turned around in his seat and glared at her. "You're in this with us," he said. "Don't you care about what happens to your boyfriend here?"

"Of course I do," Ava said. "And I have helped you guys. But I stuck a needle in John Larsen's neck. I hurt him. And I don't know what Amos has done to him. And whatever he's done, I-" Ava felt like she was going to start crying. She held back the tears and continued, "I was part of that."

"John Larsen is fine," Micah said. "He's not dead."

"He isn't," Ben added.

The tears came to Ava's eyes. "I just don't know what I believe anymore."

"Hold on," Micah said, sounding irritated. He pulled his cell phone out of his pocket and typed something. He stared at the screen in silence.

Ben watched Ava, looking as if she'd betrayed him. In avoidance, Ava glanced down at the illustration of the two teenagers embracing on the bed. She wondered if she'd one day regret losing her virginity to Ben. She dried her eyes with the back of her hand.

"Here you go," Micah said. "I asked Amos to send me this. Look who's doing just fine." He held up his phone for Ava and played a brief video. The phone showed John Larsen's head against a wooden wall. His eyes were nearly closed as if he were half asleep or intoxicated. Offscreen, Amos spoke, "John!" John looked at the camera, his eyes a little wider, and then the video ended.

"We're not the murderers," Micah told Ava. He reached deep inside his backpack and pulled out a can of black oil paint. "You're helping us get even with the murderers. You're on the right side. Now come on. This'll be easy." He got out of the vehicle and left the backpack sitting on the floor.

Ava considered the video. John Larsen was indeed alive. She hadn't assisted with a murder. Her mind once again turned to the contents of the notebook that was inside Micah's backpack. When she left the car, she made sure not to shut the door all the way.

"Looks like Chelan folks are a lot more trusting than city people," Micah said once they reached the side of the building. He grinned up at a partially open window that was about 10 feet above the ground. The window was wide but short. "Ava's small enough to fit through there."

"I don't know...." Ava said, her heartbeat quickening.

"Come on," Micah said, sounding impatient. It was clear he wouldn't tolerate more resistance from her. "We'll lift you."

Gripping the windowsill, Ava peered into the gallery's restroom. At Micah's prompting, she called out "Hello?"

Nobody responded.

Bringing one leg over the windowsill, she had the distressing thought that "breaking and entering" would be another bullet point on her criminal record. She lowered her legs onto the top of a toilet tank, and then she jumped onto the floor. She hurried out of the restroom into a hallway.

To the right was a small office with framed artworks covering its walls. Ava went to the left and entered a high-ceilinged gallery.

She gasped at the beauty of Brandon's paintings.

They were towering and brightly colored and abstract—just the opposite of the Spindly Arms drawings. Ava couldn't imagine a murderer creating such lovely paintings. One of the gallery's white walls announced:

AMENDS

Brandon Laurent

She noticed Micah waving to her beyond the glass of the gallery's front door. He looked exasperated. She quickly moved to unlock the door and let him and Ben inside.

"Don't hurry or anything," Micah snapped upon entering. He opened the can of paint and pulled a brush out of his pocket. "Ben, you hold up a Spindly Arms drawing against each painting and I'll make it stick."

"Who's going to watch outside?" Ben asked.

"I can," Ava said, remembering the car door she'd kept open. She left the gallery before Micah could propose an alternative plan.

Nobody was outside the gallery. Ava rushed across the sunlit parking lot to the Hyundai. She checked to make sure Micah and Ben were still in the building. After opening the rear door of the car, she got inside and squeezed her body between the front seats so she could snatch the notebook out of the backpack. She read part of a page as quickly as possible:

-A MAN REACHES AN AGE WHERE HE STARTS LOSING HIS POWER & THAT'S EXACTLY WHEN THOSE THREE FUCKING

*TEENS (JOHN LARSEN & BRANDON LAU-
RENT & VIVIAN CHIANG) MOVED IN TO
HUMILIATE ME FIRST WITH THAT STORY
ABOUT THE GHOOL THAT'S BASED ON ME
HE HAS NO HAIR HE HAS NO ARMS EXCEPT
FOR TREE BRANCHES HE WEARS COVER-
ALLS & LIVES ON A MOUNTAIN FARM ALL
THAT'S IN THE TOWN NEWSPAPER SO
EVERYONE CAN LAUGH AT OLD PATHETIC
ARMLESS ED*

*THEN PHOEBE STARTS BEING A WHORE
WITH BRANDON LAURENT & THAT'S
WHEN I KNOW I NEED TO DO THIS THAT
WOMAN KEPT ME GOING FOR YEARS KEPT
ME LIVING BUT WITHOUT HER I'VE GOT
NOTHING OF COURSE I'VE GOT YOU BUT
I'M NO GOOD WHEN I'M JUST A SHRED OF
A MAN THOSE FUCKING TEENS TURNED
ME INTO A SHRED-*

Ava glanced up and saw Ben leaving the gallery. He stared in the direction of the car. Ava knew she'd fail to concoct a solid excuse, and she may never have the chance to read this notebook again. She flipped through a couple of pages to the end:

*-BUT PHOEBE DESERVES IT & ULTIMITELY
I'M NOT GUILTY ULTIMITELY IT'S THOSE
FUCKING TEENS WHO ARE GUILTY MAKE
THEM SUFFER FOR ALL THE SUFFERING*

THEY CAUSED YOU'LL HAVE THE DRAW-
INGS & MAGAZINES MY FRIEND STOLE
FROM BRANDON LAURENT'S HOUSE &
YOU'VE GOT THIS EVIDINCE OF HOW
THESE TEENS RUINED LIVES & MADE ME
INTO THE GHOOL THAT I'M GOING TO BE
TODAY

I DO LOVE YOU THREE VERY MUCH I'M
SORRY I HAVE NO MORE LOVE FOR PHOEBE
OR MYSELF & ONLY HATE-

Ben banged on the front passenger-side window. "Ava, let me in now."

She reached for the handle and pushed open the door. Ben sat down and shoved the notebook into the backpack. Ava waited for him to speak about what she'd read, but he didn't say anything. He kept glancing at the entrance to the gallery.

"We need you again, Ava. You're going to lock the door and climb out the bathroom window."

"There was no ritual murder, was there?" Ava asked. "They didn't kill your grandfather or Phoebe."

"They're responsible, though," Ben snapped at her. He was glaring, and his forehead glistened with sweat. "We hold them responsible."

"What did your grandfather do to Phoebe?"

Ben shook his head. "I'll tell you later. Just promise me you won't upset Micah. It's for your own good, Ava. And for the good of you and me. Micah doesn't trust you as he did before. You don't want him against you."

Ava peered into Ben's eyes. "Tell me," she pressed him.

He moved to kiss her, but she pulled away from him and sat in the backseat. She folded her arms over her chest. "Not until you tell me, Ben," she said.

Ben glowered at her. "Don't fuck us, Ava. Not now, when we're so far into this. Now come on." He left the front seat.

Ava hesitated, remembering when Ben had tried to prevent her from being part of the scheme. Now he insisted on her involvement. She sighed and joined him outside the car. He reached for her arm, but she withdrew it from his reach.

"You'll tell me later, Ben," she said. "I want to know."

Ava felt like she gave a shoddy performance during her conversation with Brandon Laurent and the gallery owner. While she'd interacted so aggressively with John Larsen in the beer garden, wanting to expose him for his past crime, she gazed at Brandon Laurent questioningly outside the gallery, wondering what he'd been like as a teenager, what kind of relationship he'd had with Phoebe, what made him eventually switch from the terrifying Spindly Arms paintings to the almost spiritual "Amends" paintings.

He was nearly as beautiful as those paintings with his tan visage, his high cheekbones, and his thick, wavy hair. He could have been 10 years younger than John Larsen. But despite Brandon Laurent's good looks and Ava's distracted thoughts, she managed to point at her phone's screen and talk about the things Micah wanted her to talk about—the Spindly Arms posts on *Bloody Bitz* and the details of Maya Mathers's murder.

When she spoke of Maya Mathers, Brandon Laurent looked distressed. Ava didn't see any guilt in his face, though.

And maybe she'd misread John Larsen. There was a whole other story she didn't know about. And what if that other story was the truth and totally different from the one the Granley brothers had told her?

Ava tried to peer through the past decades as she stared at Brandon Laurent, but she failed. She could only see this stunning 44-year-old man looking more and more upset.

"I'm sorry, Marcia," he told the gallery owner, "but I need to get out of here. I feel sick."

"I'm going to call the police," Marcia said. "I'll have them call you so they can talk to you."

Brandon nodded. "I'll be glad to talk to them," he said. He walked away without another word to Ava.

Ava shuffled across the parking lot in the direction of the Hyundai, where Micah and Ben waited for her. She wondered if she should even get in the car. Would Ben tell her about what had happened to his grandfather and Phoebe? Her only way to find out was to go with the brothers—at least for a little while longer.

Her body dropped into the backseat. She felt exhausted from her lack of sleep and her confusing encounter with Brandon Laurent.

"Did you tell him what you were supposed to?" Micah asked.

"I did." Ava watched the crestfallen gallery owner return to the room that was full of ruined art. Ava shot Micah a defiant look in the rearview mirror. "He came off as a decent man," she said.

"Fuck you," Micah spat.

Ben spoke in defense: "Micah, she didn't-"

"No, fuck her," Micah said, glaring at Ava in the rear-view mirror. He started the engine. "Say you're sorry for your disrespect."

"I'm sorry," Ava spoke without enthusiasm. "Where are we going now?"

"Back to where we began," Micah spoke without looking at her. "Back to Glimmer Lake."

Everyone was silent during the drive west toward the Cascades. When they passed through downtown Leavenworth, Ava asked from the backseat, "How long will you keep John Larsen on that farm?"

Micah stared ahead at the road. "We can keep him there as long as we like. It's our farm. Our grandfather left it to us, and his friend maintained it for us while we were kids. We can fucking bury John Larsen on that farm if we want to."

"But you said you're not going to-"

"No," Micah said, scowling at Ava in the rearview mirror. "We're not going to kill your precious John Larsen. I told you that already. Whose side are you on again?"

Ava ignored the jab. She glanced at Ben, wondering if he might stand up for her. He gazed ahead through the windshield and didn't turn his head to look at her. Despite his distance, she guessed he wasn't going to say anything to Micah about her seeing the notebook. She wished Micah would stop somewhere so she could maybe read through Ed's letter to his grandsons some more. She wanted to know exactly what had happened between Ed and Phoebe "and those fucking teens." But she didn't think Micah would stop. He'd been driving over the speed limit for the past hour. He'd said they needed to reach Glimmer Lake by 4.

A couple of hours later, the Hyundai was once again parked in the lot outside Bowl O' Rama. Ava nodded absentmindedly while Micah rattled off instructions about what to tell Vivian Chiang inside the bowling alley. Her task of talking to the woman seemed easy—and harmless enough. She could continue along with the brothers' scheme for a little longer—at least until she found out what happened in the past.

Ben finally looked at Ava. He had a strange expression on his face as if he were trying to figure out what to say to her.

Micah spoke instead. "It's 4:30," he said. "You go." He handed her the envelope she was supposed to give Vivian Chiang.

She picked up her backpack from the car floor and pulled out the book she'd stolen from Meaghan's bedroom, *Best Short Stories of the Twentieth Century*. Micah had told her to go into the bowling alley "looking like a college student." At least he didn't say "high school student." She could handle Micah losing some faith in her, but she dreaded him finding out her true identity.

The bowling alley was decorated for Halloween with black and orange streamers arcing over the 12 lanes, and cardboard ghosts, mummies, and zombies attached to the walls. Ava frowned at the sight of a paper mâché witch head hanging above the dining area. She remembered wearing that witch mask outside John Larsen's motel room. She also recalled sticking that needle in his neck and breaking into the art gallery in Chelan. What crime would Micah want her to commit tonight?

She spotted a woman who could be Vivian Chiang sitting on a stool in the dining area. The woman was attractive—a good match for the "pretty Asian lady" Ava had written about in her *Bloody Bitz* post—and she gripped an ICEE in one hand and her cell phone in the other. She stared down at her phone with a look of distress.

Ava approached, holding her book and the envelope against her chest, and tapped the woman's shoulder. The woman gave her a startled look.

"Are you Vivian?" Ava asked. As she waited for a response, she noticed the woman seemed familiar. The Granley brothers hadn't shown her a photograph of Vivian Chiang, so she wasn't sure where she'd seen her before.

The woman nodded, and Ava handed her the envelope.

"Some guy told me to give that to the pretty Asian lady who looks like she's looking for someone," Ava said.

"'Some guy?'"

Ava tried to appear as clueless as possible as she described John Larsen's features: "A handsome man with salt-and-pepper hair. He had a mole here." She pointed to her temple.

And that's when she realized where she'd seen Vivian Chiang—in Madison Park, last spring. Vivian Chiang had been jogging, and she wore athletic shorts and a headband. Her hair was tied back into a ponytail. She approached the curbside table where the younger sister of Ava's friend Alyssa was selling Girl Scout cookies.

Ava was shocked by this recognition, and she didn't want Vivian Chiang to see her surprise. She also needed to leave because Micah wanted her out of the bowling alley before Vivian Chiang opened the envelope.

"Anyway," Ava spluttered, "my dad's picking me up. I've got to go."

Hurrying toward Bowl O' Rama's entrance, she remembered how Vivian Chiang had smiled so brightly at Alyssa's little sister on that spring day. Ava and Alyssa sat together on a patch of lawn behind the 4th-grader. Vivian Chiang pulled some cash out of one pocket of her running shorts and handed it to Alyssa's sister.

"Give me two boxes of whatever's selling the least," she'd said. "I used to help my daughter sell these. You're doing good work."

"You did everything I told you to do?" Micah asked when Ava returned to the car. He was glaring at her in the rearview mirror. The engine was already running.

Ava shot him a sulky look. She didn't feel like helping the Granley brothers anymore. She knew there'd been no ritual murder, and she doubted Vivian Chiang could have had any role in the deaths of Ed and Phoebe.

"Well?" Micah prodded, his eyes now large.

"I did what you asked," Ava said, intimidated by his intensity. "She's got the envelope."

Micah put the Hyundai in reverse, and they sped out of the parking lot. Raindrops pelted the car. It was pouring by the time they drove at a slow pace through a heavily treed residential area. "The cemetery's on that block," Micah said, pointing at a corner where willow branches hung over a high stone wall. "We need to be next to the side entrance."

Parking the car in front of a small, iron gate that interrupted the wall, he told Ava she was going to help get

Vivian Chiang into that cemetery if the woman didn't venture inside on her own. Ava would run screaming toward Vivian Chiang's car and tell her John was in there, and he'd been stabbed.

"Stabbed by who?" Ava asked with alarm. "You're not going to stab him, are you?"

"John Larsen is on the farm," Micah said, shaking his head. "You know that." He grinned. "Tell her Spindly Arms stabbed him. That'll freak her out."

Ben turned around in his seat and watched Ava with a concerned expression. He reached back and touched her leg. "You okay?"

She jerked her leg away from his hand. She suddenly became hot with anger. "I'm not doing this. I don't know what you're going to do to her."

"We're not going to hurt her," Micah said. "We're just going to scare her like we scared John Larsen."

"I want you to tell me the truth about what happened in the past," Ava told Ben. "I'm not going to wait any longer."

"What's she talking about?" Micah asked.

Ben gave his older brother a guilty look. "She read some of Grandpa's letter. While we were in the gallery."

"I know there wasn't any ritual murder," Ava said. "What did your grandfather do to Phoebe?"

Micah turned to Ben with a clenched jaw. He looked like he was going to punch his brother. "We don't have time for this bullshit." He reached inside his backpack and pulled out a moon mask and a small stack of the *Evergroan* magazines. He pushed open his door and got out into the rain. He then yanked open Ava's door. "Come on," he commanded.

"I don't want to leave the car," she said, shrinking away from him. Her previous courage was quickly fading. "Tell me the truth about what happened."

"Later," Micah barked. "We'll tell you later. Now get out."

"Just do it," Ben told her in a firm voice.

Ava unbuckled her seatbelt, but she remained sitting. Her legs were shaking from fear.

"Out now!" Micah said, and then he pulled her out of the car. He dragged her in the direction of the gate. "You're going to do what I told you. If you don't, Ben's going to get his comeuppance and you're going to get something just as bad." He squeezed her by the wrist until she yowled in pain. "You hear me?"

Ava nodded.

"You're part of this now," Micah continued. "You've helped us, and you're just as responsible as we are. We'll tell you what you want to know, but right now you've got something to do."

"All right," Ava whispered. She was too frightened to do anything other than entering the cemetery with him.

The dark and the falling rain made it difficult to see the rows of gravestones filling the block-sized cemetery. The stone wall bordered the grounds, and a couple of large, globular lamps glowed weakly atop two stone pillars that marked the entrance.

Micah took the lead and walked off the path and into a copse of trees. The limbs were thick and leafy enough to provide shelter from the rain. Ava followed him. He set the magazines in front of a gravestone, and then he pulled out his cell phone and gazed at its glowing screen. He stared at it intently, clearly waiting for a call or a message.

Ava almost spoke, but she was scared of breaking his concentration. She wondered what Micah was going to do to Vivian Chiang. No matter what it was, she knew she'd never be able to convince him to leave the cemetery right now. She told herself to just follow his instructions for at least a little longer. The brothers had said her involvement would only last through tonight.

The phone vibrated, and Micah whispered, "Yes." But then he scowled at the screen. "Fuck. She's not coming in." He told Ava, "Go!" and pointed at the cemetery's entrance.

"And you're not going to hurt her?" Ava asked.

"I told you already! Go!"

Ava started away from him.

"Wait!" he said. He kneeled and scooped up mud in one hand. Before Ava could gain greater distance from him, he smeared the mud all over her face. She winced and spit out a little dirt that had slipped through her lips.

"For effect," he said, giving her a smug grin. "Hold out your hands." When she showed him her palms, he wiped his dirty hand across them. "Now run and scream and do like I told you!"

Ava headed toward the entrance again, leaving the copse of trees.

"Scream!" Micah said.

Ava obeyed. She ran shrieking in the rain and past the pillars. She consoled herself with the thought that she wouldn't have to say much to Vivian Chiang.

A red car idled just outside the cemetery. The front passenger-side window rolled down, and Ava recognized the woman in the driver seat.

"What happened?" Vivian Chiang asked. "Are you hurt?"

"Are you Vivian?" Ava realized she'd already asked that question in Bowl O' Rama.

Vivian Chiang nodded. "How did you get here? Is John here?"

Ava gripped the windowsill. She considered telling the woman, "You need to get away from here." But instead she managed to say, "I don't know if John's still alive. He cut him! Just now." She pointed toward the cemetery. "John's still in there."

"Who cut him?" Vivian Chiang asked. She opened her door and stepped out of the car.

"Spindly Arms!" Ava screamed. She sprinted away from the vehicle and around the corner, to where Ben waited for her. He now sat behind the steering wheel. She opened one of the back doors and collapsed onto the seat. Her whole body was trembling.

"You sure he's not going to hurt her?" she asked. "Like stab her or something?"

"Why do you care so much about Vivian Chiang and the rest of them?" Ben asked. "You don't know them."

"I know they didn't do what you guys said they did." She used the sleeve of her sweatshirt to wipe the mud off her face.

Ben looked down at the steering wheel. "That doesn't mean they're not responsible for what happened to Phoebe and Grandpa Ed."

"Which was what?" Ava asked. "Please tell me now, Ben."

Ben turned around and stared at her. His lips parted as if he were about to speak.

A blaring police car siren prevented him from saying anything. The noise sounded like it was just a few blocks away. Ben looked terrified, and Ava felt just as afraid. Was this finally it—the end of her crazy weekend and the beginning of her criminal record?

Micah dashed around the corner from which she'd just come. He pulled open the passenger-side door and hopped inside. "The cunt called the fucking cops," he told his little brother. He removed the mask. "I had to get out of there. Drive now!"

Once they were in the midst of Saturday-night traffic on the commercial Lakefront Avenue, Ava said with relief, "So that's it. Vivian Chiang's out of your reach. You messed with Brandon Laurent at the art gallery. And you're going to let John Larsen go from the farm, aren't you?"

"Vivian Chiang's not out of our reach," Micah said. "Daniel was parked in front of the cemetery, watching her."

"Daniel?" Ava asked. He was their meth-head friend she'd never met. The one who shared Ben's motel room.

"He'll follow her wherever she goes next," Micah said.

Ava was suddenly furious about all the secrets and hidden plans the brothers had been keeping. She spoke in a raised voice, "Tell me what your grandfather did to Phoebe. I want to know now!"

"Pull over!" Micah shouted.

Ben steered the car into the parking lot of the Lake Town Cineplex, a colossal beige building with a trio of domes. The parking lot was bustling with cackling teenagers, young couples holding hands, and patrons of the burger restaurant next to the movie theater.

"You want me to tell you something?" Micah asked, turning around in his seat.

Ava nodded eagerly.

"So I'm not sure if Ben here told you how we grew up in a bunch of foster homes."

"He did," Ava said. She noticed Ben shoot his brother a questioning look.

"We had to go into the foster care system after our grandfather died," Micah said. He stroked his chin and stared at Ava. "You know, there are a lot of good families in that system. And there are some bad ones."

Ava gave him a look of understanding even though she couldn't relate. It was the same look she gave friends who complained about their parents being divorced.

"All it takes is one rotten foster family to make your life hell when you're a kid. Ben and Amos and I were in two bad families—and I mean bad."

Ava could see Ben's growing discomfort.

"Micah," he said.

Micah ignored him and kept on speaking to Ava. "Amos's ear, the scar on Ben's back, and the scar on my foot—that was one family."

"The scar on Ben's back?" Ava asked.

Micah chuckled. "Oh. I thought you two had fucked by now."

Ava blushed. All lights had been out that one night they slept together in Ben's motel room.

"Show her," Micah told his little brother.

"Micah, she-"

"Show her!" Micah reached upwards and switched on the overhead light.

Ben lifted his shirt, and Ava leaned forward to see three parallel scars spanning the right side of his back.

Micah turned off the light. "That comes from this pronged gardening tool our foster 'mom' liked to use," Micah said. "Our foster 'dad' used it on Ben's back and my feet the day we were running through the flowerbeds in the backyard. I was 10, and Ben was 5. Amos wasn't even 11 when our 'dad' took off part of his ear."

Ava gave a pained expression. "I'm sorry," she said.

"There was worse than that," Micah said. "Things people do or say that don't leave scars on the flesh. Things that are as ugly or scary as anything you'll see on that *Bloody Bitz* website, but they're a whole lot more real than spooks and ghouls."

Ava tried to make eye contact with Ben in the rearview mirror, but he stared through the windshield.

"None of that would have happened if those three pieces of shit left our grandfather alone," Micah said. "They fucked with him and they fucked with his wife and they fucked with all our lives." "

Ava was silent as she processed what Micah had told her. She gazed down into the shadows of the car floor. He still hadn't said what their grandfather had done to Phoebe.

"So no," Micah continued, "there wasn't any ritual murder. We told you that because it's a simple explanation and we thought it would help get you on our side. Are you still on our side, Ava?"

Ava looked up at him. She understood—or at least she thought she understood—why the brothers wanted some sort of revenge against John Larsen, Brandon Laurent, and Vivian Chiang. But she still didn't know exactly what that revenge entailed. She knew she didn't want to keep helping them. She continued to care for Ben, but did they have any future together after what they'd been through this weekend?

Before Ava could think of a response to Micah's question, his cell phone made a vibrating sound.

He pulled his phone out of his pocket. "Daniel? You're on her? Tell us where she goes and we'll meet you."

Daniel was a malnourished-looking man with sores on his face. Ava realized she'd seen Ben talking to him on that sizzling September day she first spotted Ben in Westlake Park. Now Daniel stood outside the driver-side door of a black Camaro parked on a street that ran through downtown Glimmer Lake. His gaunt cheeks glistened in the rain.

Ben brought the Hyundai to a stop next to the Camaro, and Micah rolled down his window.

"Where is she?" he asked.

Daniel pointed down the street at a diner with a glowing rooftop sign showing the words *THE HUNGRY BEAR* and a spoon dripping honey.

"Good," Micah said. "I'll drive your car. You'll duck down in the passenger seat. We'll park in front." He got out of the car. He still gripped the moon mask he'd held since leaving the cemetery. Before shutting the door, he told Ben, "Park closer than here, but not too close. You'll follow her when she leaves and keep us posted about where she goes."

"I'll get in the front seat," Ava said.

Outside the car, Daniel leered at her. Micah wrapped his arm around her back as if he were going to embrace her. "We're getting rid of these cars after tonight," he spoke into her ear in a quiet voice. "We're also getting rid of your laptop. Don't make us have to get rid of you, too. You've done good work, for the most part, Ava."

246

Chilled by his words and the rain, Ava hurried inside the front of the car. She couldn't help thinking how Micah's backpack—and Ed's notebook—was right beside her leg.

Ben parked about a block away from The Hungry Bear. Ava didn't speak to him because she was trying to think of what to say. How could she tell him she wasn't going to help the brothers anymore, even if that decision put Ben at risk of going to prison? But surely his brothers wouldn't betray him like that, would they? While she considered her words, she watched what took place across the street.

Vivian Chiang sat in a booth near one of the restaurant's front windows. Micah parked the Camaro next to Vivian Chiang's car, and Ava felt goose bumps form along her arms as she watched the masked Granley brother watch the woman he loathed. Vivian Chiang talked to a waiter, sipped from a mug, and picked at whatever food was on her plate. Through all this, she kept glancing downwards—probably at her cell phone. She suddenly shot out of her seat and came running outside the diner and into the parking lot. She faced the Camaro, which sped away.

"Is that it?" Ava whispered, sounding hopeful.

"We wait for her to go," Ben said.

Ava's leg muscles tensed when the police drove into The Hungry Bear's lot. A wide, blonde policewoman and a boyish-looking policeman with a crew cut greeted Vivian Chiang inside the diner. The woman folded her arms over her chest as she talked to them. "He beat her to death," Ben said.

"What?" Ava asked, turning to look at him. His eyes appeared to be tearing.

"Grandpa Ed. He beat Phoebe to death in the Eastern Washington desert. We all moved to Moses Lake in the spring of '93.

I guess Grandpa Ed thought leaving Glimmer Lake would be a way to jumpstart the marriage. But it didn't work. He killed her on a trail in some canyon, and then he drowned himself after dark."

"Oh, god," Ava whispered. She cupped her hand over her mouth.

"I know I should hate him for it," Ben said. His voice cracked when he said, "I loved Phoebe. And I do remember her. No matter what my brothers say."

He closed his eyes and pressed his fingers against them. When he opened them again, he no longer looked as if he were going to cry. "Grandpa Ed left his notebook with his friend Henry. Henry gave the notebook to my brothers when they turned 18. That's when Grandpa Ed wanted him to give it to them. Those teenagers did drive him to it." He sounded as if he were pleading. "You've got to see how they're at least partly guilty."

Ava opened her mouth, but she didn't know what to say. "Ben, I...." She became quiet.

"Shit." Ben stared out his window, looking in the direction of The Hungry Bear. Vivian Chiang was getting into her car.

"She's leaving," Ben said. "We need to go."

Ben didn't talk while he tailed Vivian Chiang through a residential section of Glimmer Lake. The rain had lessened. Ava noticed he kept at least a block's distance from Vivian Chiang's car, and there was often another vehicle between them. Ava wondered where the woman could be going. Perhaps a friend or family member's house? Ava was no longer distracted by Ben's story about Phoebe's death. She was ready to voice her decision.

"I want to get out," she told Ben.

He didn't look at her. He whispered, "You can't see me."

Ava realized he'd directed his words at Vivian Chiang.

"Did you hear me?" Ava asked. "I want to get out of the car. I don't want to be involved in this anymore. I'm sorry if I'm putting you at risk of your brothers turning you in. But that's between you and them."

Ben scowled. "Shut up for a second," he said.

Offended by his words, Ava gaped at him. He continued to stare ahead through the windshield.

Vivian Chiang pulled over beneath a streetlamp about a block and a half ahead of them. An old station wagon passed by her. Ben made a sharp right and turned off his headlights. He parked the car in front of a small house with a wraparound porch. Gazing out of his window in Vivian Chiang's direction, he repeated, "You can't see me, you can't see me...."

"Ben, I'm getting out," Ava said.

"Not yet you aren't," Ben said.

Vivian Chiang's car continued down the street again.

"She was checking to see if someone was following her," Ben said. "She's smart, but not that smart." He started the car and pursued her again.

"Why aren't you hearing me?" Ava asked. "I don't want to help you guys anymore."

"I get it," Ben said without emotion. "But you see there really isn't much else for you to do. You've done what we needed you to do. I'll drop you off in Seattle later tonight, and then we won't ever talk again."

"What?" Ava asked, shocked. "You made it sound like you wanted to be with me, like you wanted to be my-"

"I'm a good faker," Ben said. "Remember how I said all the girls I'd been with had some agenda?"

Though she was upset by Ben's words, Ava managed to nod. She thought of her agenda to become a better writer through this experience, and she remembered all her lies.

"That was true, what I said about those girls. And, after being played enough times, I learned how to play people, too. Don't get me wrong. I like you. You're cute and you're smart and all that. But you're just a girl, and my brothers are blood. We wanted you to help us get the Internet shit done, and you did. You were also the female presence we needed for our interactions with the fuckers."

"So you always wanted me involved in this?" Ava asked with pain in her voice.

"Sure," Ben said, "after I realized the skills you had and that you could be much more than a lay. So we made up our bullshit stories for you, including the one about me not knowing my brothers were going to rob the dollar store."

Ava suddenly felt nauseous. "And what about Maya Mathers? Are your brothers responsible for what happened to her?"

Ben didn't respond. He stared steadily through the windshield.

"Did your brothers even communicate with her? Or did they just kill her?"

Ben stayed silent, and Ava screamed, "Tell me!"

"Maya Mathers' murder is a mystery," Ben said, and Ava thought she detected the hint of a grin on his lips. "But no matter what happened to her, I guess you could say her death was a means to an end."

Ava breathed deeply so she wouldn't vomit.

"Don't worry," Ben said, patting her thigh. "It's almost over. You're a crook like us now, and we won't say anything if you don't say anything."

Vivian Chiang took a right onto a narrow road, and Ben said, "This has got to be it."

A sign on the corner read *NOT A THROUGH STREET.*

Ava still felt like she could puke on the floor of the car. She pressed both hands over her stomach.

Ben picked up his phone and dialed a number. "It's me," he said. "She's on Long Pine Lane. Looks like a dead-end street. I'm gonna get out and follow her on foot. I'll text you the house's address and if I think anyone else is there."

He pocketed his phone and pushed open his door. "Just stay here," he told Ava. "It's a long fucking walk to Seattle."

Ava didn't plan on driving anywhere else with Ben. She wanted to get out of the car now. But as she watched Ben trot down the road and across someone's lawn, she realized she was in here with the notebook. She could take one last look at Ed Granley's words.

She slipped the notebook out of the backpack and turned on her phone's flashlight. She glanced at certain words as she flipped pages to the end of the letter:

-CAUGHT HER WITH BRANDON LAURENT IN OUR OWN-

-DRAG DOWN A HANDICAPPED-

-SORRY FOR THE LANGUAGE BUT HATE MAKES ME-

Ava heard a car coming from behind her. She turned off the flashlight and glanced through the passenger-side window at the passing black Camaro. She saw Daniel's ugly face pressed up against the glass, eyeing her again.

The Camaro turned onto Long Pine Lane. Ava spotted Ben's silhouette in the distance. He was coming back to the car.

Ava knew she had to finish reading the note. She turned her flashlight back on and returned to where she'd left off the last time, near the very end:

I DO LOVE YOU THREE VERY MUCH I'M SORRY I HAVE NO MORE LOVE FOR PHOEBE OR MYSELF & ONLY HATE FOR THOSE THREE FUCKING TEENS.

I WANT YOU TO HACK OFF THEIR ARMS. AT LEAST ONE ARM FROM EACH OF THEM. AT LEAST FROM BRANDON LAURENT & JOHN LARSEN. MAKE THEM SEE HOW IT FEELS.

& I KNOW THIS IS A LOT TO ASK & I'M PROBABLY NOT IN MY RIGHT MIND FOR ASKING IT BUT I WANT ALL OF THEM DEAD. THAT'S MY TRUE WISH FROM DEEP DOWN INSIDE MY ANGRY HEART. GRANT ME THIS ONE DAY IF YOU CAN.

YOURS ALWAYS,

GRANDPA ED

Ben opened the driver-side door.

Ava didn't bother trying to hide the notebook. She stared at him with round eyes, but she was looking through him. She thought of Vivian Chiang, Brandon Laurent, and John Larsen. They had fucked up in their own ways. They gravely offended Ed. None of this weekend's events would have happened if the teenagers hadn't offended him. But Vivian Chiang, Brandon Laurent, and John Larsen were just being stupid teenagers in the early '90s—much like Ava had been a stupid teenager these past weeks.

None of them deserved to die.

And Ava could possibly still prevent Vivian Chiang from dying.

She opened her car door and stepped out into the drizzle.

"Wait," Ben said. "Where are you going?"

"I'll be right back," Ava lied. "Just stay here."

"Micah wants us in the car," Ben protested. "He might need us to pick him up if Daniel has to leave."

"I'm coming back. I just need to tell Daniel something important." She fled down the sidewalk and into the cul-de-sac. She glanced back at the car and was relieved to see Ben lowering himself into the driver seat. She looked around at the faces of the four houses on Long Pine Lane. Only one home had lights on inside. She spotted a man—Daniel—standing on the front steps of one of the dark houses. She hurried toward him and asked, "Where's Micah?"

"You should be with Ben, girly," he said.

Ava tried to open the front door, but it was locked.

"He went in the side door," Daniel said. "Did Micah send you?"

Ava ignored him and ran around the side of the house. She rushed up a set of wooden stairs to a partially open door and entered the home. She was inside a kitchen, and she was short of breath. She realized how furious Micah would be about her coming in here, but she needed to get him away from Vivian Chiang.

"Micah?" she managed to call out despite her fear.

Nobody responded. She stepped into an unlit foyer and spotted a cell phone at the bottom of the stairway to the second floor. She crouched to pick up the phone, and when she pressed its home button the screen lit up with a photograph of a smiling adolescent girl. The girl looked like she was half-Asian and half-Caucasian, and she sat criss-cross applesauce on a sunlit picnic table.

A door slammed shut upstairs.

Ava's heart was hammering against her chest as she rushed upstairs and past empty bedrooms. She heard a voice near the end of the hallway.

"Help me!" It was Vivian Chiang's voice, and it came from the last room down the hallway. Next came the sound of heavy footsteps, and then something hit a wall.

"Who are you?" Vivian Chiang asked.

"I'm Spindly Arms." Micah's voice boomed with rage. "I'm Ed Granley. I'm your past, and I've finally come to kill you."

Ava reached the doorway of the room. She saw a masked Micah standing over a cowering Vivian Chiang, who was on her knees beside a wall. Micah held a carving knife above his head.

"Micah, don't!" Ava said.

The moon mask turned toward her, and Ava had the terrifying thought it was Spindly Arms staring at her, not Micah Granley.

Vivian Chiang shot up from the floor and ran to a large, open window across the room. She lifted the window all the way and straddled the sill in an attempt to escape. Micah rushed toward her and stabbed her in the lower back.

Vivian Chiang shrieked. Her body spasmed.

Micah withdrew the knife to stab again, and Ava charged him.

"Stop, Micah!" she yelled. She grabbed his wrist so he wouldn't be able to cut Vivian Chiang, but he spun around and yanked his arm away from her. He was now facing her with his back to the window. He looked like he was debating stabbing her.

Ava was surprised to see Vivian Chiang's arms wrap around Micah's waist. The wounded woman had come back inside the room. She pulled Micah toward her and the open window, and he stumbled backward. Ava ran over to him and grabbed his right forearm with both hands, trying to shake the knife free.

It clattered on the hardwood floor.

"Leave her alone, Micah," Ava cried, still holding his wrist. "Just let her go."

Micah slammed his left fist into her cheek, and she fell back onto the floor. She shut her eyes as pain radiated through her skull, and when she opened them again she saw Vivian Chiang shoving Micah toward the window. She heard a gasp from him as he tumbled backward over the sill, and then he was gone from the room and Ava was alone with Vivian Chiang. In shock, Ava cupped a hand over her mouth.

"Is he-?" Ava whimpered.

Vivian Chiang peered outside the window with her palm pressed against her bleeding lower back.

Ava joined her at the window and looked down at Micah, who lay at the bottom of the stairs to the kitchen door. The crescent moon mask had stayed on, and he stared up at the sky with his head bent unnaturally. Ava thought she saw blood pooling beneath his head.

"Call the police," Vivian Chiang moaned. But Ava knew she couldn't call them. She'd done too much to get herself into trouble. She needed to leave.

"Here," she said, pulling Vivian Chiang's cell phone out of her pocket. She picked up the knife from the floor and handed it to the woman. "Stay in this room and you should be safe." " She ran downstairs and toward the kitchen door.

Outside, the rain had stopped. Daniel was bent over Micah's corpse. Now Ava could see the blood running from the back of Micah's head across the stone walkway and beneath a withered rosebush.

"Fucking waste," Daniel sighed, and then he started toward the Camaro. Ava left nearly as quickly, and when she reached the mouth of the cul-de-sac she paused. She stared in the direction of the Hyundai. She couldn't see Ben through the windshield.

She didn't ever want to see him again.

Ava headed toward one of the nearby dark houses and crept into its backyard. She found a rear gate that led to a narrow road shrouded by trees. She walked along that road, and her pace quickened when she heard police sirens.

The Uber driver dropped Ava off at her parents' Madison Park home around 11 P.M.—earlier than when Ava normally returned home on Saturday nights. She knew she had a bruise blooming on her right cheek, but she didn't look at her reflection in her bathroom mirror when she stripped off her clothes. While showering, she kept the water scalding hot. Afterwards, she slipped on the cupcake-patterned pajamas she hadn't worn since ninth grade. She tiptoed through the hallway outside her parents' bedroom and adjusted the digital thermostat so the heat would come on. Inside her parents' bedroom, she curled up by the vent that was on the wall near the foot of their bed. She used to lie there for warmth when she was in elementary school.

Her mother spoke in a soft voice: "Honey? I thought you were going to be with Alyssa until tomorrow. You okay?"

"I was just feeling homesick, believe it or not," Ava whispered to the comforting shadow that sat up in bed. "Go back to sleep."

Her curled position became a little tighter, and she relaxed only when the hot air came through the vent and blew against her body. She cracked open her eyes and noticed the half-moon glowing outside her parents' window. She went to that window and closed the shutters. She lifted the little metal latch that would keep them shut.

The shutters kept the moonlight out, but there was nothing Ava could do about her thoughts—or her memories.

JOHN

"Brandon, get up," John said. He looked down at his old friend, who lay sprawled on his back on a steep, ferny slope. After tripping, Brandon had tumbled about 30 feet down the hillside. John used his one remaining arm to gently shake Brandon's shoulder. "We need to keep moving."

Brandon responded to John's touch by raising his upper body. He stared toward the top of the slope, in the direction of the farm. "Is he still coming?"

John glanced back at where they'd entered the forest. He held his breath and thought to himself, *Please don't let him be there, please don't let him be there....* He saw only the half moon glowing brightly beyond the trees' leaves.

But then someone's silhouette appeared at the top of the slope. The man wielded a machete. He didn't venture into the forest. John guessed the man was trying to discern their figures in the dark, or else he was listening for them. The man didn't show any sign of being injured even though John had stabbed him inside the farmhouse.

"Hurry," Brandon whispered. He now stood, and he pulled John by the arm deeper into the forest.

John guessed the man wouldn't be able to see them in the shadows of the trees, but surely he could hear the crunching leaves beneath their feet. John was grateful when they reached a stretch of mossy ground. Their footsteps were now silent.

"I lost your arm," Brandon spoke with remorse. "I dropped it when I fell. I'm sorry."

John glanced down at the stump of his right arm, which he could barely see in the darkness. He still didn't feel any pain thanks to whatever drug he was on, but he had a tingling sensation in his shoulder. John was certain that sensation would turn into blazing agony if he didn't reach a hospital soon. He touched the bandage and realized it was soaked with blood. A wave of dizziness washed over him, and he thought he was going to faint. He wrapped his left arm around a tree trunk to brace himself.

"You okay enough to keep going?" Brandon asked.

"What if we stayed and confronted him?" John asked. "It's two against one." Of course, more than one person had been involved in what happened to John. The young couple that included the girl who stuck the needle in his neck. And the two masked guys who were in the bathroom with him when he awoke in the tub. His vision blurred, he'd watched one of the men pick up his dismembered arm and wave it at him.

"Say goodbye to normal life," the guy said in a mocking voice, and John started screaming.

One of those men left the farmhouse when the hazy morning light came through the window above the tub. The moon mask still concealed the man's face. Then a skinny man with red hair and freckles arrived. The word *YENOM* was tattooed across his forehead. John passed out and was unconscious for possibly hours, and he woke up in a nearly pitch-dark barn. The redhead and the remaining masked man eventually walked him out into the yard and tied one end of a rope around his ankle and the other around the gnarled trunk of an apple tree. The redhead started toward a car parked at the entrance to the farm and said, "I'll watch out for Laurent on Highway 2 and text you when I'm on him."

"He took my gun," Brandon now told John. "We can't confront him. We've got to head down this hill and get to my car."

John nodded. He listened for their pursuer, but all he heard was a breeze moving through the leaves above their heads. "I think he stayed at the top of the hill," he said. "Let's go."

He moved downhill from the mossy area, and the tingling feeling in his shoulder intensified into a pricking one. He continued through the trees, growing more lightheaded as he moved. He started to lean toward his left, and he felt like he was going to topple over.

"You're not doing well, buddy." Brandon took hold of John's left arm and steadied him. "But look down there," he said, pointing below them.

A one-lane forest service road cut through the trees. The moon lit the dirt road.

"It'll be easier for you to walk on that," Brandon said. "Do you think you can make it down there?"

John nodded even though he was breathless. He wasn't sure whether he'd pass out before they reached the road.

"I didn't see that when I came up through the forest earlier," Brandon said, "but I came up a different part of the hill. I'll bet if we walk east on that road it'll take us down to the road where my car's parked."

They soon left the evergreens, and John was relieved to be on a clear, wide path. He looked at the stretch of forest service road and noticed it curved sharply to the left. He figured that must be where it sloped down and connected to a paved road. The bend in the road wasn't too far ahead.

"I can do this," he said, and he could see the doubt on Brandon's face. John realized his forehead was covered in sweat, and his face must have been corpse-pale in the moonlight. But he no longer felt like he was going to faint. And he was relieved his old friend was here with him. He didn't know exactly who'd killed Maya Mathers or posted the original Spindly Arms story on that *Bloody Bitz* site, but he knew it wasn't Brandon.

As they walked, John felt Brandon's grip on his arm tighten.

"I fucked up when we were kids, buddy," Brandon said. "The thing with Vivian and me. That should never have happened. I'm sorry."

John nodded solemnly. "It's okay," he said. "We all fucked up in the past. I was a dick for not being there for you after your dad died. And all this Spindly Arms shit. This is my fault. I'm the one who linked him to the armless man."

"Ed Granley," Brandon said as if he were naming a demon.

"Ed Granley," John repeated, astounded that he'd never bothered to find out the armless man's name. He remembered when Brandon had first sketched Spindly Arms. The character didn't wear any clothes. He had a wrinkled, sexless white body.

"Give him coveralls like the ones the armless man wears," John had said.

"The armless man will know we based Spindly Arms on him," Brandon said.

John shrugged. "Who cares?"

People cared—and they'd been caring for over 25 years. John knew that now as he shuffled along the forest service road.

He recalled Vivian once saying how there's a certain part of your brain that isn't formed until you're out of your teens, and it's the part that helps you understand the long-term consequences of your actions.

A rustling sound came from the forest above the road. The sound was about 30 feet ahead of John and Brandon. It seemed to run parallel to the curve in the road. John thought he saw someone peeking at them from the trees lining the curve.

"What the hell?" he whispered when he saw what looked like a floating yellow face. He proceeded a few steps along the road even though Brandon told him to wait.

"Look!" John said when they were a little closer to the curve. "He left his mask." He pointed at the rubber crescent moon mask that dangled from the limb of a dead tree. A machete was stuck in the dirt at the base of the tree. "He's fucking with us," Brandon said. "This could be a trap." He glanced at the woods to their left. "We should be able to get to the main road if we cut downhill through these trees. "Are you up for that?"

"Let's go," John said, ignoring the increasing pain in his stump. Brandon held on to his left arm as they stumbled through the forest. John managed to avoid falling, but he was sweating even more than before, and the pain had become like an angry, stinging wasp. John bit his lower lip. He was relieved when they reached the asphalt of the main road.

"I can see it from here!" Brandon whispered, sounding elated. He pointed at a distant car parked on the opposite side of the road.

John saw where the forest service road intersected with the main road. The intersection was between them and Brandon's car. He didn't see anyone else on the asphalt or near the trees.

He hoped the man was still higher up on the hill, waiting to ambush them on the forest service road.

Brandon let go of his arm and fetched a large stick that would serve as a weapon.

John started toward the car, but he collapsed onto the asphalt. His remaining hand scraped against the surface as he tried to buffer the impact. He groaned. Rising, he experienced severe chills that made him shiver. His vertigo was returning.

"I want you to stay here," Brandon said. I'll pick you up in the car."

"I can come with you," John said. He was short of breath. He winced at the jagged pain in his shoulder.

"I'll get there faster on my own," Brandon said. "I'll be back in just a few, buddy."

John reached out to pat Brandon on the back, but his friend was already gone, jogging along the road toward the car. Watching Brandon run, John wondered if they could become close again. He pictured Brandon coming over to his house for a meal with him and Vivian. He could handle Brandon sitting across the table from her. He would enjoy having all three of them together again.

A man stepped out of the trees when Brandon was close to the car. John couldn't see the man's features, only his silhouette. He wielded a machete. Brandon paused in the middle of the road and looked in the man's direction. The man approached him, the machete raised.

Brandon immediately turned toward John and called, "Get away from here!" His eyes were large and filled with concern for his friend.

John wondered whether Brandon would try to fight the machete-wielding man with a stick. But as the man came closer to Brandon, John understood there would be no fighting. The man held a gun in his left hand, and he pointed it at Brandon.

A loud shot sent birds flying out of the forest.

In horror, John watched his friend crumple onto the asphalt.

"Brandon!" he shouted. He clenched his one remaining hand into a fist. He staggered toward his friend's prone body, but he paused when the man with the gun turned toward him. The man must have been about 100 feet away. The man lifted the machete and moved in John's direction.

"How about I cut the other one off?" he called to John.

John's legs were frozen as if he were in a nightmare. He stared at the dark figure, but he still wasn't able to discern any features.

"Nah," the man added, still walking toward John. "Too much work. Let's end this now." The main raised his arm and aimed the gun again.

Another shot, this one even louder.

John squeezed his eyes shut. He heard himself breathing quickly.

The man had missed!

John opened his eyes, but the man no longer stood in the middle of the road. His body was on the asphalt.

Someone stepped out of the woods. He wasn't far from where Brandon's killer had emerged from the trees. He carried a rifle. "Hey!" he called to John. "I'm a friend of Brandon's." Brandon's friend went to the man he'd just shot and glanced downwards at him. He then moved to Brandon's body and kneeled beside it.

John hurried toward the man, the pain in his stump now constant and excruciating. He was wheezing. *Don't pass out,* he told himself. *Don't pass out.*

As he passed the corpse on the road, he saw it was a thirty-something man with short black hair and a mangled ear. John didn't recognize him.

"Oh, Brandon," John said when he reached his dead friend. Tears immediately filled his eyes. The bullet had ripped through Brandon's neck. One of Brandon's arms was flung above his head, and John couldn't help remembering how they'd both lie in similar positions on their camping trips, staring up at the stars and musing over what they were going to do with their lives.

The man with the rifle was a stocky, balding fellow with a baby face. He glanced up at John. "Name's Ray. Brandon told me he'd be in this area. He-" Ray went silent and appeared as if he were about to start sobbing. His look of despair passed, and he continued. "I found Brandon's car, but I couldn't find him. I drove partway up the hill and parked by this burned-out building. Then I thought I heard voices at the bottom of the hill and ran down here. I guess I was too late."

John stared down at his friend again. The puddle of blood beneath Brandon's head reflected the moon. John didn't bother to wipe the tears from his cheeks. "Yeah," he said. "We're all too late."

And then he passed out.

*   *   *

Five days later—on Halloween—the nurse named Steve handed John a plastic bag filled with pain medications and a pamphlet listing wound care instructions. They stood beside the front desk of the surgery ward. Steve was a muscular guy in his twenties who made John feel more secure than the policeman who'd been stationed outside his room the first night he spent in Everett Mercy Hospital.

"He's good to go," Steve told the receptionist who sat behind the desk. The young woman wore brown mouse ears and had white whiskers painted on her cheeks. A fuzzy tan angora sweater completed her Halloween costume.

"And your ride home is here?" she asked in a cheerful voice.

"She is," John said. He glanced down the hallway and saw Vivian step out of the women's restroom. She looked as beautiful and as fit as ever, only now she had a raised, violet bruise on the right side of her forehead, and she limped slightly from the knife wound in her lower back.

She smiled as she neared him and slipped an arm around his waist. "Ready, hon?"

"Don't forget to change the wound dressings regularly," Steve told John.

"I've got my own dressings to change," Vivian said. "We can change dressings together. How sexy will that be?"

"Just call us if there are any issues," Steve said. "We'll get you fitted for the prosthetic soon enough."

"Thanks," John said. He suddenly pictured his missing arm decomposing on the forest floor in the mountains, and he distracted himself by looking at one of the posters on the hospital wall. In the poster, an elderly woman with no legs sat in a wheelchair, beaming. She was surrounded by loved ones. Above their heads was the message *The body is just a container for all that's good inside.*

"Let's get out of here," Vivian said, leading him toward the elevators. Her arm was still around his waist. John felt a pang of sadness when he remembered Brandon supporting him as he descended the hillside in the Cascades. After the police came to the scene, John gave them Brandon's sister's name. He wanted to reach out to her now to tell her how her brother had helped him, and to find out if there'd be a memorial. He'd thought about Brandon constantly since entering the hospital. He wondered what would have happened if he'd insisted on walking to the car with Brandon, or if he and Brandon had remained friends after high school, or if his paper route hadn't included Ed Granley's street....

"And have a Happy Halloween!" the receptionist called out to John and Vivian.

John glanced back and noticed Steve give her a disapproving look. John had told Steve that the men who were responsible for the Spindly Arms murder in Pioneer Square were also responsible for his missing arm and the death of his former best friend. But the receptionist didn't know all that.

"Happy Halloween!" John replied in a weak voice.

Outside the hospital, it was dark and the air was crisp with autumn. Vivian said she'd parked just across the street. When John asked why she didn't leave her car in the lot beneath Everett Mercy, she said, "I wanted to see something near the hospital."

They crossed the street in the direction of a large park. John saw Vivian's Honda Accord, but she led him beyond the vehicle and toward the edge of the park. A cement path curved past a bench, a dim lamp, and cedar trees. John didn't like how dark it was in there.

"I want to show you something," Vivian said.

John froze on the sidewalk. "I don't know."

He was unsure about entering the park because he knew some of the people who'd come after him, Vivian, and Brandon were still at large. Yes, Amos and Micah Granley were dead, and the police had caught two ex-cons who'd helped the brothers with their revenge scheme. One was Daniel Graffle, who'd assisted the Granley brothers in robbing a dollar store in the past, and the other was someone who called himself "Count Red." According to Detective Garcia, he'd served time for raping a woman in Spokane. But the police still hadn't located the youngest brother, Benjamin Granley, or the mysterious teenage girl who'd stuck the needle in John's neck.

"C'mon," Vivian said in a soothing voice. "We'll be fine. I came to this park earlier by myself." She grinned at him. "And I have my cell phone, a can of mace, and a gun in my purse."

"Where'd you get a gun?" John asked, shocked she had the weapon.

"Ralph let me borrow it until everything's calm again. He gave it to me two nights ago, when I took Maggie out for dessert."

John relented and entered the park with her. They walked between the cedar trees until they reached a large clearing. Vivian took him by the hand and led him to a lamppost beside a fence. Beyond the fence was a moonlit amphitheater. John gazed down at the small and empty stage.

"Do you know where you are?" Vivian asked.

"Wait," John said. On the block beyond the stage was a tall brick building with the faded words *IRMA'S SUNDRIES* on its side. That was the building that had housed the concert hall John, Vivian, and Brandon sometimes went to in high school. But back in the early '90s there was no amphitheater. The park sloped down to the street and only contained dirt paths and trees—including the huge sequoia on which John and Vivian had carved their initials one evening before a show.

John remembered bringing up the tree to Vivian at the high school reunion: "We said we'd meet there in 20 years if we were unhappy in our lives."

"The sequoia's gone," Vivian now said with a sad smile. "I came to check before picking you up at the hospital."

"A lot of things are gone now that we're midlife," John said. "And there's just nothing we can do about it." He realized he was at peace with his second statement.

"The past is past," Vivian said in agreement with John's sentiment. "It's powerful, but we can try not to let it overpower us."

John felt Vivian's grip around his waist tighten. She was looking to their right, in the direction of the amphitheater's upper benches. Sitting on the end of the uppermost bench was someone wearing an enormous crescent moon mask. The mask was bigger than any of the others John had seen last week, and glitter made it glimmer in the moonlight. The person looked down at his or her lap, and then the screen of a cell phone lit up. The figure tapped the screen and blurted, "You assholes were supposed to meet me here half an hour ago." He sounded like a teenager. "Are you guys actually trick-.or-treating? Oh, man."

Vivian grinned at John. "Shall we go home now?"

"Please," John said. He felt more at ease as they strolled past the cedar trees.

Vivian brought her arm away from his waist and squeezed his left hand. "You know, you could write about all this," she said.

John looked at her questioning face. He had the thought that he hadn't written creatively in decades—not since his early twenties. He wasn't sure he remembered how to do it.

But then he said, "I could...."

ACKNOWLEDGEMENTS

Thank you, Montag Press and publisher Charlie Franco, for launching Novel Number Three! I'm truly grateful for your backing over the years. Thanks to my ace editor, Kathryn Sargeant, for pushing me to go deeper with each character, and your ability to catch every detail that isn't quite right or true. My writers group has encouraged and improved my fiction for over two decades. Thank you, Sasha Mastroianni, Colin McArthur, Kevin O'Brien, and Garth Stein, for sticking with me on the journey through each of my books. I'm grateful to my longtime pals Christie Lavin and Josh Rogin for providing critical and constructive reads of *Grave Regrets*. Cheers to Jamison Oishi for once again serving as my crime scene consultant. Thank you to Stafford Lombard for always supporting my fiction and driving me through those hills of "Glimmer Lake" where I first imagined Ed Granley living in his dilapidated home. Finally, love and gratitude to my family—the Massengills, Keatings, Kings, and Lombards—for your unwavering appreciation of my weird fiction.

Made in the USA
Middletown, DE
10 November 2022

14556078R00168